THE 3 BUTTON TRICK
and
Other Stories

NOVELS BY NICOLA BARKER

Wide Open

Small Holdings

Reversed Forecast

THE 3 BUTTON TRICK
and
Other Stories

Nicola Barker

THE ECCO PRESS

THE ECCO PRESS
100 West Broad Street
Hopewell, New Jersey 08525

Published simultaneously in Canada by
Publishers Group West Inc., Toronto, Canada
Printed in the United States of America

Library of Congress Cataloging-in-Publication Data

Barker, Nicola, 1966–
The three button trick and other stories /
Nicola Barker.
p. cm.
ISBN 0-88001-677-9
1. England—Social life and customs—
20th century—Fiction.
I. Title.
PR6052.A64876A6   1999
823'.914—dc21   98-50624
CIP

9   8   7   6   5   4   3   2

FIRST EDITION 1999

CONTENTS

THE 3 BUTTON TRICK
and
Other Stories

Layla's Nose Job

Layla Carter was just about as happy as it was possible for a sixteen-year-old North London girl to be who possessed a nose at least two centimetres longer than any nose among those of her contemporaries. As with all subjects of a sensitive nature, the length of Layla's nose was an issue of great topicality and contention. Common clichés such as 'Don't be nosy' or 'You're getting up my nose,' even everyday phrases like 'Who knows?'—especially when uttered by an errant younger brother with a meaningful glance at the relevant part of Layla's physiognomy—would cause an atmosphere of hysterical teenage uproar in the Carter's semi-detached in the leafy suburbs of Winchmore Hill.

Layla sensed that the source of her problem was genetic, but neither of her parents, Rose and Larry Carter, possessed noses of any note. Her three siblings were blessed with lovely, truffling pink snouts with snub ends and tiny nostrils. They had nothing to complain about.

Her nose had always been big. On family occasions like Christmas or Easter when her grandparents and great aunts descended on the Carter household for a roast lunch and a glass of Safeways own-brand port, the family photo albums would be dragged out of the cabinet under the television and all tied by blood and name would pore over them and sigh.

No one sighed louder than Layla. Her odyssey of agony and

self-consciousness began with her christening snaps and continued well after the visitors had gone home, the washing-up had been done and the living-room carpet hoovered.

As far as she could tell, her nose had always been disproportionate. She had often had recourse to see other people's christening photographs, and in none of them that she could remember had so many profile shots been taken to so much ill effect. Her nose emerged like a shark's fin from between the delicate folds of her fine, pearly-white shawl, and the sight of it cut into her stomach like a blade.

She struggled to remember a time when the size of her nose hadn't been a full-time preoccupation. As a young child in her first weeks at school, after a particularly violent spate of playground jousting—little boys shouting 'big nose' at her for a period in excess of fifteen minutes—her class teacher had bustled her, howling, into the staff-room and had dried her eyes, saying softly, 'When you grow older you'll study the Romans. They were the people who built all the best, long, straight roads in Britain, many, many years ago. Now just you guess what all of the Romans had in common? They all had fine aquiline noses. Long, straight, proud noses like yours. One day you'll learn to be proud of your nose too. You'll learn that all the best people have strong, bold, expressive faces and strong, proud, dignified noses.' She offered Layla a tissue and said, 'Now go on, blow.' Layla pushed her face forward and then felt a pang of intense misery as her nose poked a hole through the centre of the tissue; like a dog jumping through a paper hoop. Nothing could console her.

People are so cruel, children are so cruel. In the school playground as she grew older, worse humiliations were in store. Her nose became her central signifier. Whenever her best friend Marcy was deputized to approach a handsome young buck for whom Layla had developed a girlish passion, she would always see him turn to Marcy with a frown and say, 'Layla? Who's she?'

By way of explanation Marcy would invariably point her out as she stood skulking in the corner of the playground closest to the girls' toilets and say, 'That's her there. You know, the one with the big nose.'

Marcy always apologized for her indiscretions. She was a sympathetic girl, but she came from a big family where sensitivity and tact often had to be abandoned in the arena of attention-grabbing. She would say to Layla, 'I'd much rather have a big nose than no nose at all.'

Neither of them had ever seen anyone without a nose before, but as the years dragged by Layla regularly stood in front of her bedroom mirror with her hand covering this offending part of her face in an attempt to perceive herself, and her other features, without its overwhelming presence. The result was often quite gratifying. Whenever she tried moaning to her mother, Rose would say, 'Just be grateful for what you have got. You've got pretty blue eyes and lovely soft, brown, curly hair. You've got a good figure too. Be grateful. Try not to be so negative.' In return, Layla would grimace and shout, 'God! It's bad enough having a nose like Mount Everest—I'd hardly tolerate being fat as well. I have to make the best of myself, but that doesn't make things any better. In some ways that makes things worse. If I was truly ugly, what would I care if I had a big nose?'

She wished she could chop it off. When she was twelve, a short burst of appointments with the school therapist brought more light to this preoccupation. The therapist told Rose and Larry that Layla's regular association in her conscious and unconscious mind with chopping and removal implied a rather unusual and boyish adherence to what is commonly called the castration complex. He said, 'Layla wants to be a man. She wants to rival her father, Larry, for Rose's love and attention. Unfortunately she has no penis. This makes the penis a hate object. She wants to castrate Larry's penis because she is jealous of it. She feels guilty about her aggressive impulses towards Larry and so turns these feelings of violence on to herself. To Layla, her nose is a penis. Her hatred of her nose is symbolic of her hatred of her own sexuality. When she comes to terms with that, she'll be a happier and more complete person.'

After their appointment the Carters took Layla for a hamburger at the McDonalds in Enfield's town centre as a treat. She sipped her milkshake and frowned. She said, 'What difference does all this make to me? Talking won't change the size of my nose, will it? Why does everyone have to pretend that my nose isn't the problem but that I am? It's as if everyone who wants to help me is determined to believe that my nose isn't all that big at all. But it is. It is!'

She had made her point. The family paid no heed to the therapist's recommendations. Except Larry, who took to locking the bedroom and the bathroom doors whenever he happened to undress; especially when shaving. He must have felt guilty about something.

By the time that she was fifteen, Layla knew everything conceivable about dealing with an outsize nose. She knew how to react when boys got on to the school bus in the afternoons and laughed at her and gesticulated, she knew how to comb and style her hair in a way that helped to accentuate her better features as opposed to her worse, she knew how to avoid having her photograph taken on family occasions (on holiday and at home), she knew how to spend hours every morning with a make-up brush and facial foundation, shading the sides of her nose and lightening its centre in a way she'd seen depicted in hundreds of teenage girls' magazines. Most of all she knew how to focus on this one, single thing. She made herself into a nose on legs.

She could not read a magazine without studying the nose of every model on its waxy, paper pages. If a model had a slightly larger nose than usual she would tear out the picture and put it into a scrapbook or stuff it in the drawer of her desk. At night she would list in her mind successful people who had big noses. She counted them like sheep in her pre-dream state; Chryssie Hynde, Margaret Thatcher, Barbra Streisand, Bette Midler, Dustin Hoffman, Rowan Atkinson, Cher. She thought about Cher quite a bit, because Cher had had her nose fixed.

In her dreams she visualized a scalpel, and its sharp edge touched her face like a kiss. It sliced her nose away so that her face felt light and radiant. But when she tried to bring her hand to her face to feel her new nose, her arms felt terribly heavy and could not be lifted. She used all her energy and willpower to attempt to lift them but they would not move. At this point she would awake from her dream and discover that she was actually trying to lift her arms, her real arms. In an instant she could then lift them to her face, and feel her face, and feel that everything was still the same. Even in her dreams, wish-fulfilment had its limits. Nothing ever went all the way.

Layla's problems were more than just cosmetic when she was fifteen. At this time Marcy began going out with her first serious boyfriend. Although they remained best friends this meant that Marcy grew less supportive towards Layla and increasingly preoccupied with her new ▸relationship. She also became enthusiastic about the idea of Layla becoming involved in a relationship herself. Layla had very high standards. All the boys who supposedly found her attractive did so (she firmly believed, with some grounds), because they were universally unattractive themselves.

But the pressure was on. Marcy visualized the 'double date' as the height of teenage sophistication and sociability. 'Imagine how much fun we could have if you and someone else could come out with me and Craig,' she'd say.

One warm summer Wednesday afternoon after school, Layla and Marcy went for a brisk stroll around the precinct in the town centre, looking at clothes, talking about teachers and drinking root beer. They ended up at Waitrose, where they bought a packet of Yum-Yum doughnut twists. Marcy suggested that they eat them on a bench in the park.

It was a set-up. Layla had barely taken the first bite of her doughnut when Craig turned up with one of his friends, Elvis. Her heart plummeted. After mumbling hello she walked a short distance to feed the rest of her Yum-Yum to a wayward duck. After a minute or so Marcy came over to her. She took her arm and said, 'Don't you like Elvis? Craig and I thought you'd get along.'

Layla baulked at this. She said, 'You thought we'd get along because we both have big noses, is that it?'

Marcy laughed nervously. 'Of course not. He's Jewish. Lots of Jewish men have big noses, it's natural.'

Layla forgot herself and wiped her sticky hands on her school dress. When she spoke again, her voice was dangerously calm. 'Of all the boys in the school you choose the one with the biggest nose to match me up with. You're supposed to be my best friend.'

'Lots of women think that Jewish men are very sexy, that their big noses are sexy,' Marcy interrupted.

Layla exploded, 'I hate big noses. I hate my nose. Why the hell should I want to go out with someone with an enormous nose?'

The two boys had turned to face them from their position by the bench. Elvis looked flush and irritated. Craig was laughing. He called over, 'You know what they say about men with big noses, don't you, Layla? They've got the biggest pricks.' He turned to Elvis. 'You'll vouch for that, won't you?'

Elvis was extremely angry. He said, 'You know what they say about girls with big noses, don't you, Layla? They say that they're very, very, very ugly, and that no one wants to go out with them.' He showed her one finger.

Her face went crimson. Marcy tried to defuse the situation. She rubbed Layla's arm apologetically. 'He's normally quite nice. I think he overheard us. He was upset, he didn't mean what he said.'

Layla pulled her arm away with great violence, the force of which pushed her a step backwards and sent the duck skittering off. 'Thanks a lot. Thanks for really humiliating me. I thought you were my friend. I suppose you and Craig had a real laugh planning this.'

Elvis had marched off in disgust, but Craig had made his way over to Marcy's side and put his arm protectively around her shoulders. 'Marcy was only trying to be nice. You make a mistake in thinking that everyone else is as interested in your stupid nose as you are. Elvis would've been a fool to want to go out with you, anyway. You're too self-obsessed.'

Layla strode over to the bench where she had left her school bag, and picked it up by its strap. Then she turned and said, 'Just because I have a big nose you all feel you've got the right to look down on me. I can just imagine Elvis and I going out on a date. Everyone who saw us would say, "Isn't it nice that two such strangely deformed people have found each other." I suppose it's like two dwarves going out together or two blind people, or two people with terrible speech impediments who could spit and stutter at each other over Wimpy milkshakes. Well, I want better than that. I'm more than just a big nose. I thought I was your best friend, Marcy, but in fact I'm just your big-nosed friend. That's all I am.'

Marcy said nothing as Layla sped away across the park.

That night when she got home Layla went straight to her bedroom. She locked the door and wouldn't come out. Rose left her a dinner-tray outside the door. She was concerned for Layla. The previous week she had seen a programme on teenage suicide. Layla was so volatile. Larry told her not to worry.

Layla sat alone and did a lot of thinking. She tried to analyse her world view. She tried to get outside herself and to see her situation from all angles. One central problem faced her: had other people made her self-conscious about her nose, or was she just vain, as Craig had implied? Had she created the problem for herself, or had society made her nose into a monster? Obviously her nose had always been in the centre of her face and it had always been big, but was that in itself enough to destroy her life?

She thought about Elvis and wondered how much consideration he gave to the size of his nose. But his was a Jewish nose. Hers was just a big nose. She knew that the size of Elvis's nose fitted into a larger scheme of things. It had a cultural space. It meant something. She thought, 'If you're Jewish and have a big nose it's like being Barbra Streisand or Mel Brooks. It means that you have a history, that you belong. The shape of my nose is just a mistake. My problem is stuck right bang in the centre of my face, and it has no wider implications than that. My problem is my nose. I didn't make the problem, the problem made me.'

It was so simple. It had to come off.

Late that evening she went downstairs into the living room and switched off the television. She stood in front of the screen—like a wonderful character from a film or a soap—and she announced firmly, 'Either I have a nose job or I kill myself. I can't go on like this any longer. I've heard that you can have one on the National Health. If you both love me you will help me.' She swayed gently as though she were about to swoon, then gathered herself up and strode from the room like Boadicea approaching her chariot: a woman with swords on her wheels.

Rose made an appointment with their local GP the following afternoon. Layla took an hour off school. She explained her problem to the GP and he agreed to book her in with a specialist.

Five months later Layla met the specialist. He was called Dr Chris Shaben and was a small, vivacious, balding man with a crooked face and yellowy teeth. Apparently he had a very beautiful wife. His surgery was on Harley Street and the gold plaque on his door said, 'Dr Chris Shaben, Plastic Surgeon' in a beautiful flowing script.

Layla sat in his office and discussed her nose at great length. For the first time ever she felt as though she was actually talking to someone who cared, someone who understood, and best of all, someone who could do something. It was as a dream to her. Entering his surgery had been like a scene of recognition in a book or a film; that moment when everything falls into place. It was an ecstatic moment. Layla was like a newborn child finding its mother's milky nipple for the first time.

It took a while to convince Dr Shaben that she was desperate and sincere. He said, 'Normally we only do plastic surgery treatments on the National Health if the problem involved is more than just cosmetic, but I'm willing to make an exception in this instance, Layla. Although you're young, you're very articulate and intelligent. I realize that your concerns go deeper than mere vanity.'

Layla nodded. She said slowly, 'For a while I tried to make myself believe that I had made the size of my nose into an issue, that the problem was to do with me, on the inside, not the out. My parents encouraged this line of thought, although my Mum has always been supportive, and my analysis did the same thing. But now I know that the problem is on the outside too. People judge one another visually; I should know, I do it myself. I want to be normal. I want to stop being on the outside, the periphery.'

Dr Shaben nodded and smiled at Layla. His bald head and short stature made him look like a tiny, benign, laughing Buddah as he sat hunched and serene in his big, leather, office chair.

Before the operation Layla abandoned her GCSE course work and concentrated instead on the leaflets, diagrams and information surrounding the surgery that she was about to undertake. She read how modern technology now meant that some nose operations could be undertaken entirely through the nostrils without any recourse to external incisions and unsightly scarring. The nose was chiefly made up out of bone and gristle, but was also extremely sensitive because of the large number of nerve endings at its tip. She tested this theory by smacking her nose with a pencil and then smacking other parts of her face like her cheeks and eyebrows. The nose was much more delicate. After the operation, a certain amount of swelling and bruising was to be expected.

Four days after her sixteenth birthday Layla awoke in a large and unfamiliar room. Her duvet was tightly stretched across her chest and felt unusually harsh and full of static. She was dopey. Her throat felt weird and dry. Her nose was numb but ached. She thought for an instant that she was dreaming her nose dream, that she wanted to put her hands to her face but her hands were restricted, yet after a few minutes she realized that she was in a strange bed in a strange environment. It was no dream, but her arms were restricted by the tightness of her sheets and blankets. She wriggled her body gently to create some room and worked her hands free. She placed them on her face. Her nose hurt. Her hands touched soft, filmy bandage and Band-Aid. It was done.

For the next five days her head felt light. Dr Shaben said that it was simply psychological, but she felt the lightness of a person who once had long hair and then cut it short, the roomy strangeness of someone who has had their arm broken and set in plaster and then has the plaster removed so that their arm floats up into the air because it feels so odd and weightless and light.

At first her face looked swollen and ugly. In hospital she wore no make-up and was blue with bruises. But she could see the difference. In the mirror her nose looked further away. Dr Shaben was pleased for her. He was well satisfied.

Throughout her stay in hospital, Rose had been in to see her every day. Larry preferred to stay away. Before she had gone in on her first night he had said to her, 'Remember how when you were small I would sit you on my knee and bounce you up and down and call you my little elephant girl? You always laughed and giggled. It's not like that any more. Now you've grown up into someone I don't recognize. I can't approve of what you are doing. God made you as you are. That should be enough.'

This came as a great shock to Layla. She had completely forgotten Larry's pet name for her. When she heard him say it again it was like a blow to her face, a blow to her nose, making it ache, making her numb. It was a kind of violent anaesthetic.

She was being pulled in so many directions. Everyone had a different opinion as to the whys and wherefores. Rose simply said, 'Do whatever will make you happy.'

After five days she came home. Although she was still slightly bruised, the mirror was her friend. Her three brothers greeted her at the front door with euphoric whoopings. Larry sat in the living room, watching the cricket. He turned after a minute or so and saw her, standing nervously by the door, her hands touching the bookcase for support. First he smiled, then he laughed, 'Five days away, all that money spent, and look at you. No difference! You look no different.' He laughed on long after she had left the room, but when he'd finished his stomach felt bitter.

Later Marcy visited. She smiled widely and hugged Layla like a real friend. Then she looked closely at her nose and said, 'Maybe your nose looks slightly different, but to me you are still the same old Layla. In my mind's eye you are exactly the same person. Nothing has changed.' She thought that she was saying the right thing.

Layla sat alone upstairs in her room, staring into the mirror. She felt sure that she looked different. She felt sure that she was now a different person, inside. But the worry now consumed her that other people would not be able to see how different she looked. It felt like a conspiracy. She thought, 'Maybe I've become the ugly person I was outside, inside. Perhaps that can never be changed.' She felt like Pinocchio.

That night she had a dream. In her dream she was a tiny little elephant, but she was without a trunk. She had four legs and thick grey skin, but flapping ears and a thin end-tassled tail. But she had no nose. Because she had no nose she couldn't pick things up—to eat, to wash, to have fun—all these things were now impossible. It was like being without arms. She kept asking for help. Her mother smiled and stroked her, but everyone else just laughed and pointed.

She slept late. When she awoke she felt battered and exhausted. When she looked into the mirror, her old face looked back at her. Nothing had changed. She felt utterly helpless. Her mind rambled and a thousand different images moved through the space behind her eyes. Her head was full of colour. She saw different people too, pointing their fingers, wiping her nose, holding her arm, bouncing her up and down on their knee, up and down, up and down.

In the kitchen she looked for a small knife to cut the top off her boiled egg. Instead she found that she had a chopping knife in her hand and it was as long as her arm. She cut the egg in half and its yolk hit the wall. She placed the blade near to her nose and felt tempted to move it closer. She stopped. For hours she remained stationary.

Larry had forgotten his sandwiches. He drove home in his lunch hour and let himself into the quiet house. He went upstairs for a quick pee. For once he neglected to shut and lock the door. He whistled contentedly.

Downstairs in the kitchen Layla's mind started to turn again. She considered her options.

Inside
Information

Martha's social worker was under the impression that by getting herself pregnant, Martha was looking for an out from a life of crime.

She couldn't have been more wrong.

'First thing I ever nicked,' Martha bragged, when her social worker was initially assigned to her, 'very first thing I ever stole was a packet of Lil-lets. I told the store detective I took them as a kind of protest. You pay $17\frac{1}{2}$ per cent VAT on every single box. Men don't pay it on razors, you know, which is absolutely bloody typical.'

'But you stole other things, too, on that occasion, Martha.'

'Fags and a bottle of Scotch. So what?' she grinned. 'Pay VAT on those too, don't you?'

Martha's embryo was unhappy about its assignment to Martha. Early on, just after conception, it appealed to the higher body responsible for its selection and placement. This caused something of a scandal in the After-Life. The World-Soul was consulted—a democratic body of pin-pricks of light, an enormous institution—which came, unusually enough, to a rapid decision.

'Tell the embryo,' they said, 'hard cheese.'

The embryo's social worker relayed this information through a system of vibrations—a language which embryos alone in the Living World can produce and receive. Martha felt these conversations only as tiny spasms and contractions.

Being pregnant was good, Martha decided, because store detectives were much more sympathetic when she got caught. Increasingly, they let her off with a caution after she blamed her bad behaviour on dodgy hormones.

The embryo's social worker reasoned with the embryo that all memories of the After-Life and feelings of uncertainty about placement were customarily eradicated during the trauma of birth. This was a useful expedient. 'Naturally,' he added, 'the nine-month wait is always difficult, especially if you've drawn the short straw in allocation terms, but at least by the time you've battled your way through the cervix, you won't remember a thing.'

The embryo replied, snappily, that it had never believed in the maxim that Ignorance is Bliss. But the social worker (a corgi in its previous incarnation) restated that the World Soul's decision was final.

As a consequence, the embryo decided to take things into its own hands. It would communicate with Martha while it still had the chance and offer her, if not an incentive, at the very least a moral imperative.

Martha grew larger during a short stint in Wormwood Scrubs. She was seven months gone on her day of release. The embryo was now a well-formed foetus, and, if its penis was any indication, it was a boy. He calculated that he had, all things being well, eight weeks to change the course of Martha's life.

You see, the foetus was special. He had an advantage over other, similarly situated, disadvantaged foetuses. This foetus had Inside Information.

In the After-Life, after his sixth or seventh incarnation, the foetus had worked for a short spate as a troubleshooter for a large pharmaceutical company. During the course of his work and research, he had stumbled across something so enormous, something so terrible about the World-Soul, that he'd been compelled to keep this information to himself, for fear of retribution.

The rapidity of his assignment as Martha's future baby was, in part, he was convinced, an indication that the World-Soul was aware of his discoveries. His soul had been snatched and implanted in Martha's belly before he'd even had a chance to discuss the matter rationally. In the womb, however, the foetus had plenty of time to analyse his predicament. *It was a cover-up!* He was being gagged, brainwashed and railroaded into another life sentence on earth.

In prison, Martha had been put on a sensible diet and was unable to partake of the fags and the sherry and the Jaffa cakes which were her normal dietary staples. The foetus took this opportunity to consume as many vital calories and nutrients as possible. He grew at a considerable rate, exercised his knees, his feet, his elbows, ballooned out Martha's belly with nudges and pokes.

In his seventh month, on their return home, the foetus put his plan into action. He angled himself in Martha's womb, at just the right angle, and with his foot, gave the area behind Martha's belly button a hefty kick. On the outside, Martha's belly was already a considerable size. Her stomach was about as round as it could be, and her navel, which usually stuck inwards, had popped outwards, like a nipple.

By kicking the inside of her navel at just the correct angle, the foetus—using his Inside Information—had successfully popped open the lid of Martha's belly button like it was an old-fashioned pill-box.

Martha noticed that her belly button was ajar while she was taking a shower. She opened its lid and peered inside. She couldn't have been more surprised. Under her belly button was a small, neat zipper, constructed out of delicate bones. She turned off the shower, grabbed hold of the zipper and pulled it. It unzipped vertically, from the middle of her belly to the top. Inside, she saw her foetus, floating in brine. 'Hello,' the foetus said. 'Could I have a quick word with you, please?'

'This is incredible!' Martha exclaimed, closing the zipper and opening it again. The foetus put out a restraining hand. 'If you'd just hang on a minute I could tell you how this was possible . . .'

'It's so weird!' Martha said, closing the zipper and getting dressed.

Martha went to Tesco's. She picked up the first three items that came to hand, unzipped her stomach and popped them inside. On her way out, she set off the alarms—the bar-codes activated them, even from deep inside her—but when she was searched and scrutinized and interrogated, no evidence could be found of her hidden booty. Martha told the security staff that she'd consider legal action if they continued to harass her in this way.

When she got home, Martha unpacked her womb. The foetus, squashed into a corner, squeezed up against a tin of Spam and a packet of sponge fingers, was intensely irritated by what he took to be Martha's unreasonable behaviour.

'You're not the only one who has a zip, you know,' he said. 'All pregnant women have them; it's only a question of finding out how to use them, from the outside, gaining the knowledge. But the World-Soul has kept this information hidden since the days of Genesis, when it took Adam's rib and reworked it into a zip with a pen-knife.'

'Shut it,' Martha said. 'I don't want to hear another peep from you until you're born.'

'But I'm trusting you,' the foetus yelled, 'with this information. It's my salvation!'

She zipped up.

Martha went shopping again. She shopped sloppily at first, indiscriminately, in newsagents, clothes shops, hardware stores, chemists. She picked up what she could and concealed it in her belly.

The foetus grew disillusioned. He re-opened negotiations with his social worker. 'Look,' he said, 'I know something about the World-Soul which I'm willing to divulge to my earth-parent Martha if you don't abort me straight away.'

'You're too big now,' the social worker said, fingering his letter of acceptance to the Rotary Club which preambled World-Soul membership. 'And anyway, it strikes me that Martha isn't much interested in what you have to say.'

'Do you honestly believe,' the foetus asked, 'that any woman on earth in her right mind would consider a natural birth if she knew that she could simply unzip?'

The social worker replied coldly: 'Women are not kangaroos, you cheeky little foetus. If the World Soul has chosen to keep the zipper quiet then it will have had the best of reasons for doing so.'

'But if babies were unzipped and taken out when they're ready,' the foetus continued, 'then there would be no trauma, no memory loss. Fear of death would be a thing of the past. We could eradicate the misconception of a Vengeful God.'

'And all the world would go to hell,' the social worker said.

'How can you say that?'

The foetus waited for a reply, but none came.

Martha eventually sorted out her priorities. She shopped in Harrods and Selfridges and Liberty's. She became adept at slotting things of all conceivable shapes and sizes into her belly. Unfortunately, the foetus himself was growing quite large. After being unable to fit in a spice rack, Martha unzipped and addressed him directly. 'Is there any possibility,' she asked, 'that I might be able to take you out prematurely so that there'd be more room in there?'

The foetus stared back smugly. 'I'll come out,' he said firmly, 'when I'm good and ready.'

Before she could zip up, he added, 'And when I do come out, I'm going to give you the longest and most painful labour in Real-Life history. I'm going to come out sideways, doing the can-can.'

Martha's hand paused, momentarily, above the zipper. 'Promise to come out very quickly,' she said, 'and I'll nick you some baby clothes.'

The foetus snorted in a derisory fashion. 'Revolutionaries,' he said, 'don't wear baby clothes. Steal me a gun, though, and I'll fire it through your spleen.'

Martha zipped up quickly, shocked at this vindictive little bundle of vituperation she was unfortunate enough to be carrying. She smoked an entire packet of Marlboro in one sitting, and smirked, when she unzipped, just slightly, at the coughing which emerged.

The foetus decided that he had no option but to rely on his own natural wit and guile to foil both his mother and the forces of the After-Life. He began to secrete various items that Martha stole in private little nooks and crannies about her anatomy.

On the last night of his thirty-sixth week, he put his plan into action. In his arsenal: an indelible pen, a potato, a large piece of cotton from the hem of a dress, a thin piece of wire from the supports of a bra, all craftily reassembled. In the dead of night, while Martha was snoring, he gradually worked the zip open from the inside, and did what he had to do.

The following morning, blissfully unaware of the previous night's activities, Martha went out shopping to Marks and Spencer's. She picked up some Belgian chocolates and a bottle of port, took hold of her zipper and tried to open her belly. It wouldn't open. The zipper seemed smaller and more difficult to hold.

'That bastard,' she muttered, 'must be jamming it up from the inside.' She put down her booty and headed for the exit. On her way out of the shop, she set off the alarms.

'For Chrissakes!' she told the detective, 'I've got nothing on me!' And for once, she meant it.

Back home, Martha attacked her belly with a pair of nail scissors. But the zip wasn't merely jammed, it was meshing and merging and disappearing, fading like the tail end of a bruise. She was frazzled. She looked around for her cigarettes. She found her packet and opened it. The last couple had gone, and instead, inside, was a note.

Martha, [the note said] *I have made good my escape, fully intact. I sewed a pillow into your belly. On the wall of your womb I've etched and inked an indelible bar-code. Thanks for the fags.*
Love, Baby.

'But you can't do that!' Martha yelled. 'You don't have the technology!' She thought she heard a chuckle, behind her. She span around. On the floor, under the table, she saw a small lump of afterbirth, tied up into a neat parcel by an umbilical cord. She could smell a whiff of cigarette smoke. She thought she heard laughter, outside the door, down the hall. She listened intently, but heard nothing more.

The Butcher's Apprentice

If he had come from a family of butchers maybe his perspective would have been different. He would have been more experienced, hardened, less naïve. His mum had wanted him to work for Marks and Spencers or for British Rail. She said, 'Why do you want to work in all that blood and mess? There's something almost obscene about butchery.'

His dad was more phlegmatic. 'It's not like cutting the Sunday roast, Owen, it's guts and gore and entrails. Just the same, it's a real trade, a proper trade.'

Owen had thought it all through. At school one of his teachers had called him 'deep.' She had said to his mother on Parents' Evening, 'Owen seems deep, but it's hard to get any sort of real response from him. Maybe it's just cosmetic.'

His mum had listened to the first statement but had then become preoccupied with a blister on the heel of her right foot. Consequently her grasp of the teacher's wisdom had been somewhat undermined. When she finally got home that evening, her stomach brimming with sloshy coffee from the school canteen, she had said to Owen, 'Everyone says that you're too quiet at school, but your maths teacher thinks that you're deep. She has modern ideas, that one.' Owen had appreciated this compliment. It made him try harder at maths that final term before his exams, and leaving. At sixteen he had pass marks in mathematics, home economics and the whole world before him.

In the Careers Office his advisor had given him a leaflet about prospective employment opportunities to fill out. He ticked various boxes. He ticked a yes for 'Do you like working with your hands?' He ticked a yes for 'Do you like working with animals?' He ticked a yes for 'Do you like using your imagination?'

When his careers guidance officer had analysed his preferences she declared that his options were quite limited. He seemed such a quiet boy to her, rather dour. She said, 'Maybe you could be a postman. Postmen see a lot of animals during their rounds and use their hands to deliver letters.' Owen appeared unimpressed. He stared down at his hands as though they had suddenly become a cause for embarrassment. So she continued, 'Maybe you could think about working with food. How about training to be a chef or a butcher? Butchers work with animals. You have to use your imagination to make the right cut into a carcass.' Because he had been in the careers office for well over half an hour, Owen began to feel obliged to make some sort of positive response. A contribution. So he looked up at her and said, 'Yeah, I suppose I could give it a try.' He didn't want to appear stroppy or ungrateful. She smiled at him and gave him an address. The address was for J. Reilly and Sons, Quality Butchers, 103 Oldham Road.

Later that afternoon he phoned J. Reilly's and spoke to someone called Ralph. Ralph explained how he had bought the business two years before, but that he hadn't bothered changing the name. Owen said, 'Well, if it doesn't bother you then it doesn't bother me.'

Ralph asked him a few questions about school and then enquired whether he had worked with meat before. Owen said that he hadn't but that he really liked the sweet smell of a butcher's shop and the scuffling sawdust on the floor, the false plastic parsley in the window displays and the bright, blue-tinged strip-lights. He said, 'I think that I could be very happy in a butcher's as a working environment.'

He remembered how as a child he had so much enjoyed seeing

the arrays of different coloured rabbits hung up by their ankles in butcher shop windows, and the bright and golden-speckled pheasants. Ralph offered him a month's probationary employment with a view to a full-time apprenticeship. Owen accepted readily.

His mum remained uncertain. Over dinner that night she said, 'It'll be nice to get cheap meat and good cuts from your new job, Owen, though I still don't like the idea of a butcher in the family. I've nothing against them in principle, but it's different when it's so close to home.'

Owen thought carefully for a moment, then put aside his knife and fork and said, 'I suppose so, but that's only on the surface. I'm sure that there's a lot of bloodletting and gore involved in most occupations. I like the idea of being honest and straightforward about things. A butcher is a butcher. There's no falseness or pretence.'

His dad nodded his approval and then said, 'Eat up now, don't let your dinner get cold.'

Owen arrived at the shop at seven sharp the following morning. The window displays were whitely clean and empty. Above the windows the J. Reilly and Sons sign was painted in red with white lettering. The graphics were surprisingly clear and ornate. On the door was hung a sign which said 'closed'. He knocked anyway. A man with arms like thin twigs opened the door. He looked tiny and consumptive with shrewd grey eyes and rusty hair. Owen noticed his hands, which were reddened with the cold, calloused and porkish. The man nodded briskly, introduced himself as Ralph then took Owen through to the back of the shop and introduced him to his work-mate, Marty. Marty was older than Ralph—about fifty or so—with silvery hair and yellow skin. He smiled at Owen kindly and offered him a clean apron and a bag of sawdust. Owen took the apron and placed it over his head. Ralph helped him to tie at the back. Both Marty and Ralph wore overalls slightly more masculine in design. Owen took the bag of sawdust and said, 'Is this a woman's apron, or is it what the apprentice always wears?'

As Ralph walked back into the main part of the shop he answered, 'It belongs to our Saturday girl, so don't get it too messy.

We'll buy you a proper overall at the end of the week when we're sure that you're right for the job.'

As he finished speaking a large van drew up outside the shop. Ralph moved to the door, pulled it wide and stuck a chip of wood under it to keep it open. He turned to Owen and by way of explanation pointed and said, 'Delivery. The meat's brought twice a week. Scatter the sawdust, but not too thick.'

Owen put his hand into the bag of dust and drew out a full, dry, scratchy handful which he scattered like a benevolent farmer throwing corn to his geese. The delivery man humped in half of an enormous sow. She had a single greenish eye and a severed snout. He took it to the back of the shop through a door and into what Owen presumed to be the refrigerated store-room. Before he had returned Ralph had come in clutching a large armful of plucked chickens. As Owen moved out of his way he nodded towards the van and said, 'I tell you what, why not go and grab some stuff yourself but don't overestimate your strength and try not to drop anything.'

Owen balanced his packet of shavings against the bottom of the counter and walked out to the van. Inside were a multitude of skins, feathers, meats and flesh. He grabbed four white rabbits and a large piece of what he presumed to be pork, but later found out was lamb. The meat was fresh and raw to the touch. Raw and soft like risen dough. He lifted his selections out of the van and carried them into the shop, careful of the condition of his apron, and repeated this process back and forth for the next fifteen or so minutes. While everyone else moved the meat, Marty busied himself with cutting steaks from a large chunk of beef. When finally all of the meat had been moved Ralph went and had a cigarette outside with the delivery man and Owen picked up his bag of shavings and finished scattering them over the shop floor. On completing this he called over to Marty, 'Do I have to spread this on the other side of the counter as well?'

Marty smiled at him. 'I think that's the idea. It should only take you a minute, so when you've finished come over here and see what I'm doing. You never know, you might even learn something.'

Owen quickly tipped out the rest of his bag over the floor at the back of the counter and scuffed the dust around with his foot. It covered the front of his trainer like a light, newgrown beard. Then he walked over to Marty and stood at his shoulder watching him complete his various insertions into the beef. Marty made his final cut and then half turned and showed Owen the blade he was using. He moved the tip of the blade adjacent to the tip of Owen's nose. 'A blade has to be sharp. That's the first rule of butchery. Rule two, your hands must be clean.' He moved the knife from side to side and Owen's eyes followed its sharp edge. It was so close to his face that he could see his hot breath steaming up and evaporating on its steely surface. Marty said thickly, 'This blade could slice your nose in half in the time it takes you to sneeze. Aaah-tish-yooouh!'

Then he whipped the knife away and placed it carefully on the cutting surface next to a small pool of congealing blood. He said, 'Rule three, treat your tools with respect.'

Owen cleared his throat self-consciously. 'Will I be allowed to cut up some meat myself today, or will I just be helping out around the shop?' Marty frowned. 'It takes a long time and a lot of skill to be able to prepare meat properly. You'll have to learn everything from scratch. That's what it means to be the new boy, the apprentice.'

Ralph came back into the shop and set Owen to work cleaning the insides of the windows and underneath the display trays. Old blood turned the water brown. Soon the first customers of the day started to straggle into the shop and he learned the art of pricing and weighing. The day moved on. At twelve he had half-an-hour for lunch.

After two o'clock the shop quietened down again and Owen was sent into the store-room to acquaint himself with the lay-out, refrigeration techniques and temperatures. As he looked around and smelt the heavy, heady smell of ripe meat, he overheard Ralph and Marty laughing at something in the shop. Ralph was saying, 'Leave him be. You're wicked Mart.' Marty replied, 'He won't mind. Go on, it'll be a laugh.'

A few seconds later Ralph called through to him. Owen walked into the shop from the cool darkness of the storeroom. The light made his eyes squint. The shop was empty apart from Ralph and Marty who were standing together in front of the large cutting board as though hiding something. Ralph said, 'Have you ever seen flesh, dead flesh, return to life, Owen?' Owen shook his head. Marty smiled at him. 'Some meat is possessed, you know. If a live animal is used as part of a satanic ritual at any point during its life, when it dies its flesh lives on to do the devil's work. After all, the devil's work is never done.'

As he finished speaking he stepped sideways to reveal a large chunk of fleshy meat on the chopping board. It was about the size of a cabbage. Everyone stared at it. They were all silent. Slowly, gradually, almost imperceptibly, the meat shuddered. Owen blinked to make sure that his eyes were clear and not deceiving him. After a couple of seconds it shuddered again, but this time more noticeably. It shivered as though it were too cold, and then slowly, painfully, began to crawl across the table. It moved like a heart that pumped under great duress, a struggling, battling, palpitating heart.

Owen's face blanched. His throat tightened. Ralph and Marty watched his initial reactions and then returned their gazes to the flesh. By now it had moved approximately five or six inches across the cutting board. Its motions were those of a creature in agony, repulsive and yet full of an agonizing pathos. Owen felt his eyes fill, he felt like howling.

Ralph turned back to look at Owen and saw, with concern, the intensity of his reactions. He said, 'Don't get all upset, it's only a joke. It's got nothing to do with the devil, honest.'

He smiled. Owen frowned and swallowed hard before attempting to reply. 'Why is it moving? What have you done to it?'

Marty reached towards the piece of convulsing flesh with his big butcher's hand and picked it up. As he lifted it the flesh seemed to cling to the table. It made a noise like wet clay being ripped into two pieces, like a limpet being pulled from its rock. He turned it over. Underneath, inside, permeating the piece of meat, was a huge round cancer the size of Marty's fist. A miracle tumour, complete, alive. The tumour was contracting and then relaxing, contracting and relaxing. Maybe it was dying. Owen stared at the tumour in open-mouthed amazement, at its orangy, yellowy completeness, its outside and its core. Marty said, 'Sometimes the abattoir send us a carcass that shouldn't really be for human consumption. They know that an animal is ill but they slaughter it just before it dies. They have to make a living too, I suppose.'

With that he threw the meat and its cancerous centre into a large half-full refuse bag and began to wipe over the work surface as though nothing had happened. Owen could still make out the movements of the cancer from inside the bag. A customer came into the shop and Ralph walked over to serve her. Owen felt over-whelmed by a great sense of injustice, a feeling of enormous inten-sity, unlike anything he had ever experienced before. He felt as though his insides were tearing. He felt appalled. Then instinctively he grabbed at the back of his apron and yanked open its bow. He pulled it over his head and slammed it on to the counter. He said, 'I'm going home now. I'm going home and I'm taking this with me.'

Before anyone could respond Owen had grabbed the heavy refuse bag full of bones and gristle and off-cuts and had struggled his way out of the shop. When he had gone, Ralph turned to Marty and said, 'He was a nice enough kid.'

Marty shrugged.

Owen got out of the shop and walked a short distance down the road before placing the bag on the pavement and opening it. He reached inside and felt for the cancer. When he finally touched it, it sucked on his finger like a fish or a baby. He took it out of the bag, pulled off his sweater and bundled the cancer up inside it. He car-ried it on the bus as though it were a sick puppy. It moved very slightly. When he got home he crept upstairs and locked himself in his room. He closed the curtains and then sat on his bed and un-bundled the tumour. He placed it gently on his bedside table under the warm glow of his lamp. It was growing weaker and now moved only slowly.

Owen wondered what he could do for it. He debated whether to pour water on it or whether to try and keep it warm. He wondered whether it might be kinder to kill it quickly, but he couldn't work out how. He wondered if you could drown a tumour (that would be painless enough), or whether you could chop it in half. But he couldn't be sure that tumours weren't like the amoebas that he'd studied in biology at school that could divide and yet still survive. He couldn't really face destroying it. Instead he decided to simply stay with it and to offer it moral support. He whispered quietly, 'Come on, it'll be all right. It'll soon be over.'

After a few hours the tumour was only moving intermittently. Its movements had grown sluggish and irregular. Owen stayed with it. He kept it company. He chatted. Eventually the tumour stopped moving altogether. Its meaty exterior was completely still. He knew that it was dead. He picked it up tenderly and cradled it in his arms as he carried it downstairs, out of the house and into the garden. Placing it gently on the grass, he dragged at the soft soil in the flower-beds with both his hands until he had dug a hole of significant proportions. Then he placed the still tumour into the hole and covered it over. In a matter of minutes the soil was perfectly compacted and the flowerbed looked as normal.

He went inside and lay on his bed awhile. At six he went downstairs to the kitchen where his mother was beginning to prepare dinner. As he poured himself a glass of water she said, 'I didn't know that you were home. How did your first day go?'

Owen gulped down the water and then placed his glass upside down on the draining board. He said, 'I think I'm going to be a postman.'

Then he dried his hands on a kitchen towel and asked what was for dinner.

G-String

Ever fallen out with somebody simply because they agreed with you? Well, this is exactly what happened to Gillian and her pudgy but reliable long-term date, Mr Kip.

They lived separately in Canvey Island. Mr Kip ran a small but flourishing insurance business there. Gillian worked for a car-hire firm in Grays Thurrock. She commuted daily.

Mr Kip—he liked to be called that, an affectation, if you will— was an ardent admirer of the great actress Katharine Hepburn. She was skinny and she was elegant and she was sparky and she was intelligent. Everything a girl should be. She was *old* now, too, Gillian couldn't help thinking, but naturally she didn't want to appear a spoilsport so she kept her lips sealed.

Gillian was thirty-four, a nervous size sixteen, had no cheekbones to speak of and hair which she tried to perm. God knows she tried. She was the goddess of frizz. She frizzed but she did not fizz. She was not fizzy like Katharine. At least, that's what Mr Kip told her.

Bloody typical, isn't it? When a man chooses to date a woman, long term, who resembles his purported heroine in no way whatsoever? Is it safe? Is it cruel? Is it downright simple-minded?

Gillian did her weekly shopping in Southend. They had everything you needed there. Of course there was the odd exception:

fishing tackle, seaside mementos, insurance, underwear. These items she never failed to purchase in Canvey Island itself, just to support local industry.

A big night out was on the cards. Mr Kip kept telling her how big it would be. A local Rotary Club do, and Gillian was to be Mr Kip's special partner, he was to escort her, in style. He was even taking the cloth off his beloved old Aston Martin for the night to drive them there and back. And he'd never deigned to do that before. Previously he'd only ever taken her places in his H-reg Citroën BX.

Mr Kip told Gillian that she was to buy a new frock for this special occasion. Something, he imagined, like that glorious dress Katharine Hepburn wore during the bar scene in her triumph, *Bringing Up Baby*.

Dutifully, Gillian bought an expensive dress in white chiffon which didn't at all suit her. Jeanie—twenty-one with doe eyes, sunbed-brown and weighing in at ninety pounds—told Gillian that the dress made her look like an egg-box. All lumpy-humpy. It was her underwear, Jeanie informed her—If only! Gillian thought—apparently it was much too visible under the dress's thin fabric. Jeanie and Gillian were conferring in The Lace Bouquet, the lingerie shop on Canvey High Street where Jeanie worked.

'I tell you what,' Jeanie offered, 'all in one lace bodysuit, right? Stretchy stuff. No bra. No knickers. It'll hold you in an' everything.' Jeanie held up the prospective item. Bodysuits, Gillian just *knew*, would not be Mr Kip's idea of sophisticated. She shook her head. She looked down at her breasts. 'I think I'll need proper support,' she said, grimacing.

Jeanie screwed up her eyes and chewed at the tip of her thumb. 'Bra and pants, huh?'

'I think so.'

Although keen not to incur Jeanie's wrath, Gillian picked out the kind of bra she always wore, in bright, new white, and a pair of matching briefs.

Jeanie ignored the bra. It was functional. Fair enough. But the briefs she held aloft and proclaimed, 'Passion killers.'

'They're tangas,' Gillian said, defensively, proud of knowing the modern technical term for the cut-away pant. 'They're brief briefs.'

Jeanie snorted. 'No one wears these things any more, Gillian. There's enough material here to launch a sailboat.'

Jeanie picked up something that resembled an obscenely elongated garter and proffered it to Gillian. Gillian took hold of the scrap.

'What's this?'

'G-string.'

'My God, girls wear these in Dave Lee Roth videos.'

'Who's that?' Jeanie asked, sucking in her cheeks, insouciant.

'They aren't practical,' Gillian said.

Jeanie's eyes narrowed. 'These are truly modern knickers,' she said. 'These are what *everyone* wears now. And I'll tell you for why. No visible pantie line!'

Gillian didn't dare inform her that material was the whole point of a pantie. Wasn't it?

Oh hell, Gillian thought, shifting on Mr Kip's Aston Martin's leather seats, 'maybe I should've worn it in for a few days first.' It felt like her G-string was making headway from between her buttocks up into her throat. She felt like a leg of lamb, trussed up with cheese wire. Now she knew how a horse felt when offered a new bit and bridle for the first time.

'Wearing hairspray?' Mr Kip asked, out of the blue.

'What?'

'If you are,' he said, ever careful, 'then don't lean your head back on to the seat. It's real leather and you may leave a stain.'

Gillian bit her lip and stopped wriggling.

'Hope it doesn't rain,' Mr Kip added, keeping his hand on the gearstick in a very male way, 'the wipers aren't quite one hundred per cent.'

Oh, the G-string was a modern thing, but it looked so horrid! Gillian wanted to be a modern girl but when she espied her rear-end engulfing the slither of string like a piece of dental floss entering the gap between two great white molars, her heart sank down into her strappy sandals. It tormented her. Like the pain of an old bunion, it quite took off her social edge.

When Mr Kip didn't remark favourably on her new dress; when, in fact, he drew a comparison between Gillian and the cone-shaped upstanding white napkins on the fancily made-up Rotary tables, she almost didn't try to smile. He drank claret. He smoked a cigar and tipped ash on her. He didn't introduce her to any of his Rotary friends. Normally, Gillian might have grimaced on through. But tonight she was a modern girl in torment and this kind of behaviour quite simply would not do.

Of course she didn't actually *say* anything. Mr Kip finally noticed Gillian's distress during liqueurs.

'What's got into you?'

'Headache,' Gillian grumbled, fighting to keep her hands on her lap.

Two hours later, Mr Kip deigned to drive them home. It was raining. Gillian fastened her seatbelt. Mr Kip switched on the windscreen wipers. They drove in silence. Then all of a sudden, *wheeeuwoing!* One of the wipers flew off the windscreen and into a ditch. Mr Kip stopped the car. He reversed. He clambered out to look for the wiper, but because he wore glasses, drops of rain impaired his vision.

It was a quiet road. What the hell. Mr Kip told Gillian to get out and look for it.

'In my white dress?' Gillian asked, quite taken aback.

Fifteen minutes later, damp, mussed, muddy, Gillian finally located the wiper. Mr Kip fixed it back on, but when he turned the relevant switch on the dash, neither of the wipers moved. He cursed like crazy.

'Well, that's that,' he said, and glared at Gillian like it was her fault completely. They sat and sat. It kept right on raining.

Finally Gillian couldn't stand it a minute longer. 'Give me your tie,' she ordered. Mr Kip grumbled but did as she'd asked. Gillian clambered out of the car and attached the tie to one of the wipers.

'OK,' she said, trailing the rest of the tie in through Mr Kip's window. 'Now we need something else. Are you wearing a belt?'

Mr Kip shook his head.

'Something long and thin,' Gillian said, 'like a rope.'

Mr Kip couldn't think of anything.

'Shut your eyes,' Gillian said. Mr Kip shut his eyes, but after a moment, naturally, he peeped.

And what a sight! Gillian laboriously freeing herself from some panties which looked as bare and sparse and confoundedly stringy as a pirate's eye patch.

'Good gracious!' Mr Kip exclaimed. 'You could at least have worn some French knickers or cami-knickers or something proper. Those are preposterous!'

Gillian turned on him. 'I've really had it with you, Colin,' she snarled, 'with your silly, affected, old-fashioned car and clothes and *everything*.'

From her bag Gillian drew out her Swiss Army Knife and applied it with gusto to the plentiful elastic on her G-string. Then she tied one end to the second wiper and pulled the rest around and through her window. 'Right,' she said, 'start up the engine.'

Colin Kip did as he was told. Gillian manipulated the wipers manually; left, right, left, right. All superior and rhythmical and practical and dour-faced.

Mr Kip was very impressed. He couldn't help himself. After several minutes of driving in silence he took his hand off the gearstick and slid it on to Gillian's lap.

'Watch it,' Gillian said harshly. 'Don't you dare provoke me, Colin. I haven't put my Swiss Army Knife away yet.'

She felt the pressure of his hand leave her thigh. She was knickerless. She was victorious. She was a truly modern female.

The
Three
Button
Trick

Jack had won Carrie's heart with that old three button trick.

At the genesis of every winter, Jack would bring out his sturdy but ancient grey duffel coat and massage the toggles gently with the tips of his fingers. He'd pick off any fluff or threads from its rough fabric, brush it down vigorously with the flat of his hand and then gradually ease his way into it. One arm, two arms, shift it on to his shoulders, balance it right—the tips of the sleeves both perfectly level with each wrist—then straighten the collar.

Finally, the toggles. The most important part. He'd do them one-handed, pretending, even to himself, some kind of casualness, a studied—if fallacious—preoccupation, his eyes unfocused, imagining, for example, how it felt when he was a small boy learning to tell the time. His father had shown him: ten past, quarter past, see the little hand? See the big hand? But he hadn't learned. It simply didn't click.

So Jack's mother took over instead. She had her own special approach. The way she saw it, any child would learn anything if they thought there was something in it for them: a kiss or a toy or a cookie.

Jack's mother baked Jack a Clock Cake. Each five-minute interval on the cake's perimeter was marked with a tangy, candied, lemon segment. The first slice was taken from the midday or midnight point at the very top of the cake and extended to the first lemon segment on the right, which, Jack learned, signified five minutes past the hour. 'If the little hand is on the twelve,' his mother told him, 'then your slice takes the big hand to five minutes past twelve.'

Jack wrinkled up his nose. 'How about if I have a ten past twelve slice?' he suggested.

He got what he'd asked for.

Jack was born in Wisconsin but moved to London in his early twenties and got a job as a theatrical producer. He'd already worked extensively off-off Broadway. He met Carrie waiting for a bus on a Sunday afternoon outside the National Portrait Gallery. It was the winter of 1972. He was wearing his duffel coat.

Carrie was a blonde who wore her hair in big curls, had milk-pudding skin and breasts like a roomy verandah on the front of her body's smart Georgian townhouse frame. Close up she smelled like a bowl of Multi-flavoured Cheerios.

Before Jack had even smelled her, though, he smiled at her. She smiled in return, glanced away—as girls are wont to do—and then glanced back again. Just as he'd hoped, her eyes finally settled on the toggles on his coat. She pointed. She grinned. 'Your buttons . . .'

'Huh?'

'The buttons on your coat. You've done them up all wrong.'

He looked down and pretended surprise. 'I have?'

Jack held his hands aloft, limply, gave her a watery smile but made no attempt to righten them. Carrie, in turn, put her hand to her curls. She imagined that Jack must be enormously clever to be so vague. Maybe a scientist or a schoolteacher at a boys' private school or maybe a philosophy graduate. Not for a moment did it dawn on her that he might be a fool. And that was sensible, because he was no fool.

Carrie met Sydney two decades later, while attending self-defence classes. Sydney had long, auburn ringlets and freckles and glasses. She was Australian. Her father owned a vineyard just outside Brisbane. Sydney was a sub-editor on a bridal magazine. She was strong and bare and shockingly independent. On the back of her elbows,

Carrie noticed, the skin was especially thick and in the winter she had to apply Vaseline to this area because otherwise her skin chapped and cracked and became inflamed. The reason, Sydney informed Carrie, that her elbows got so chapped, was that she was very prone to resting her weight on them when she sat at her desk, and also, late at night, when she lay in bed reading or thinking, sometimes for hours.

Sydney was thirty years old and an insomniac. Had been since puberty. As a teenager she'd kept busy during the long night hours memorizing the type-of-grape in the type-of-wine, from-which-vineyard and of-what-vintage. Also she collected wine labels which she stuck into a special jotter.

Nowadays, however, she'd spend her wakeful night-times thinking about broader subjects: men she met, men she fancied, men she'd dated, men she'd two-timed, and if none of these subjects seemed pertinent or topical—during the dry season, as she called it—well, then she'd think about her friends and their lives and how her life connected with theirs and what they both wanted and what they were doing wrong and how and why.

Carrie appreciated Sydney's attentiveness. If Jack had been working late, if Jack kept mentioning the name of an actress, if Jack told her that her skin looked sallow or her roots were showing, well, then she would tell Sydney about it and Sydney would spend the early hours of every morning, resting on her elbows and mulling it all over.

Sydney had a suspicion that Jack was up to something anti-matrimonial and had hinted as much to Carrie. Hinted, but nothing more. Carrie, however, took only what she wanted from Sydney's observations and left the rest. In conversational terms, she was a fussy eater.

Jack walked out on Carrie after twenty-one years of marriage, two days before her forty-fourth birthday. The following night, after he'd packed up and gone, she and Sydney skipped their karate class and sat in the leisure centre's bar instead. Sydney ordered two bottles of Bordeaux. She wasn't in the least bit perturbed by Carrie's

predicament. In fact, she was almost pleased because she'd anticipated that this would happen a while ago and was secretly gratified
by the wholesale accuracy of her prediction.

'You're still a babe, Carrie,' Sydney whispered, pouring her
some more wine. 'You could have any man.'

'I don't want any man,' Carrie whimpered. 'I only want Jack.
Only Jack. Only him.'

'That guy Alan,' Sydney noted, 'who takes the Judo class. I
know he likes you. Sometimes it seems like his eyes are stuck to your
tits with adhesive.'

'Please!'

'It's true.'

'Jack only walked out yesterday, Sydney, probably for a girl fifteen years my junior. You really think I care about anything else at
the moment?'

Sydney had great legs; long and lithe and small-kneed. Gazelle
legs, llama legs. She crossed them.

'I'm simply observing that Jack isn't the only shark in the
ocean.'

Carrie took a tissue from her sports bag and dusted her cheeks
with it.

'I remember the very first time I ever met Jack, waiting for a bus
outside the National Portrait Gallery. A Sunday afternoon. He had
his coat buttoned up all wrong and I pointed it out to him and we
started talking . . .' Carrie stopped speaking and hiccuped.

Sydney chewed her bottom lip. That old three button trick, she
was thinking. The slimy bastard.

'You know, Carrie,' she said sweetly. 'You're still so beautiful.
You're still the biggest lily in the pond. You're still floating on the
surface and bright enough to catch the attention of any insect or am-
phibian that might just happen to be passing.' She paused. 'Even a
heron,' she added, as an afterthought.

Carrie scrabbled in her sports bag. She grabbed her purse,
opened it, took out a twenty-pound note to pay the barman for the
bottles of wine.

'My treat,' Sydney interjected.

Carrie paid him anyway. She was about to shut her purse but then paused and delved inside it.

'Look,' she said, her voice trembling, holding aloft a blue card.

Sydney put out her hand. 'What is it?'

'Our season ticket to the ballet. We went every week. It was one of those routines . . .'

'Well,' Sydney took the ticket and perused it, 'you shall go to the ball, Cinders.'

'What?'

'You and me. We'll go together. When is it?'

'Wednesday.'

Sydney handed the card back. 'Fine.'

As it turned out, Sydney couldn't make it. She rang Carrie at the last minute. Carrie answered the phone wrapped up in a towel, pink from a hot bath.

'What? You can't make it?'

'But I want you to go, anyway. Find someone else.'

'There is no one else. It doesn't matter, though. I wasn't really in the mood myself.'

'Carrie, you've got to go. Alone if needs be. It's the principle of the thing'

'I know, but it's just . . .'

'What?'

'It's kind of like a regular box and we share it with some other people and if I go alone . . .'

'So? That's great. It means you won't feel entirely isolated, which is ideal.'

'And then there's this fat old man called Heinz who's always there. A complete bore. We really hate him.'

'Heinz?'

'Yes. Jack always found him such a pain. We even tried to get a transfer . . .'

'Bollocks. Just go. Ignore him. What's the ballet?'

'*Petrushka.*'

'Yip!'

'I've seen it before. It's not one of my particular favourites.'

'Go anyway. You've got to start forging your own path, Carrie. You'll thank me after. Honestly.'

She'd made a special effort, with her hair and her make-up. She was wearing a dress that she'd bought for the previous Christmas. It was a glittery burgundy colour. Her lips matched. The box was empty when she arrived. She felt stupid. She sat down.

After five minutes, a couple she knew only to say hello to arrived and took their seats. They smiled and nodded at Carrie. She did the same in return. She then paged through her programme and pretended that she wasn't overhearing their conversation about the kind of conservatory they should build on to the back of their house. He wanted a big one that could fit a table to seat at least six. She wanted a small, bright retreat full of orchids and tomato plants.

Carrie kept reading and rereading the names of the principal dancers. The orchestra's preparatory honking and parping jangled in her throat and with her nerves. She closed her eyes. I will count to ten. One, two, three, four . . .

'Ooof! Here we go, here we go!'

Heinz, squeezing his way over to his seat, pushing his considerable bulk between the two rows of chairs.

'Oi! Hup! There we are.'

Carrie opened her eyes and stared at him. He had a box of chocolate brazils in one hand and a bulging Selfridges bag in the other, which he almost, but couldn't quite, fit into the gap between his knees and the front of the box.

Carrie's gut rumbled her antipathy. He smelled, always—as Jack had noted on many an occasion—of wine gums and Deep Heat. An old smell. He must have been in his eighties, wore a grey-brown toupee and weighed in, she guessed, like a prize bull, at around three hundred and twenty pounds.

Carrie converted this weight into stone and then back again to occupy herself.

Heinz nodded at her. She nodded back. He always wore a

sludge-coloured bow tie. It hung like a shiny little brown turd, poised under his chin.

Heinz endeavoured, with a great harrumphing, to find adequate room by his knees for his bag. 'Uh-oh! Uh-oh!'

Carrie gritted her teeth.

'If you haven't room for your shopping, this chair is empty.' She indicated Jack's empty seat which separated them.

'Empty? Really? That lovely man of yours isn't with you tonight? Empty, you say?' He wheezed as he spoke, like an asthmatic Persian feline, which made his German accent even more pronounced.

You'd think, Carrie speculated, that a wheeze would take the hard edges off a German accent, but you'd be wrong to think so.

'Would you mind'—close to her ear—'if I sat next to you and put my bag on the other seat?'

My God! Carrie thought, fixing her eyes on the stage curtains and breathing a sigh of relief at their preliminary twitchings.

'Brazil?'

Ten minutes in, Heinz was whispering to her.

'What?'

'Brazil? Go on. Have one.'

'No, thank you.'

'Go on!'

'No. I don't actually like brazils. Nuts give me hives.'

Heinz closed the box and rested it on his lap.

During the intermission, Heinz regaled Carrie with tales about the relative exclusivity of the Turner and Booker prizes. He liked the opera, it turned out, especially Mozart. He found camomile tea to be excellent for sleeplessness. He was a widower of seven years.

Carrie noticed how the box's other regulars smiled at her sympathetically whenever they caught her eye. It was odd, really, because actually, with increased acquaintance, Heinz wasn't all that bad. In fact, if anything, he'd made her the centre of attention in the box. The focus, the axis. She felt rather like Princess Margaret opening a day care centre in Fulham.

As the safety curtain rose for the second half, Heinz was

telling Carrie how he'd just been to Selfridges to buy a cappuccino maker. He loved everything Italian. He'd been stationed there during the war.

As the stage curtains closed, Heinz mopped something from the corner of his eye and muttered gutturally, 'Poor, poor old Petrushka!'

During the curtain calls Heinz told Carrie that he often felt that it was sadder to be a sad puppet than a sad person.

'Pardon?'

'Petrushka, the puppet. Sometimes it feels like the ballet is sadder because he is a puppet and not a living being.'

'Oh, right. Yes.' Carrie finished applauding and leaned over to pick up her bag. Heinz stayed where he was.

'How will you be getting home then, Carrie?'

'I brought my car.'

'Really?'

'Yes.'

'So maybe, maybe you wouldn't mind joining an old man for a cup of coffee somewhere before you make your way back?'

'Uh?' Carrie was agog.

'Oh! Um . . .' She thought about it for a long moment. She imagined her quiet house, her empty bed. 'OK,' she said cheerfully, 'love to.'

Sydney was late for Thursday's class so they didn't have a chance to chat beforehand. Afterwards though, in the sauna, they had plenty of opportunity for exchanging news. Carrie wore a white towel around her essentials and sat on the lower bench. Sydney wore nothing and sat on the upper.

'How'd it go then?'

'Pardon?'

'Last night.'

'Fine.'

'Yeah?'

'Yes.' Carrie cleared her throat. 'I mean, you know how it is when you do something alone for the first time when you're accustomed to doing it with someone else . . .'

'I guess so.'

Sydney lay down flat on her back. Whenever she lifted her shoulders or her buttocks, they stuck to the wooden boards, aided by the natural glue of her body's moisture. The noise this made reminded Carrie of the sound of an emery board against a ragged nail.

'Actually,' Carrie said, grinning, '*La Fille Mal Gardée* is my favourite ballet.'

'Really? You like an element of slapstick, huh?'

'I suppose I must do.'

'Myself, I prefer a tragedy. I find that tragedy best reflects my emotional and psychological state.'

Carrie turned and stared straight into Heinz's frogspawn eyes. 'You're kidding.'

'Me? Kidding? Not at all. Not at all.'

Heinz offered Carrie his family-size box of Maltesers.

'Thanks.'

Carrie took one and popped it into her mouth. 'That's the strangest part . . .' she said, chewing and enjoying the sensation of chocolate and malt on her tongue. 'I've been to four ballets with you and never for a moment did I think you seemed like a sad or a dissatisfied person.'

It was the interval. Heinz and Carrie were propping up the theatre bar. Heinz had discovered that Carrie's favourite winter tipple was port and lemon. He'd taken to ordering her one before the show. This meant they didn't have to wait to be served during the intermission.

Heinz smiled at Carrie. 'You see the best in everyone.'

'Maybe I'm just insensitive.'

'You? Insensitive? Never. You're an angel.'

A man standing just to Carrie's left turned and stared at them. Carrie caught his eye. His expression was a mixture of amusement and confusion. Carrie took a sip of her drink. People were so funny, the way they stared. Their quizzical expressions. It had begun to dawn on her that when she was out with Heinz she became a puzzle. She became mysterious.

Alone, at home, in life, she felt like something dried-up, wrung-out and innocuous. Out with Heinz, she felt like she was transformed into something much less explicable.

Heinz was bossy and opinionated but he wasn't entirely unobservant. He rolled his eyes at Carrie. 'Probably thinks you're my daughter.'

Carrie shrugged. 'And I could be too, easily.'

Carrie often found Heinz to be genuinely perceptive. At their second ballet together he'd said, 'And your husband . . . ?'

To which she'd responded, 'I don't ever want to talk about him.'

'Very well.'

And they'd never spoken about him since. It was almost like, Carrie decided, Jack had never even existed.

Sydney was plaiting her hair, trying, but failing, to include the front bang-like bits into the weave so that they didn't keep falling into her eyes. Their class was due to start at any minute. Carrie stood behind her, scowling to herself, intensely discomfited.

'I was only saying,' Sydney observed, still plaiting, 'that it seems a bit strange for you not to want me to come with you when you said yourself on several occasions that there was a spare ticket going begging.'

'There is a spare ticket,' Carrie said, caught distinctly off her guard. 'It's only that next week I promised someone else . . .'

'Who?'

'A friend called Sue,' Carrie said, too quickly, and then widened her eyes when she'd finished speaking as if the words she'd just uttered were indigestible.

'Who?'

'I told you about her, surely? She's the one who thinks I should open my own interior design shop.'

'Sue?'

'Yes. Remember? I said I was thinking about starting work again, now that Jack's gone. The money's tight and everything.'

'Interior design? That's the first I've heard of it. How could you afford to open an interior design shop? You don't know anything about retail . . .'

Sydney finished her plaiting and turned to face Carrie. Carrie's cheeks were red, she noted, and she was scratching her neck as though she'd been bitten.

'It was just an idea.'

'Where would you get the money from to start a business with? You're broke.'

'I know.'

'Interior design, you said?'

Carrie nodded.

'Sue? Sue who?'

Carrie blinked and then swallowed. 'The Sue who's coming to the ballet with me next week. We were at school together. I surely must've mentioned her before.'

'No.'

People had started to filter their way gradually into the gym. Carrie pointed, 'I think the class is due to start.'

'OK, next time.'

'Pardon?'

Sydney smiled. 'Next time I want to come with you, so make sure you keep the ticket spare, all right?'

'Yes. Fine.'

Sydney led the way. Carrie looked down at her trainers and silently incanted a Hail Mary.

They'd become so engrossed in their conversation that they hadn't noticed everyone else going back inside. Carrie was so engrossed in what Heinz was saying that she almost hadn't noticed his hand on her shoulder. Almost.

'What else do I have to spend my money on? Huh? There's nothing. I want for nothing. It would give me enormous pleasure to help you out.'

'I don't know.' Carrie, for some reason, couldn't stop thinking about Sydney.

'Actually, Heinz, next time I come to the ballet I'll be bringing someone with me . . .'

Heinz's hand slipped from Carrie's shoulder. His voice was suddenly flat. 'Oh. That's good. It seems such a shame to waste the seat every week like you do.'

'Exactly. We go to the same evening class together.'

'Does this person have a name?'

'Sydney.'

'I see. I see.'

Carrie noticed that Heinz's face was pale and doughy. 'Is something wrong?'

'Nothing at all. Nothing.'

Carrie continued to stare at Heinz. Was he all right? He didn't look it. She suddenly became nervous and she didn't know why. She started to babble. 'She's Australian. I had to invite her. She asked.'

Heinz put his hand to his bow tie. 'She's a girl?'

'Yes.'

Carrie watched with ill-concealed amazement as Heinz burst out laughing. He laughed so hard and loud that his toupee slipped. Then he plucked it from his forehead with his meaty hand, tossed it into the air with a great whoop and then caught it, just as deftly.

The sauna. Sydney sat bolt upright, her eyes as wide as saucers, each hand enfolding a single breast as though her amazement endangered them in some way.

'You're sleeping with this guy?'

Carrie's towel was wrapped as tight as it could be but still she hitched it closer. 'Not exactly. I didn't spend the night . . .'

'You fucked this man?'

'Please! He's eighty-three!'

'Exactly! He's eighty-fucking-three and you shagged him. My God! How did this happen? How does it happen that an attractive forty-four-year-old woman, in her prime, great body, big hair, the lot, shags an eighty-three-year-old man who she was the first to admit . . .'

'It wasn't . . .'

'Who she was the *first* to admit is the fattest and most boring old loudmouth in the whole damn universe. How? Huh?'

'Sydney! *Please* . . .'

'Jesus, I can just imagine it.'

'Imagine what?'

'You know what I mean.'

'Don't!'

'Guess what I'm visualizing, Carrie. I am visualizing this grey slug of a man with an enormous pale belly and a tiny penis like a party-time Mars Bar hanging down below . . .'

'Stop it!'

Carrie was on the brink of crying. She was so ashamed. It wasn't even the act, the fact of it, that shamed her, only Sydney's perception of it and then *her* perception of it as a result of Sydney's. That was all. And if Sydney hadn't insisted on the second ballet ticket it would never have been a problem, she could have hidden it. She could have pretended . . .

'He must be loaded.'

'What?'

'Money. Why else would you want him? Is he loaded? Is he going to, maybe, give you a little bit of money to start off your interior design business? Is that it?'

Carrie was mortified. 'It isn't like that at all!'

'No? How is it then?'

'I don't know!' Carrie started crying.

Sydney was unmoved. She said softly, 'You know, I kept thinking you were taking this whole Jack thing too well.'

'I don't want to talk about Jack!'

'What would Jack think, huh? What would Jack actually think if he knew what you were doing?'

Carrie stood up, covered her cheeks with her hands, bolted out of the sauna, through the changing rooms and into the showers.

There she turned the tap to cold, ripped off her towel and pushed her burning face into the jet.

Sydney crossed her llama legs at the knee and then dialled Jack's number.

'Hi Jack. It's Sydney.'

'Sydney? Well, hello. What can I do for you?'

'I want to see you. It's about Carrie.'

After Jack had put down the phone, he picked up his duffel coat and brushed it off. He was keenly looking forward to a cold snap.

It was a nightmare. Just as she'd imagined. Heinz wore his toupee and his turd-coloured tie. He kept regaling them with terrible stories about his late wife's beloved red setter which had died—following several years of chronic incontinence—after swallowing a cricket ball. Carrie supposed that he must be nervous. Poor lamb.

Sydney was horribly polite. She kept staring at Heinz's stomach as she spoke to him, like she expected, at any minute, that something might explode out of it.

When Carrie drove her home, she didn't talk for the first ten minutes of the journey. She merely said, 'Carrie. Leave me. I have to digest.'

Carrie left her. Eventually, after she'd digested sufficiently, Sydney said, 'He belched throughout the ballet. It was like sitting next to an old pair of bellows. Christ, the orchestra should recruit him for the wind section.'

Carrie's heart sank. 'He wasn't belching. He swallowed a toffee too quickly. It went down the wrong way. He kept apologizing.'

'And that fucking dog! His dead wife's dead fucking dog! Does he really think I'm interested in how they fed it a diet of fresh chicken to try and quell its chronic flatulence? Are *you* interested, Carrie? Huh?'

'No.'

'Pardon?'

'No! No, I'm not interested. I'm not.'

'And I just can't believe . . .'

'What?' Carrie tried to keep her eyes on the road, but Sydney's expression . . .' What?!'

'The two of you . . .'

'What?'

Sydney's eyes were glued to the road ahead. It was starting to rain. Carrie turned on the windscreen wipers just in time with Sydney's next pronouncement.

'Fucking.'

Carrie said nothing. They both stared at the road. Eventually Sydney turned her eyes towards Carrie. 'Well?'

Carrie said nothing. She focused on the road and the wipers and the rain and the way that the light from the streetlamps reflected in the drops of water on the windscreen before each harsh stroke brushed it away. Where do they go? She wondered. Where do those moments go? The rain falling in just such a way, the light, the wiper. Something there and then something gone.

Sydney found she was boiling. Not hot, but something *inside*. What else could she do? What else could she say? Carrie had closed down, shut up, like a clam. Sydney cursed herself. She was too impetuous. Too quick to judge. If only she'd tried to be nice, to be supportive. Maybe then Carrie might have provided her with some details. Something to ponder, to mull over, fat to chew on. Damn! Sydney crossed her arms, stared at the road, *boiled*.

'I got your number from the book,' Heinz said.

'Didn't I give it you?'

'No.'

'I should've.'

'She didn't like me.'

'No. Actually, I think she really hated you.'

'Sometimes I can be overwhelming. It's a fault of mine. I know that. But I am simply myself. When you get old . . .'

'You tried your best.'

'But did I? One tends to forget how it is to . . . uh . . . to play the game.'

'Never mind.'

'Can I see you?'

'Pardon?'

'Tonight?'

Carrie rubbed her eyes with her spare hand. 'I only just got in. It's raining outside . . .'

'Tomorrow?'

Sydney lay on her stomach and rested the weight of her head on her hands. What was wrong? It was just . . . she couldn't imagine. Carrie and that fat old man. My God! She just couldn't *picture* it. Not properly. Not graphically. She rolled on to her back. Couldn't imagine. But my Lord, *my Lord*, how she longed to!

Sydney stared at Jack's buttons. Jack pretended not to notice. Sydney sighed.

'Jack,' she said, 'you haven't a hope in hell of winning me over with that old three button trick.'

Jack's eyes blinked and then widened. 'What do you mean, ma'am?'

'Nor that Courtly American Gentleman shite.'

Jack scowled. 'What's the axe you've got to grind, Sydney?' he asked, not charming any longer.

'No axe,' Sydney said. 'I just thought you should know . . .' She paused. What did she want to say, exactly? Would she tell Jack about Heinz? She looked into Jack's face and knew that the notion of an eighty-odd-year-old man sleeping with his wife was hardly going to incite him to jealousy.

'Is it Carrie?' Jack asked.

'Yep.' Sydney rubbed the corner of her eyes.

'You look washed out,' he said.

'Tired. Haven't been sleeping.'

'Really?'

Sydney uncrossed her legs. 'Carrie's got someone new.'

Jack looked surprised. 'Already?'

'Yeah.'

'Who?'

Sydney cleared her throat. 'Someone she's known for a while.'

'She met them at the gym? Who is it? Do I know them?'

Sydney shrugged. 'That's not the point.'

'So I do know them?'

'I didn't say you knew them.'

'Are they younger than me?'

Sydney squirmed. 'I just thought . . .'

'Why are you telling me this?'

Sydney picked up her briefcase. 'Not for any reason, really.' She frowned and then asked out loud. 'Why am I telling you? I don't know.' She stood up. 'That three button thing you do,' she said finally, 'I just wanted to tell you that it's a real cheap trick.'

Half a bottle of Jim Beam later, it finally clicked. The only thing that made sense. Carrie was having an affair with Sydney. And Sydney was terrified of what exactly his response might be. She was intimidated by him. She was *threatened*. Naturally. And she'd really wanted to tell him too, to throw it in his face, debilitate him. Only then . . . only then she just didn't have the nerve. That was it! Had to be. Carrie and Sydney. Sydney and Carrie. Wow.

'You won't believe this, Sydney. Something so odd happened . . .' They were pulling on their leotards and tying up their laces.

'Try me.'

'Jack rang. He left a message on the machine. He wants to drop by. On Wednesday.'

Sydney pulled the bow stiff on her lace. She straightened up.

'But Wednesday!' she exclaimed. 'Isn't that ballet night?'

Carrie looked uneasy, momentarily, like she didn't know quite what Sydney was getting at. 'Uh, yes . . .'

'So you won't be needing your tickets?'

'I suppose not, unless . . .'

'So I could have them both, maybe?'

'You?'

'Yeah. I quite got a taste for it the other night. How about it, huh?'

Heinz started when he saw her. He wondered whether Carrie had come with her but had popped to the Ladies for some reason, or to the bar. He squeezed his way over to his seat.

'Hello there.'

Sydney looked up. 'Oh, hi. How are you?'

'Not too bad. Not too bad at all.'

He sat down, adjusted his position, pulled at his little bow tie which constricted him, reached into his jacket pocket and pulled from its depths a Cadbury's Chocolate Orange. He unwrapped the foil and offered the orange to Sydney.

'Dark chocolate,' he said.

Sydney tried to pull off a slice but it wouldn't come loose. Heinz intervened, knocked at the chocolate orange with the centre of his palm and then offered it to her again.

'Thanks,' Sydney said, smiling, showing him what fine, straight teeth she had and just how sweet and obliging she could be.

Jack had brought flowers. Lilies. Her favourites.

'Look, Carrie, I met up with Sydney the other day.'

Carrie was putting the flowers in water, but preparing each stem first by slicing an inch off the bottom at a sharp angle. That way, she knew, the flower could drink so much more.

'Sydney?'

'Yeah.'

'She didn't mention it.'

'No?'

Jack was actually relieved. He'd been worried in case Sydney might have blotted his copybook with Carrie by suggesting things about him, by exaggerating or maligning. Sydney could bitch with the best when she felt the urge. She was dangerous.

'Let me tell you something,' Jack said, leaning his back up against one of the kitchen cupboards.

'What?' Carrie was wide eyed and restless. What had Sydney said? Had she been indiscreet? Had she mentioned Heinz?

'I know what's been going on,' Jack said, 'and I'm here to tell you that I don't care. I've given it some thought . . .'

'What do you know?'

'About you and Sydney.'

'What about us?'

He put out both his hands. 'Just tell me,' he said, 'that it's over. Because my suitcase,' he couldn't hide his smile, 'my suitcase, darling, is lying packed in the boot of my car.'

'I'll tell you something else,' Sydney said, lounging on Heinz's sofa and drinking her fourth martini.

'What?'

Heinz was sitting on his comfy chair sipping a cup of tea.

'I went and saw Jack the other day, right? A private *tête à tête*, and he came into the café where we'd arranged to meet with the buttons on his coat done up all . . .' Sydney made a higgledy-piggledy movement with her hands, 'like so . . .'

'He's missing her?' Heinz interjected, almost sympathetic.

'No. Not at all. That's my point. It's the three button trick.'

'The what?'

'Men do it. Some men. To make them look . . .' she burped, 'vul-ner-a-ble. And this is the best bit . . .' She put her hand over her mouth. 'Pardon me.'

'The best bit?'

'Yeah. Turns out, he only pulled that trick the very first time he ever spoke to Carrie. 1972. Outside the National Portrait Gallery. Took her in completely. Beguiled her, absolutely. And there he was, large as life, trying it on with me!'

'Did you tell her?'

Sydney knocked back the rest of her drink. 'Who?'

'Carrie.'

'Nope. Seemed a shame.'

Heinz nodded.

'Nice flat,' Sydney said, looking around her.

'It suits me well enough.'

'Come and sit over here.' Sydney patted the sofa to her left. 'Come on.'

Heinz smiled. 'I am perfectly comfortable where I am, thank you.'

Sydney stared at him, balefully. 'What's wrong?'

Outside the sound of a faint car horn was just audible.

'Nothing is wrong,' Heinz said, pushing his great bulk up from his comfy chair and walking over to the window. While his back was turned, Sydney unbuttoned the grey silk shirt she was wearing and took it off. Heinz turned and said, 'I think that's your cab.'

'Huh?'

'Outside.'

'What cab?'

'I called for one a little while back.'

'A cab? Can't I stay here?'

'What for?'

Sydney started grinning but only half her mouth worked properly. 'Sex, stupid.'

Heinz picked up Sydney's pale silk shirt from the arm of the sofa and handed it to her. 'I'm eighty-three years old,' he said gently, 'and entirely impotent.'

'What's wrong?' Carrie asked, for the umpteenth time. 'I can tell something's bothering you. I only wish you'd tell me.'

Sydney had still not yet quite recovered. It was Thursday night at the gym.

'Nothing's wrong.'

She hadn't been sleeping. Her elbows were hurting. She couldn't stop thinking . . .

'I only got out of the house tonight because Jack's at a conference. I swore not to come here any more. He seems to have got the idea into his head that you're some kind of . . .' Carrie couldn't think of the appropriate word.

Sydney was staring at Carrie with an odd expression. Either Carrie lied, she was thinking, or Heinz lied.

'So Jack doesn't know about Heinz yet?'

'No.'

'Well, let's just hope he doesn't get to find out, either.'

Carrie shook her head. 'I spoke to Heinz on the phone. I explained that I didn't want Jack knowing. He was so good about it.'

'Knowing what?'

'Knowing anything.'

Sydney smiled at this, and Carrie, for some reason, had cause, she sensed, to feel a sudden dart of disquiet. In her stomach. In her gut.

'I told you not to ring me!' Carrie exclaimed, terrified at the possibility of discovery.

'Is it safe to talk?'

'Jack's in the bath. He's listening to the cricket on the radio.'

'You know I miss you terribly. You know that, don't you?'

'Heinz, there's no point . . .'

'But this isn't about that. It is about your friend, Sydney.'

'What?'

'She keeps calling around and she also keeps writing to me. She phones me . . .'

'Sydney?'

'I just want you to talk to her. I simply want her to leave me in peace.'

'My God. How odd.'

'I miss you so much.'

Carrie's cheeks glowed an unnaturally bright colour as she said goodbye and then gently placed down the receiver.

She waited until the last person had left the sauna. 'Carrie,' she said, 'I've done something I think you should know about.'

'What?'

'I had sex with Heinz.' She'd expected Carrie to blush or blanch. One or the other.

'What happened?'

'Straight sex. Nothing fancy.'

Carrie frowned, 'I'm afraid I don't believe you, Sydney.'

'Why not? It's true.'

'He's impotent.'

'He isn't. You slept with him.'

'I didn't sleep with him.'

'You said you did.'

'He's impotent.'

'So what . . .'

'He's in love with me. He'll do *anything*.'

Sydney stared at Carrie, confounded. Carrie was round and soft and lily white. She seemed peculiarly full of herself.

'So let me get this straight . . .' Sydney said, wanting details so badly.

'He just wants you to leave him in peace.'

'Does Jack know yet?' Sydney asked, knowing she was routed and turning nasty.

'He doesn't know.'

Carrie appeared unperturbed. Sydney shrugged. 'Better make sure he doesn't find out, then.'

Carrie only smiled.

'Jack made a move on me, when we met up recently,' Sydney said. 'He tried that old three button trick of his.'

'What do you mean?'

'So you don't even know about that one yet?' Sydney asked. 'Oh, you'll just love it. It's so cheap.' And she set about putting Carrie straight on that particular matter.

He'd kept on nagging so in the end she'd been forced to give in to him. 'It's a terrible waste,' he said, 'to keep on leaving the seats empty.'

Anyhow, Carrie was bored of sitting at home every night with nothing to do and no proper conversation. Sometimes he mentioned the name of a new actress. Sometimes he wasn't too tactful and inadvertently made her feel her age.

When Heinz finally entered the box, a little late, without his tie, pale-faced, dishevelled, Jack muttered, 'Christ, I'd almost forgotten about him.'

Carrie said nothing, but she hadn't forgotten.

Sydney was sitting on her bed and in front of her was a pile of scrap books. She opened the first one. Dry red wines from the Perth region. She touched the wine label and wondered about her mummy and her daddy. Her elbows were itchy. She reached for a tub of Vaseline. She dipped in her fingers.

Heinz had had several options: to forget about her, to confront her and tell her what a bastard Jack was, to be a kind of bastard himself. He was old. If he'd learned anything along the line, he'd learned that the little things didn't matter, at the end of the day, but the big things mattered, and sometimes you had to compromise yourself, however slightly, to try to maintain that bigger picture.

In the interval they bumped into one another at the bar. Jack was several feet away ordering drinks. Heinz had given plenty of thought to this moment. He'd had several options available. He'd taken the cheapest. Arriving late, no tie, the business.

'You look terrible,' she said, glancing over towards Jack, her lips barely moving. She stared at his shirt. 'And your buttons,' she added, 'are done up all wrong.'

He looked down at himself. 'Really?' he said, wheezing, like he'd barely noticed. But when he looked back up again his old heart began pumping.

Jack was walking over towards them holding two glasses. A whisky, a port and lemon. He was walking over. He was close and he was closer.

Carrie put out her hand and touched Heinz's buttons. 'Oh God,' she said softly, 'that stupid three button trick, you old hound,' and her eyes started sparkling.

Wesley

BLISTERS

Look,' Trevor said, 'you've got to serve from the back, see?'

Wesley dropped the orange he'd just picked up.

'Put it where it was before,' Trevor said sniffily. 'Exactly.'

Wesley adjusted the placement of the orange. There. Just so. It was neat now. The display looked hunky-dory.

'Let me quickly say something,' Wesley said, as Trevor turned to go and unload some more boxes from the van.

'What?'

'It's just that if you serve people from the back of the stall they immediately start thinking that what you're giving them isn't as good as what's on display.'

Trevor said nothing.

'See what I mean?'

'So what?'

'Well, I'm just saying that if you want to build up customer confidence then it's a better idea to give them the fruit they can see.'

'It's more work that way,' Trevor said, shoving his hands into his pockets.

'Well, I don't care about that,' Wesley responded. 'I'm the one who'll end up having to do most of the serving while you're running the deliveries and I don't mind.'

Trevor gave Wesley a deep look and then shrugged and walked off to the van.

Another new job. Selling fruit off a stall on the Roman Road. Wesley was handsome and intelligent and twenty-three years old and he'd had a run of bad luck so now he was working the markets. No references needed. Actually, on the markets a bad temper was considered something of a bonus. Nobody messed you around. If they did, though, then you had to look out for yourself.

Trevor had red hair and a pierced nose. Wesley looked very strait-laced to him in his clean corduroy trousers and polo-neck jumper, and his hands were soft and he spoke too posh. What Trevor didn't realize, however, was that Wesley had been spoilt rotten as a child so was used to getting his own way and could manipulate and wheedle like a champion if the urge took him. Wesley had yet to display to Trevor the full and somewhat questionable force of his personality.

Wesley pulled his weight. That, at least, was something, Trevor decided. After they'd packed up on their first night he invited Wesley to the pub for a drink as a sign of his good faith. Wesley said he wanted something to eat instead. So they went for pie and mash together.

Trevor had some eels and a mug of tea. Wesley ate a couple of meat pies. Wesley liked the old-fashioned tiles and the tables in the pie and mash shop. He remarked on this to Trevor. Trevor grunted.

'My dad was in the navy,' Wesley said, out of the blue.

'Yeah?'

'He taught me how to box.'

'Yeah?'

'Last job I had, I punched my boss in the face. He was up a ladder. I was on a roof. Broke his collar bone.'

'You're kidding!' Trevor was impressed.

'Nope.'

'Fuck.'

'Yeah.'

'What did he do?'

'Tried to prosecute.'

'What!?'

'I buggered off. I live my life,' Wesley said plainly, 'by certain rules. I'll do my whack, but when push comes to shove, I want to be treated decent and to keep my mind free. See?'

Trevor was mystified. He ate his eels, silently.

'I had a brother,' Wesley said, 'and I killed him when I was a kid. An accident and everything. But that's made me think about things in a different way.'

'Yeah?' Trevor was hostile now. 'How did you kill him?'

'Playing.'

'Playing what?'

'None of your fucking business.'

Trevor's eyebrows rose and he returned to his meal.

'I want to do the decent thing,' Wesley said. 'You know? And sometimes that'll get you into all kinds of grief.'

Trevor didn't say anything.

'Watch this.'

Trevor looked up. Wesley had hold of one of the meat pies. He opened his mouth as wide as he could and then pushed the pie in whole. Every last crumb. Trevor snorted. He couldn't help it. Once Wesley had swallowed the pie he asked Jean—the woman who served part-time behind the counter—for a straw. When she gave him one, he drank a whole mug of tea through it up his left nostril.

Trevor roared with laughter. He was definitely impressed.

After a week on the job Wesley started nagging Trevor about the quality of the fruit he was buying from the wholesalers. 'The way I see it, right,' Wesley said, 'if you sell people shit they won't come back. If you sell them quality, they will.'

'Bollocks,' Trevor said, 'this ain't Marks and fucking Spencer's.'

Wesley moaned and wheedled. He told Trevor he'd take a cut in his money if Trevor spent the difference on buying better quality stuff. Eventually Trevor gave in. And he took a cut in his wages too.

After a month, Wesley used his own money to repaint the stall a bright green and bought some lights to hang on it to make it, as he said, 'more of a proposition.'

'Thing is,' Wesley observed, fingering the little string of lights,

'we have to get one of the shops to let us tap into their electricity sup-
ply, otherwise we can't use them.'

Trevor didn't really care about the lights but he was grudgingly
impressed by the pride Wesley seemed to take in things. He went to
the newsagents and the bakery and then finally into the pie and
mash shop. Fred, who ran the shop, agreed to let them use his power
if they paid him a tenner a week. Wesley said this seemed a reason-
able arrangement.

Things were going well. Wesley would spend hours juggling
apples for old ladies and did a trick which involved sticking the
sharpened end of five or six matches between the gaps in his teeth
and then lighting the matches up all at once. He'd burned his lips
twice that way and had a permanent blister under the tip of his nose.
He'd pick at the blister for something to do until the clear plasma
covered his fingers and then he'd say, 'Useful, this, if ever I got lost in
a desert. Water on tap.'

After six weeks things had reached a point where Trevor would
have done anything Wesley suggested. The stall was flourishing.
Business was good. Wesley worked his whack and more so. He kept
everyone amused with his tricks and his silly ideas. The customers
loved him. He was always clean.

What it was that made Wesley so perfect in Trevor's eyes was the
fact that he was a curious combination of immense irresponsibility—
he was a mad bastard—and enormous conscientiousness. He wanted
to *do* good but this didn't mean he had to *be* good.

One morning, two months after Wesley had started on the
stall, Trevor got a flat tyre on his way back from the wholesalers and
Wesley was obliged to set up on his own and do a couple of the early
deliveries himself into the bargain.

He took Fred at the pie and mash shop his regular bundle of
fresh parsley and then asked him for the extension cord so that he
could put up his lights on the stall. Fred was busy serving. He indicated with his thumb towards the back of the shop. 'Help yourself,
mate. The lead and everything's just behind the door. That's where
Trevor stashes them each night.'

Fred liked Wesley and he trusted him. Same as Trevor did and all the others. Wesley, if he'd had any sense, should have realized that he was well set up here.

Wesley wandered out to the rear of the shop. He pulled back the door and picked up the extension lead. Then he paused. It was cold. He looked around him.

A big room. Red, polished, concrete floors. Large, silver fridges. And quiet. He could hear the noise from the shop and, further off, the noise from the market. But in here it was still and the stillness and the silence had a special *sound*. Like water.

Wesley closed his eyes. He shuddered. He opened his eyes again, tucked the lead under his arm and beat a hasty retreat.

He was in a world of his own when Trevor finally arrived that morning. On two occasions Trevor said, 'Penny for them,' and then snapped his fingers in front of Wesley's unfocused eyes when he didn't respond.

'I'm thinking of my dad,' Wesley said. 'Don't ask me why.'

'Why?' said Trevor, who was in a fine good-humour considering his tyre hold-up.

'I was just in the pie and mash shop getting the extension lead for the lights. Out the back. And then I was suddenly thinking about my dad. You know, the navy and the sea and all the stuff we used to talk about when I was a kid.'

'Your dad still in the navy?' Trevor asked.

Wesley shook his head. 'Desk job,' he said.

'Probably those bloody eels,' Trevor said, bending down and picking up a crate of Coxes.

'What?'

'Those eels out the back. Making you think of the sea.'

'What?'

'In the fridges. He keeps the eels in there.'

'How's that?' Wesley's voice dipped by half an octave. Trevor didn't notice. He was wondering whether he could interest Wesley in selling flowers every Sunday as a side-interest. A stall was up for grabs on the Mile End Road close to the tube station. Sundays only.

'You're telling me he keeps live eels in those fridges?'

'What?'

'Live eels?' Wesley asked, with emphasis.

'In the fridges, yeah.' Trevor stopped what he was doing, straightened up, warned by the tone of Wesley's voice.

'What, like . . .' Wesley said, breathing deeply, 'swimming around in a big tank?'

'Nope.' Trevor scratched his head. 'Uh . . . like five or six long metal drawers, horizontal, yeah? And when you pull the drawers open they're all in there. Noses at one end and tails at the other. Big fuckers, though. I mean, five foot each or something.'

A woman came up to the stall and wanted to buy a lemon and two bananas. She asked Wesley for what she needed but Wesley paid her no heed.

'Hang on a second,' he said gruffly, holding up his flat hand, 'just shut up for a minute.'

He turned to Trevor. 'You know anything about eels?' he asked. Trevor knew enough about wild creatures to know that if Wesley had been a dog or a coyote his ears would be prickling, his ruff swelling.

'Not to speak of . . .' he said.

'Excuse me,' Wesley said to the customer, 'I'll be back in a minute,' and off he went.

Wesley strolled into the pie and mash shop. Fred was serving. Wesley waited patiently in line until it was his turn to be served.

'What can I get you, Wesley?' Fred asked, all jovial.

Wesley smiled back at him. 'Having a few problems with the lights on the stall,' he said. 'Could I just pop out the back and see if the plug's come loose or something?'

'Surely,' Fred said, thumbing over his shoulder. 'You know the lie of the land out there.'

Wesley went into the back room and up to one of the fridges. He took hold of the top drawer and pulled it open. The drawer contained water, and, just as Trevor had described, was crammed full of large, grey eels, all wriggling, eyes open, noses touching steel, tails touching steel. Skin rubbing skin rubbing skin.

Held in limbo, Wesley thought, in this black, dark space. Wanting to move. Wanting to move. Wanting to move. Nowhere to go. Like prison. Like purgatory.

Wesley closed the drawer. He shuddered. He covered his face with his soft hands. He breathed deeply. He hadn't been all that honest. What he'd said about his dad and everything. True enough, his dad had been in the navy, he'd travelled on ships the world over, to India and Egypt and Hong Kong. Only he never came back from the sea. Never came back home. Sort of lost interest in them all. Only sent a card once, a while after . . . a while after . . . to say he wouldn't ever be back again.

Wesley knew all about the sea, though. Knew all about fishes and currents and stingrays and everything. His mum had bought him a book about it. For his birthday when he was six. And so he knew about eels and how they all travelled from that one special place in the Sargasso Sea. Near the West Indies. That's where they were spawned and that's where they returned to die.

But first, such a journey! Feeding on plankton, the tiny, little transparent eels, newborn, floated to the surface of that great sea from their deep, warm home in its depths, drifted on the Gulf Stream, travelled over the Atlantic, for three summers, then into European waters, in huge numbers, swam upriver, from salt to freshwater. What a journey. And man couldn't tame them or breed them in captivity or stop them. Couldn't do it.

How did they know? Huh? Where to go? How did they know? But they knew! They knew where to go. Moving on, living, knowing, remembering. Something *in* them. Something inside. Passed down through the generations. An instinct.

Wesley uncovered his face and looked around him. He wanted to find another exit. He walked to the rear of the fridges and discovered a door, bolted. He went over and unbolted it, turned the key that had been left in its lock, came back around the fridges and strolled out into the shop.

'Thanks, mate,' Wesley said as he pushed his way past Fred and sauntered back outside again.

Trevor shook his head. 'No way,' he said. And he meant it.

'You've got to fucking do this for me, Trev,' Wesley said.

'Why?'

'You know how old some of those eels are?'

'No.'

'Some could be twenty years old. They've lived almost as long as you have.'

'They get them from a farm,' Trevor said. 'They aren't as old as all that.'

'They can't breed them in captivity,' Wesley said. 'They come from the Sargasso Sea. That's where they go to breed and to die.'

'The what?'

'Near the West Indies. That's where they go. That's what eels do. They travel thousands of miles to get here and then they grow and then they travel thousands of miles to get back again.'

'Sounds a bit bloody stupid,' Trevor said, 'if you ask me.'

'I'm a travelling man,' Wesley said, 'like my dad was. Don't try and keep me in one place. Don't try and lock me away.'

'They're eels, Wesley,' Trevor said, almost losing patience.

'Imagine how they're feeling,' Wesley said, 'caught in those fridges. Needing to travel. Needing it, needing it. Like an illness, almost. Like a fever. Dreaming of those hot waters, the deep ocean. Feeling cold steel on their noses, barely breathing, crammed together. Nowhere to go. No-fucking-where to go.'

'Forget it,' Trevor said, 'I've got no argument with Fred. Forget it, mate.'

'Take the van, Trevor,' Wesley said calmly. 'Drive it round the back, where they make the deliveries. I already unlocked the door.'

Off Wesley strode again. Trevor jangled the keys in his pocket, swore out loud and then ran after him.

Wesley crept in through the back entrance. He stood still a while. He could hear the chattering of customers in the shop and he could hear the sound of a van pulling into the delivery passage. He went outside, smiling wildly, happy to be fucking up, same as he always was.

'OK, Trev,' he said. 'Open the back doors but keep the tail up so's when I dump them in there they don't escape.'

Trevor looked immensely truculent but he did as Wesley asked.

Wesley went back inside, opened up one of the big, silver drawers, pushed his arms in, down and under all that silky, scaleless eel-flesh. He curled his arms right under, five eels, all wriggling, closed his arms around them and lifted. Water splashed and splattered. He looked over to the doorway leading into the shop, bit his lip, couldn't pause. The eels were whipping and lashing and swerving and writhing. He headed for the exit at top speed.

Trevor stood by the tailgate. When he saw the eels he swore. 'Fuck this man! Fuck this!'

Wesley threw the eels into the back of the van. 'Ten minutes,' he said, 'to get them back to water, otherwise they'll suffocate.'

Trevor watched the eels speeding and curling in the back of his van, swimming, almost, on air. He turned to say something but Wesley was gone. A minute later Wesley re-emerged. More eels. Like snakes. Faces like . . . faces like cats or otters or something. Little gills. Seal eyes.

As Wesley turned to go back in Trevor caught him by his shirt sleeve. 'I'm not doing this,' he said. 'Things are going well for us here. He's kept eels in this place for years, gets a delivery every week.'

Wesley turned on him. 'Give me the keys.'

'What?'

'Give me the shitting keys and I'll drive them to the canal myself.'

'This is stupid!'

'Don't call me fucking stupid. No one calls me that. Give me the fucking keys.'

Trevor took the keys out of his pocket and dropped them on the floor. He walked off. His eyes were prickling. 'Fuck it!' he shouted, and his voice echoed down the passageway.

Back inside, Wesley pulled open the third drawer, shoved his arms in, took hold of the eels. Water was everywhere now. Thank God it was lunchtime and Fred was busy. He held the fish tight and straightened up. He headed for the back door.

Outside, he met Fred. He was holding the five eels. He looked at Fred.

'What the hell are you doing?' Fred said.

'Why aren't you in the shop?' Wesley asked, stupidly.

'Jean's in,' Fred said, eyeing the eels. 'She's covering.'

'Oh. I didn't know that.'

'What are you doing with my eels?' Fred put out his arms. 'Give them to me.'

'No,' Wesley said. 'You can't own a wild thing.'

As he spoke he took a step back. Fred moved forwards and put himself between Wesley and the tailgate. The eels were itching to get free. Wesley's arms were aching. Fred took a step closer. He was short and square and tough as a boxing hare.

Wesley opened his arms. The eels flew into the air, landed, skidded, flipped, whipped, scissored, dashed. At top speed, they sea-snaked down the passageway, into the market, on to the main road.

'Down the Roman Road,' Wesley yelled. 'Back to the water, back to the frigging sea!'

Fred punched Wesley in the mouth. Jesus, Wesley thought, feels like all my teeth have shifted. He staggered, righted himself, clenched his hands into fists, by way of a diversion, then kicked Fred in the bollocks. Fred buckled.

Wesley skipped past him and sprang into the van. Got the keys in the ignition, started the engine, roared off in a cloud of black exhaust fume.

Beale's Place, Wright's Road, St Stephen's Road. Bollocks to the One Way! Sharp right at the tip of the market. Back on to the Roman Road, screw the traffic, on to the pavement, over the zebra crossing, past the video shop, the church, the intersection, Mile End Park. Sharp left. Over the grass. Tyre tracks. Mud-cut. Foot flat. Brakes.

How long had he taken? He didn't know. He could see the canal, just below. Dirty, dark waters. Dank and littery.

Down with the tailgate! The eels were like flying fish. The air made them pump and shudder. Like spaghetti in a heated pan, boiling and bubbling.

'Get in there!' Wesley yelled at them. 'The Grand Union Canal, the Thames, the Channel, the Ant-bloody-arctic.'

A cluster of eels shuddered down into the grass, rippled on to the concrete path, and then One! Two! Three! Four! Five! Six! Seven! Eight! Into the canal.

One eel split from the others, turned right and darted towards some undergrowth. One stayed in the back of the van, smaller than the others and less agile. Wesley grabbed it by its tail. He swung it in his arms. He ran to the edge of the canal. He threw it. The eel made a whip-cracking motion in the air, shaped itself like a fancy ribbon, just untied from a box of something wrapped and precious. Then splosh! It was under.

Wesley stood by the canal for several minutes. He inspected his hands, he sniffed, he stopped shaking. He started walking. He walked. He walked. He passed by a fisherman. He stopped walking. He looked over his shoulder. 'Which way is it to the sea?' he asked casually. 'From here, I mean?'

The fisherman gave this question some consideration while sucking his tongue and rolling his rod between his two hands.

'I should think,' he said, eventually, 'I should think it's in the exact opposite direction from the one you're travelling.' Then he turned, stared down along the path Wesley had just trodden, and pointed.

BRACES

After she'd eaten her sandwiches, Joy would push her hand into her mouth, manipulate her fingers—Wesley could hear the clink as her short nails touched steel—and grunt and puff as she laboriously pulled her braces out. She'd had problems with her top row ever since she'd lost her first set of milk teeth. The main front incisor was buckled and protrusive, had a gap to its left but partially covered its neighbour to the right.

To rectify this problem, a dentist had fitted Joy with a thin wire which circled her front teeth and was held in place by a large, plastic disc.

This disc had been specifically modelled to the contours of the roof of Joy's mouth. Not modelled well enough, though, by every indication, because bits of bread and fruit and food and sweet-stuff always got lodged under it while she ate. They snook and snuck and jostled against the wire and the roof of her mouth. They stuck around and niggled her, even after gargling.

Wesley watched as Joy sucked her teeth and then inspected the brace as it lay on her hand. It was semi-transparent. It made him think of jelly fish and the middle of an oyster. 'Ruff! Ruff!' he barked, and bounced around like a dog so that he didn't have to watch her as she picked at the residue on her brace with her fingers and then licked them clean with her tongue. It was like she was eating a second meal, he thought, feeling intimate twinges in his gut.

Joy, distracted from her brace by Wesley's barking, glanced over at him. 'Shut up, big mouth!' she yelled, and then, 'Crunchy peanut butter!' she glowered. 'Tell your mum to buy smooth next time. It's easier.'

Wesley stopped bouncing and barking. He stood perfectly still, like she'd asked, and nodded submissively. 'Will do,' he said.

Wesley had invented a series of rules for himself. He was nine years old and had a terrible strawberry-coloured nerve rash on his right cheek which he'd had for so long that even his mother acted like it was a birthmark and told the people at his new school—his teacher, the dinner ladies—that it was simply something he was born with.

His mother let him do just as he pleased. If he wanted sweets she would give him some money. If he wanted a gun or a sword or a portable television she would buy it for him. She didn't like Joy, but she couldn't stop him from seeing her. She wouldn't dare, she wouldn't.

Wesley was so busy and there were so many things to do. Joy would come with him. She was a little bit older than him and she had a bad temper. Sometimes she tripped him up or spat at him and often she gave him Chinese burns.

'Stupid, stupid boy! Stupid boy!'

There were several children at his new school who asked him to play with them, but Joy told him that they were ignorant. 'They don't know,' she'd say, 'all the things we know.' And then she'd tell him to do something naughty as a dare and he'd do it because otherwise, Joy told him, he would break his arm or his mum would be in a car accident.

Joy was so pretty. She wore her yellow hair in a pony tail and she had blisters on her ankles and bruises on her knees.

One of his new friends at school was called Simon. Simon liked to play basketball and he could walk on his hands. Wesley liked Simon and even asked his mother to buy him a basketball jacket like the one Simon wore. Joy didn't like Simon, though, and she didn't like basketball.

'There's a new rule, Wesley,' she said, as they walked home from school one afternoon. 'If you play with Simon again then I'll hit you in the face. Like this.' Joy hit Wesley in the face. 'See?'

Wesley nodded. He touched his cheek where it stung.

'Good.' Joy smiled. She was happy again.

Wesley's mother was angry about the jacket. He brought it home and it was ripped and muddy. She held it up and inspected it.

'What happened, Wesley?'

Wesley didn't want to get Joy into trouble. He said nothing.

'Did someone at school do this to your jacket?'

He nodded.

'Who?'

He shrugged.

It was half past ten and Wesley's mother was walking past Wesley's bedroom. He'd been in bed for almost an hour and he should have been asleep by now. She stood outside his door and listened. It sounded as though Wesley was clapping his hands. Clap! Clap! Clap!

She pushed his door ajar and peered inside. Wesley was sitting up in bed and he was slapping his own face. Slapping his cheek. Slap, slap, slap! His eyes were blank as she approached but his cheeks were wet with tears. She caught hold of his hand. She kissed it. 'Lie down,' she whispered, and later, once he was sleeping, 'I love you.'

The week before the end of term, Wesley's mother had been called to the school to speak to Wesley's teacher. Wesley had attacked one of the other children with a broken tree branch. The boy was called Simon and could walk on his hands. Wesley had attacked him while he was performing this trick and had knocked him over and then hit him in the face with the broken branch. He had grazed his hands and his face was scratched.

Wesley's mother was embarrassed and confused and concerned and she didn't quite know what to do. Eventually she said, 'I thought Wesley and Simon were friends . . .'

The teacher nodded. 'They were a while ago but lately Wesley has become rather withdrawn.'

Wesley's mother scratched her forehead. 'You know, a few weeks back I bought Wesley a new basketball jacket and then he came home from school a couple of days later and it was muddy and ripped and torn. Do you think it's possible that Simon might have been bullying him?'

The teacher sighed. 'I don't know. I don't think so.'

'But it's possible?'

The teacher shrugged. 'Possible, but unlikely. About Wesley's father . . .'

'He's away at sea most of the time.'

'Maybe Wesley misses him . . . ?'

'It's not that.' Wesley's mother's face seemed to glisten under the classroom's fluorescent light. 'It's not his father he's missing.' She paused. 'It's his brother.'

The teacher put her head to one side but said nothing.

'His brother died four years ago when Wesley was five. He got shut in an old discarded refrigerator and suffocated. Wesley was out playing with him when it happened.'

'I see.'

'But he's all right now. He's a perfectly normal little boy and he knows that I'm always here for him and that I love him . . .'

'It's only five days,' Wesley told Joy, 'until the school holidays, and then we can play together all the time.'

Joy was very full of herself lately, but it seemed like the more success she had with her high-handed techniques and her bullying, the less content she felt about things.

'Wesley,' she said, picking at the blister on her ankle until white plasma squirted out of it and slid into her sock. 'You are my special friend, aren't you? You will look after me, won't you?'

'I will, I will,' Wesley said, passionately, his eyes filling.

His mother had picked him up in the car because it was the last day of school and he had some books and some drawings to take home with him.

'So, Wesley,' his mum said, 'what shall we do in the holidays?

Shall we go to the cinema? Shall we go to Whipsnade Zoo?' She stopped off at their local Wimpy Bar on the way home and bought him a burger and a milkshake.

They were almost home and then Wesley became tense and distracted.

'Mum,' he said, 'we must go back.'

'Where?'

'School.'

'Why?'

'Joy. I left her in the classroom.'

'What?'

'I left Joy in the classroom. That was the last time I saw her and now she's gone.'

Wesley's mother pulled the car over to the side of the road. 'Wesley,' she said softly, 'I'm sure Joy can easily find you if she wants to.'

Wesley's eyes were wide and frightened. 'But she's in the classroom! We must get her! If she stays in the classroom she'll starve over the summer and she'll die!'

His mother smiled. 'Maybe a cleaner will go in there later and she'll get out then. Or maybe the teacher left a window open. She'll find her own way home.'

Wesley started sobbing. He was inconsolable.

Wesley's teacher met Wesley's mother in the school car park. It was eight o'clock and Wesley had been crying for four and a half hours. He was sitting in the car, still crying.

'You must think I'm a fool,' Wesley's mother said, 'but I can't stand seeing him so distressed. He's just got it into his head that his little friend is locked in the classroom and nothing I can say . . .'

The teacher looked over towards the car. Wesley's face was puce with sobbing. 'When his brother died,' she said gently, 'how did he react?'

Wesley's mother shook her head. 'Just quiet and frightened. Not a tear.'

The teacher sighed. 'This is his way of grieving for his brother,' she said. 'If we unlock the classroom, it'll be almost like we're pretending that we can bring his brother back. Do you know what I mean?'

Wesley's mother was scowling but she sort of understood. She said, 'Wesley makes up little games and little rules for himself all the time . . .'

'And why,' his teacher added, 'would he have decided to lock this invisible friend of his in the classroom if he hadn't wanted, in his heart of hearts, to finally be rid of her?'

The car door slammed. Wesley was out of the car and racing towards the school buildings, in the dark, towards his classroom. His mother, his teacher, called out and then followed him.

They found Wesley with his face pushed up against the window of the schoolroom. He was looking for Joy but he couldn't see her in the darkness. 'Open it!' he screamed. 'Let her out! Open it! Open it!'

And when they wouldn't open it he started slapping his face on his bad cheek. His teacher tried to hold him and his mother tried to hug him. But they wouldn't open it. His teacher kept saying, 'She's not in there. You don't need her. You lost her because you wanted to.'

And his mother kept saying, 'It's not Christopher. Christopher is dead now, Wesley. Christopher is dead now.'

Wesley broke free. He ran from them, screaming, his arms windmilling, so angry that they'd mentioned Christopher, so angry that Joy was stuck in the classroom and they wouldn't let him have her back. And he'd never been angry before, not really. Joy was the angry one. Joy was the cross one who made him do bad things but now Joy was gone and he was angry. They had taken her. They had taken her. And now she would starve during the summer holidays. Oh, his throat—oh, his chest—oh, his *heart*.

Joy sat at a desk. Now what? She was bored. It was dark in here. There was nothing to do. She found some chalk and scribbled on the blackboard. She drew a big white rectangle. She stared at it for a while. 'Christopher,' she whispered, 'come and play with me. Christopher, Christopher, come and play.'

Nothing happened. She scratched at the blisters on her ankles. She closed her eyes. And then she moved herself, in an electric current, in a bolt of static, in an electrical pulse, out of that classroom and into Wesley's brain.

Wesley was still running and shouting and screaming. He was making so much noise that he didn't even know Joy had come back to him. She moved herself, her braces and her blisters and her bruises, into the darkest corner of Wesley's mind, that place where Christopher was. And they played together then, Joy and Christopher, the two of them, quietly, silently. Bitter, ugly, cruel little games which nobody knew about.

Even Wesley stopped remembering who they really were.

MR
LIPPY

The first time Iris met Mr Lippy he was in Hunstanton, sitting on the ocean wall, watching the tide from the Wash as it lapped away at the concrete just below his feet. His right fist was wrapped up in a thick, white gauze. Iris guessed straight away that he must have sustained this injury in a fight. She should have avoided him. Naturally. If only she'd known what was good for her. Perhaps she didn't know. Or if she did, she didn't care.

'Hi,' she said.

'I don't talk to girls,' he responded.

'You from the West Country?' she asked, brutally, registering some kind of rural burr in his voice.

He said nothing.

'How'd you hurt your hand, then?'

He ignored her.

'Live around here?'

She sat down next to him and swung her legs. She was eighteen and liked a challenge. She wore sandals and a halter-neck top even though it was late October.

His bottom lip stuck out while she spoke to him. He pouted without thinking, like he was sulking about something, only he didn't know what, didn't know, even, that he was sulking.

'What's a good-looking man like you got to sulk about?' she said.

'Pardon?' He turned and looked at her.

'Mr Lippy!' She laughed. She stuck her bottom lip out, mimicking him.

'I wasn't doing that!'

'Wanna bet?'

'I wasn't!' He switched on his brain and stared at her properly, for the first time.

From that moment onwards, Iris always called him Mr Lippy if he scowled or sulked or swore at her. His real name was Wesley but she called him Wes. She always wanted things different from the way they were.

Wesley had yearned all his life to be close to the sea. His dad had been a sailor. But he was born inland and had lived there until he'd arrived at the Wash under his own steam aged twenty-four. Now he was twenty-eight.

Sometimes he worked on the funfair in Hunstanton. Sometimes he went potato picking. He worked in the sugar beet factory until they closed it, and then, after a spate in the arcade, got a job ferrying tourists across the Wash in an open-topped, antiquated hovercraft to visit Seal Island.

Iris didn't know that Wesley's broken fist had been sustained, not in a fight as she'd imagined, but in an accident at work: one of the other lads had reversed the hovercraft too close to the ocean wall where Wesley was stationed at the back of the craft, ready to put out the gang-plank. The lad's foot had slipped off the brake on to the accelerator, and Wesley's hand had been crushed that way.

An accident. But Wesley relished the pain. He liked punishment. And anyhow, he'd received several hundred pounds in compensation, just like that. A gift from the gods. So he opened a bank account and nested it there.

Iris was living in a bed and breakfast facing the seafront. She was a bully but he thought it was because life had been hard on her. He was wrong. They made love under a single duvet. If Wesley got carried away, if he threatened to come before she was ready, then she'd squeeze his bad fist until he saw only stars. It was good, she thought, to keep him distracted. Just a little bit.

He'd known her for a month when she told him she was pregnant. She didn't know anything about him.

'I don't care,' he said, 'what happens, really, so long as I can stay close to the sea.'

'Why?' She was only two weeks pregnant but already she felt different about things and she wanted Wesley to feel different too.

'I don't know. My dad was a sailor.'

'Really? And your mum?'

'She lives in Gloucester.'

'Yeah? Think she'll be pleased?'

Wesley shrugged. Iris waited for Wesley to ask about her mum and dad. He didn't ask. She wanted him to.

'Do you love me?'

'I'm used to being on my own.'

'Don't you have any plans? For the future, I mean?'

Wesley rearranged the gauze on his fist.

'Not me,' he said.

'Why not?'

Wesley closed his eyes.

Seal Island. In the summer the boat was packed to its gills with children. Clutching their packed lunches and their cans of fizzy pop. They'd all passed the morning on the big wheel and the dodgems, eating candy-floss and bags of sticky honeycomb. And now they were headed for Seal Island. They had dreams of palm tress and Captain Hook and hidden treasure to help them over the brown sea and the lurching waves. An island, full of basking seals.

When the tide was out, you might see the sluttish brown outline of the sandbank. You might see a lethargic seal, on its edge, rolling to the bank's perimeter, and then the flip of its tail as it swam off and under. If the tide was in, you were lucky to see that much.

Seal Island. Wesley loved it. Every day. The tears, the screams, the disappointment. He loved that stuff. He'd turn and he'd look at the children, the occasional mum, the odd uncle. And he'd think, 'Good, they should learn that life is shit. Good they should know it.'

Iris became worried about Wesley's motivation. 'That's cruel,' she'd say, 'to lead the little buggers into thinking that they're getting more for their money than they've a right to expect.'

'No crueller,' Wesley said, 'than leading them into thinking that life is anything better than a bitch.'

One day Wesley came back to Iris's room to discover her parents there. They weren't at all as he'd imagined.

'Mum and Dad want me to come home again,' Iris said, 'and I want you to come with me, Wes.'

'Home, where?' he asked, shifting his weight from foot to foot.

She'd promised him it was close to the sea. In the back of the car, they sat. One suitcase between them. 'Nearly there,' she kept saying. 'Nearly, nearly.'

Iris's father showed Wesley the shop, the nursery, the rabbit pen, the pet section, the field with the ponies, the café. The whole kit and caboodle. Finally he showed him the owl sanctuary. Twenty cages.

'What's it mean?' Wesley asked. 'Sanctuary?'

'Couldn't survive in the wild,' Iris's father said. 'Some come from exotic places.'

Wesley stared at the owls. They stared back. Not blinking.

'You never told me,' Wesley said, that night, in their bedroom, 'that your parents were rich like this.'

'Never asked,' Iris said.

'I don't understand,' Wesley said, 'why anyone should want to run away from something that's as good as here.'

Iris shrugged. 'I'm back, aren't I?' she said, all saucy.

'It's far from the sea,' Wesley said.

'Fuck that shit.'

He turned to look at her.

'You don't even like the sea,' she said, 'not really. It just makes you sad and angry. It's all mixed up in your head with some stupid fantasy about your dad.'

Wesley was injured by this. It was almost as though, he thought, Iris didn't respect his reasons. Like his reasons weren't good enough.

Big eyes. Big wings. Big beaks. He'd feed them little chicks and small white mice. Their keeper, Derek, told Wesley all about them. 'See those big eyes,' he'd say. 'Well, that leads people into thinking that they're wise and all, but they aren't.'

'No?'

'No. Their eye sockets take up much of the space in their skulls, so their brain is as tiny as a hazelnut, just about.'

Wesley would stare at the owls for hours on end, unblinking, but only during the week. At weekends he avoided the sanctuary because then it was crowded with tourists who whistled and screamed and pointed. Some of the cages had little notices which read: MIND FINGERS AND NOSES. THESE ARE WILD ANIMALS. DO NOT TOUCH WIRE MESH.

Wesley worked in the nursery. Sometimes he helped out in the cafeteria. Iris would trail around after him, trying to make him smile.

'Aren't you happy here?' she'd ask. 'Don't you love me?'

He did quite like her, actually.

'Do you resent me being pregnant?'

'Nope.'

'Will we ring your mother yet and tell her about it?'

'Nope.'

'Why not? Why *not*?' It had started to gall Iris, his inability to celebrate *anything*.

One owl especially. He'd stare and stare. It was as big as a spaniel. Grey feathered. Pop-eyed, crazy-looking. Like an emu. Like something unimaginable.

Wesley wondered what would happen if he set the bird free. When he was younger he'd dreamed about freedom, but now he was resigned to a life of drudgery. Free, he'd whisper, and then, die. Free. Die. Free. Die. Free. Die.

Derek had told him, you see, that if the owls were released they would starve to death or some of them would freeze. They were too bloody conspicuous, Wesley thought, for their own safety.

'Why don't you want me to meet your family? Are you ashamed of me? Am I too young?'

Wesley stood up, picked up his coat, as if to leave the room.

'Where are you going?'

'Outside.'

'Where? To look at those bloody owls again. I swear you spend more time looking at those owls than at me.'

He left her. She followed him, in her slippers, barely dressed. It was dark out. He ignored her. He went to the owl pens.

In the dark he could hardly see them, only the white ones. He made his way to the pen of his favourite. If he stared and he stared he could make out the pale moon-slip of her beak.

'What are you doing?' Iris whispered.

Wesley tried to see the owl more clearly but his eyes weren't yet adapted. He could hear the others, though. Ghostly trills. Occasional squeals.

'It's worse at night, don't you think?' he asked. 'To keep them here?'

'What?'

'People watch them during the day and they don't seem too bad, but at night, that's their time. That's when they wake and want to fly.'

Iris crossed her arms over her chest. It was cold out here.

'I'm haunted,' Wesley said, eventually, 'by things that happened in the past.'

'What things?' Iris asked. 'Why won't you tell me, Wes?'

'I lost my right hand,' Wesley said.

'What?' Iris was confused now.

'People kept leaving me. When I was a boy.'

'Your dad?' she said, trying to follow him.

'And all the time,' he said, 'I wanted to try and find the thing I'd lost. Searching. Searching. Punishing everyone.'

'What?' She was shivering now. It was cold. It was cold.

'But I'll tell you,' he said, 'that I've finally realized something.

All the time I thought I was punishing others I was actually only punishing myself, but not *properly*.'

He was trying to see the owl in the darkness. He could make out her shape now.

'Let's go in,' Iris said. 'Let's talk inside.'

He turned to face her. 'I must do something,' he said, 'to show you how much I love you.'

'What?' He had lost her, completely.

'For the baby,' he said.

He stretched open his right hand in front of her face. For a moment she was frightened that he might try to hurt her. He might hit her or smother her with that hand. But then he turned from her and slowly, deliberately, finger by finger, he pushed his hand into the wire mesh of that giant and wakeful emu-owl's cage.

He could see his white fingers in the darkness, and finally, too, he could see her. She could see him. She was still. She was silent. He heard one of the other birds calling and then she was on him. Ripping and tearing with her beak like a blade.

Iris screamed.

She couldn't forgive him. On his right hand was left only a thumb. She griped that she'd almost lost their child with the shock of it. He apologized. Over the following months he kept apologizing. He stopped pouting. He couldn't stop smiling now. Sometimes she'd catch him touching his spoiled hand with his good one, talking to himself, but so softly, like it was a child's face he was stroking.

On the night their baby was born he left her. An envelope lay on the bed. Her parents found it and brought it to her. Inside was a cheque for several hundred pounds and a note which said only: 'Heading Inland.' That was all.

Skin

Stephanie was over fifteen minutes late. Jane sat in a window-seat and read her paperback (bought for exactly this kind of occasion), intermittently sipping her half pint of lager.

They had arranged to meet in the Red Lion at seven o'clock. Jane hated sitting in pubs alone, she felt conspicuous, although in fact she was no more conspicuous than any woman who sat in a pub alone might be. She was reading an early Jilly Cooper which she had bought second-hand from a book stall outside the Festival Hall during the previous summer.

In general (since her 'A' levels) she had preferred to read magazines rather than novels, but in certain situations she felt that magazines created an unnecessarily promiscuous impression. Girls on the tube who read them often had long, painted fingernails, smart shoes and sheer tights. Magazines represented a disposable lifestyle; Jane preferred the idea of an indispensable lifestyle: at twenty-four, she worked in a bank and was rather conservative.

She looked up from her novel and stared momentarily out of the window—through a pair of yellowy nets—hoping to catch a glimpse of Stephanie trotting down the road towards her, but instead, all she saw was the reflection of a nearby street-light in the glass of the window, a bleary, streaky, visual sludge. Her eyes returned to the words on the page.

The pub was empty apart from two men slouching at the bar, a young couple, who seemed to be recovering from a recent argument, sitting in an alcove, and over towards the door a pensioner who was reading a late edition of the *Evening Standard*. Someone had put some money into the juke box, which was playing 'Suspicious Minds.' Jane imagined that it might have been the male half of the young couple.

As her eyes sped across the page, Jane thought for a moment about her boyfriend Mitch and Stephanie's boyfriend Chris. She wondered what they were doing. Maybe they were watching the football on television, or maybe they were playing snooker.

The pub's doors swung open. Everybody turned towards them. Jane had earlier been engaged in a heated debate with herself about how to react when the doors opened. Initially she had decided that it was best if she ignored the various comings and goings around her. She had endeavoured to create the impression of calculated indifference, preoccupation, oblivion. Later, however, she had decided that it might be appropriate to look up fleetingly from her book towards the door so that people who might be looking at her would know immediately that the only reason for her continuing presence in the pub was the fact that she was waiting for someone. She was expecting someone. It made her feel less vulnerable, also less approachable.

On this occasion she was glad she had looked up. Stephanie stood in the doorway, looking ruffled and indecisive. Jane waved at her and smiled. Stephanie caught her eye, smiled back, relieved, then pointed her finger towards the bar. Jane nodded. Stephanie then pointed a finger towards Jane's drink. Jane shook her head and placed a prim, flat hand over the top of her glass. Stephanie walked to the bar and ordered a gin and tonic.

Jane watched her, at last relaxing in the pub's worn, red velvet environs, putting down her book and leaning back in her chair. She watched Stephanie as she waited for her drink and then paid for it. Stephanie was still wearing her uniform—she worked in John Lewis, the Oxford Street branch—and her hair was tied back in a ponytail. She looked young for twenty-four. Jane thought it must be the way that she had tied back her hair. As Stephanie approached her Jane said ironically, 'I'm surprised the barman served you, Steph, you don't look eighteen with your hair tied back like that.'

Stephanie put her spirits glass down and squeezed in between the table and the seat. As she sat down she touched her hair with a free hand and looked unnecessarily self-conscious, then said, 'I think the barman'd serve a large squirrel if it appeared at the counter and asked for a pint of lager. He doesn't look too discriminating.'

Jane shrugged. Stephanie pointed towards Jane's book. 'Jilly Cooper. Good?'

Jane picked up the book and put it into her bag. 'Something to read. It's not like you to be late.'

Stephanie frowned, 'I know. I've had a bit of a strange day. Sorry.'

Jane raised her eyebrows, professionally interested. 'Busy?'

Stephanie shrugged. 'Not too bad. You?'

Jane shook her head. 'So so.'

They both picked up their drinks and took a sip. On returning her glass to the table Stephanie put her hands to the back of her head and pulled her hairband out. She then shook free her hair which fell about her shoulders in semi-curls. Jane watched her as she did this and couldn't help thinking that Stephanie was looking particularly well, strangely spruce, as though she had just had a shower, an odd post-swimming clean-washed look. She sniffed the air for a trace of chlorine but could smell none. 'You haven't been swimming, have you? Marshall Street pool?'

Stephanie looked guilty, 'No. Well, yes. Well, I had a shower, that's all.'

Jane frowned. 'Where's your towel? Why did you have a shower? That's odd. Are you wearing any make-up? Why did you have a shower?'

Stephanie looked overwhelmed, 'I . . . I needed a shower. I hired a towel.'

Jane began to pull a fastidious expression.

'Honestly, it was perfectly clean.' Stephanie's face crumpled. 'Oh God! I feel . . . I don't know. I was going to say I feel awful, but in fact I feel almost the opposite.' She thought for a moment. 'I feel rather, almost hysterical. Pent up. I've done the strangest thing.'

Jane was frowning. 'Is everything all right at work?'

Stephanie nodded wordlessly.

'Chris? Nothing's happened between you and Chris?'

Stephanie shook her head, 'No, Chris is fine.' She frowned. 'I don't feel as if I can tell you . . .'

Jane clucked her tongue, exasperated. 'What can't you tell me? You always tell me everything. What's going on?'

They had been best friends since primary school. Jane had always been dominant and Stephanie softer, better intentioned but easily swayed. She saw life as a set of rules which she obeyed. Jane saw life as a set of rules which she supported. She thought Stephanie's passivity occasionally subversive, but knew her well enough to be sure of her back-up and understanding in most situations. They came from the same stock, a simmering, warm if unadventurous stew of suburban values; their schooling the same, parents the same, boyfriends the same, and their ambitions . . . ?

Jane stared at Stephanie across the table and wondered what it was that she had done. She shoved around a set of geometric boundaries in her mind, a variety of fully contained and containable possibilities. 'Pregnant?'

Stephanie grimaced. She looked up at Jane and felt almost helpless; she must tell her because who else could she tell? (God knows, not her mother.) And the notion of saying nothing was virtually inconceivable. She knew that all acts suffered in the doing because of the inevitability of the telling. She must tell her.

Jane watched, waiting. Stephanie took a further sip of her drink, laced her hands together on her lap and then took a deep breath. 'I'm downstairs in the Men's Knitwear Department this week, occasionally on the till, but mainly involved with stock, pricing, you know . . .'

Jane nodded, she had a picture of the knitwear department in her mind, and a cardigan that she wanted to buy for Mitch. 'Knitwear Department. So?'

Stephanie looked down at her hands. 'Well, I was . . . It was dead during the last hour, you know how it can be, hardly anyone about, and I was tidying up, straightening jumpers on hangers and refolding . . . I don't know if it's the same in the bank, but the last hour is always the worst and the best, the way the minute-hand keeps you in but the hour-hand points towards the door . . .'

Jane was nonplussed by Stephanie's attempts to wax lyrical. 'The last hour. Right.'

Stephanie took a deep breath. She knew this wasn't going to be easy. 'I was folding up some vests and socks when I noticed a man near by, well, I think that initially there were two of them, but the other one wandered off. They were skins, really tall in puffy green jackets and tight, short jeans and boots . . .'

Jane frowned. 'White trash.'

Stephanie bit her lip and nodded. 'Really short hair, just like, just really short, soft, like a coloured shadow on the scalp. But smart, not like normal skins, with bleached trousers and tatoos on their necks, like ugly roosters, dirty. This one was smart . . .'

Jane reiterated her earlier point, which made a class distinction as opposed to a value judgement. 'White trash. Yuk. Shoplifting I bet. Pringle jumpers or long socks for under their boots.'

Stephanie nodded. 'Socks.'

She was silent for a moment. In her mind she outlined what she was going to say and felt her stomach contract with the extremity of it. She thought momentarily of not telling and then knew that she must tell. She tried a different approach. 'Do you ever have that feeling sometimes when everything feels sort of, strong, like soup or evaporated milk, sort of condensed, as though some things just must happen in a specific way, like a recipe . . . ?'

Jane looked uncomprehending. 'Like what? No, I don't think so.'

Stephanie frowned. 'Like when you first fell in love with Mitch, like when you first decided to have your hair cut, or the feeling you get when you want to dive into a pool but know that the water is cold, but you want to dive in anyway.'

Jane sipped her lager and watched as one of the men at the bar walked over and put some money into the juke box. Doris Day started singing 'Move Over Darling.' She tapped her foot in time and tried to respond appropriately to what Stephanie was saying.

'I don't know what you mean. Did you go swimming after all? Why all this talk about swimming all of a sudden?'

Stephanie looked crestfallen. She knew that she was already losing Jane's sympathy. 'That was a simile. Remember? Like Gerard Manley Hopkins or someone. I was trying to explain a feeling.'

Jane rolled her eyes. 'Just tell me what you *mean*. What about that skinhead, the shoplifter. Did you catch him?'

Stephanie nodded. 'Yes, I caught him.'

'And then?' Jane drained her glass of lager and placed it decisively down on a beermat. Stephanie studied her own glass, watched the condensation on the exterior of its bowl and around its base. The glass left a ring of moisture on the surface of the table when she picked it up. She took a sip and replaced it, but in a different place so that she could study the damp ring on the table's surface, moisten her finger in the dampness and then draw on the polished wood. She drew another circle. 'I walked over to him and told him that I knew he had placed some socks inside his jacket. I asked whether he intended to pay for them.'

'What did he say? Didn't you try and call the store detective? I would have.'

Stephanie drew two dots inside the circle and then a straight line. The circle was now a face, a round, rather simple but glum-looking face. 'No, I didn't call the store detective. It was almost twenty-to-six. I didn't want the hassle.'

'Weren't you frightened?'

She nodded. 'I suppose so. He was tall. At first he just stared at me. Then he turned, as if he was going to walk away.'

'And then?'

'I put out my hand and grabbed his arm. He had one of those weird jackets on, a puffy green jacket. He must've been almost six feet tall. Mean-looking.'

Jane stopped tapping her foot as the Doris Day song finished on the juke box. She looked over to see if the two young men at the bar were going to put another song on but they had recently been joined by a third man and were deep in conversation. Stephanie smiled at her. 'Can I get you another drink yet?'

Jane shook her head. 'Not yet. Wait a while. So what happened then?'

Stephanie looked down at the table again, at the face she had drawn, which was already evaporating. She picked up some more moistness from the ring left by the glass and cut across the face with several rapid strokes. 'I took hold of his arm and said, "You can't leave here until you put those socks back." He grinned at me and said, "Which socks? I haven't got any." '

'Did he pull his arm away?'

Stephanie looked disconcerted. 'Um. No. I don't think he pulled his arm away. It was all very quick. The aisle was empty. The whole shop seemed empty.'

'What did you say then?'

Stephanie took another sip of her drink. 'I said, "You have got socks there, I saw you pick them up. I'm not stupid. Please just put them back and I'll leave you alone." '

'And did he?'

She shook her head. 'No. He looked down at my hand on his arm and started to smile. He said, "I haven't got any socks, only on my feet." I said, "I know you've got them," and indicated with my other hand towards a bulge in his jacket where I'd seen him put the socks.'

'Why didn't you call one of the store detectives? I'm surprised they didn't notice him come in. Probably on a tea break.'

Jane created her own scenarios; scrupulous and disapproving. Stephanie shrugged. 'I don't know where they were. Anyway, I could handle it. He didn't turn nasty. I think he was surprised. I wouldn't let him go.'

Jane smiled. 'You're small but ferocious, like a terrier. Did he give you the socks?'

Stephanie tried to smile back. 'After a while, yes. He put his hand inside his jacket and produced the socks. He threw them on to the nearest shelf. The shop seemed so quiet. He was still smiling at me.'

Jane wrinkled up her nose. 'Yuk. Creepy.'

Stephanie continued, 'And then he started to apologize. I don't know why. I hadn't expected him to. He started to apologize like he'd offended me somehow. It was strange.'

Jane nodded. 'At least he had some manners. Did you let him go? I would've called the store detectives. I suppose it was too late by then though, but he shouldn't have got away with it. Did he just leave?'

Stephanie took a deep breath. 'Well, while he was apologizing I realized that I still had my hand on his arm. We sort of realized at the same time. And then, and then . . .'

Jane raised her eyebrows, 'And then?'

Stephanie bit her lip. 'Then we, sort of, kissed.'

Jane looked so shocked that Stephanie wanted to laugh, but couldn't quite bring herself to.

'What? A proper kiss? A kiss?'

Stephanie nodded. 'It just happened.'

Jane fought down two competing impulses in her gut, the first of total disapproval, the second of total fascination. Stephanie watched this conflict translate itself on to Jane's face and said, 'It didn't mean anything.'

Finally Jane asked, 'What sort of a kiss? A French kiss? What did you say after?'

Stephanie blushed. 'A French kiss. His mouth tasted of cough sweets and smoke. We didn't really say anything. If he did say something, it was only to apologize about the socks again.'

Jane frowned. 'So what did you do? After?'

Stephanie shrugged. 'I . . . I suppose I put my hand under his shirt. He was wearing a T-shirt.'

'You were looking for more socks? You were, weren't you?'

Stephanie burst out laughing. She had recovered from her earlier embarrassment. 'No. By then I had forgotten about the socks. I was feeling his stomach and his chest. His chest was hairless, but surprisingly firm.'

Jane was silent for a moment, trying to understand what this situation meant. Stephanie had never been a promiscuous person. She stared at her face across the table and looked for any perceptible signs of distress. There were none. After a while she said, 'Why did it happen? You've never done this sort of thing before. I thought you were faithful to Chris. I don't understand you.'

Stephanie sighed. 'I was trying to explain earlier. Of course I've never done anything like this before. It was strange, as though . . . like a compulsion. Inevitable. Dangerous but compulsive. I don't know. I can't understand it myself. It's not as though we were immediately physically attracted. It was more the situation itself, the differences between us . . .'

Jane interrupted. 'I suppose it was only a kiss. Maybe it was just mutual attraction.'

Stephanie looked momentarily indecisive and then said, 'No, that's the whole point. It wasn't just a kiss. We had sex.'

To fill the following silence she added, 'The more I think about it, the more I'm convinced that it was just a power thing. There was something explosive about the situation, the confrontation, something strangely . . . well, strange. Erotic.'

Stephanie looked down at her hands. She had never used the word 'erotic' before. Especially in front of someone like Jane. Using the word was almost as much fun as the sex had been. She felt like D. H. Lawrence.

Jane was devastated. She looked at Stephanie and couldn't understand her, she couldn't contain what she had done in the relevant compartments of her brain. She wondered whether Stephanie was now a slag. A slut. Finally she said, 'You behaved like a slut, with some big, ugly skinhead.'

Stephanie shrugged. 'If you mean "slut" in a good way, then yes, I did. The shop was so quiet. We made love behind some racks of mohair jumpers. Nobody came.'

She smiled at her unintentional pun. Jane missed the joke. Her ideas of Stephanie had now been so radically altered that any coherent discussion about motivation and intent seemed entirely fruitless. But she was like a small, common bird, like a sparrow, a pack creature, something that acts on impulse. She wanted to know the details, but this desire compromised her and she knew it. Eventually she said, 'How was he?' She had never been able to ask this question about the sexual relations between Stephanie and Chris, but this was different. Stephanie looked for a moment like she wasn't going to reply, then she said, 'Good. Strange. Condensed . . .'

'Did he have . . . ?'

Stephanie frowned. 'Don't ask. It wasn't like that.'

Jane felt coarse and embarrassed. She snapped defensively, 'I'm not particularly interested in what it was like. Don't flatter yourself.' She was silent for a second and then added, 'How can we even discuss it? How can we talk about it? There's nothing to say.'

Stephanie frowned, trying to understand what Jane meant. She said, 'I thought I should tell you.'

Jane raised her eyebrows and tried to look ironic. 'Tell me? Tell me what? I think you should consider telling Chris. I don't think he'll be too sympathetic, though.'

Stephanie cupped the bowl of her glass in both hands. She was temporarily confused. She had known that Jane would be disapproving, surprised, maybe even shocked, but the coherence and simplicity of what she had experienced . . . She repeated the word silently to herself and felt it to be totally appropriate. Simplicity. That expresses it best. It was so simple, unadulterated, natural and yet unnatural.

She tried to articulate her thoughts. 'It wasn't sordid, just natural and kind of obvious, that's why it's so hard to describe . . .'

Jane shrugged. 'Just sex. Are you seeing each other again?'

Stephanie sighed and shook her head. 'I shouldn't think so. I hadn't thought about it like that. It wasn't like that.'

Jane seemed unimpressed. 'So you won't be seeing him again. But will you have sex with other people at work? When it's quiet, just before closing?'

She was smirking. Stephanie felt at once angry and misunderstood. She spoke instead of thinking, before thinking. 'Maybe this has changed me. I didn't feel immediately different, but I think that I might actually be. I knew you wouldn't approve, but I thought you'd be . . .' She tried to collect her thoughts.

Jane turned away from Stephanie and looked over her shoulder and towards the juke box. It was silent. She wondered whether she could be bothered to go over and put some money into it. It then struck her that this might in fact be a good idea, a means to walk away from the conversation, to bring about a hiatus, a gap, a space, so that when she returned they could discuss other things. She took her purse from her bag and stood up. She said, 'I'm going to put some music on the juke box.'

Stephanie didn't reply. She nodded. She watched Jane walk over to the juke box and thought, 'Suddenly we have no common ground. When she comes back to the table she won't discuss this with me again. It's as though nothing can be expressed between us which will make sense, which we can both understand. When she comes back to the table she will be assured in her own mind that she is now better than me, that she has something over me, and yet . . .'

She sighed and pushed a piece of hair that had fallen across her face behind her ear. 'And yet something so incredible has happened.' She felt sad, almost bitter, but in her heart she knew that the space that had sprung up between them, the vacuum, had now opened up inside her, and it was a positive space that could be filled with so many things; ideas, possibilities. She thought, 'Words are like gifts, some people are generous and some frugal.' She decided to make herself a present by keeping quiet.

Symbiosis: Class Cestoda

The first thing they did after saying hello was to move straight into Shelly's bedroom and have sex. They had been voluntarily apart for five months. During this entire period Sean had seen Shelly on only one single occasion, and that had been at Sainsbury's where he had been trying to get hold of some Turkish Delight for his mother. He had seen her by the bread counter buying a French stick. She was chatting to the young girl who was serving her. He couldn't imagine what about. His first impulse was to think, 'She's lost so much weight, she seems so cheerful', as an afterthought, 'without me.' His second impulse was to duck behind a stack of soup tins as she turned in his direction and then to scurry away when he was sure that she would not notice him. He didn't want to see her, to speak to her, but equally he didn't want her to see him making a quick get-away. That would hardly seem dignified for either party.

He was twenty-seven and she was twenty-five. They had been 'seeing' each other for four years and for the last two of those four years they had been living together. She rented a flat in Wood Green close to the tube station. He had opted to move in with her and initially things had been fine.

She had never been thin. She was what most dietitians would call pear-shaped, but she was five feet and eight inches tall, which is a good size for a woman, and that height somehow undermined the size of her hips and made her shape seem less obvious. Unfortunately, within a year of their practical union she had begun to gain weight.

Sean knew that he was hardly the perfect partner, that his idea of faithful was to try and think of her when he was screwing other women. But he firmly believed that in other respects he was an excellent mate. He helped with the housework, he bought her flowers, he told her that she was beautiful.

It would be a lie to say that when she gained weight he didn't find her any less attractive. Her eating was perpetual and compulsive. Invariably she had something in her mouth; if not part of a jam tart or a sausage roll then some chewing gum or a boiled sweet. Sometimes he felt that her eating was a way of distancing herself from him; as though the layers of fat were an attempt to keep him away. Even so, she was always saying that she loved him, always saying that she needed him.

Her doctor had recommended a trial separation, a cooling-off period so that they could both analyse their feelings at a sensible distance. By this time she was well over fourteen stone and what the medical profession might describe as clinically depressed. He had been more than willing to accept this new development in their relationship. His mother had clucked her tongue at him when he had arrived home again with a suitcase and several carrier bags, and had told him that he just wasn't willing to stick things out, to sort things out.

Shelly had a theory about something called Symbiosis. She had learned about this word at school in her biology lessons. It had always been a word with great significance and relevance to her life. She loved the feel of the word in her mouth as she said it out loud. She thought, 'Everyone has words that are particular to them, that are significant to them, and this word, this idea is the most important factor in my life.'

She dreamed a lot about love. She wanted to be in a situation in the future where she could literally not survive without the love, kindness and care of a man and he, similarly, would feel the same way about her. Symbiosis (*sim-bi-ō'sis*) n. *the living together of two kinds of organisms to their mutual advantage.*

Shelly believed that men were altogether a different kind of organism to women. She had tried to make things work out with Sean but he had wanted everything his own way. He still told her that he found her attractive, but he also still told her that he found other women attractive too. After sex he would regularly disappear off into the bathroom with a girlie magazine and she would lie alone in bed and try to think of something else. She didn't say anything because she wanted it to work out, she wanted him to need her and she knew that she needed him, someone, something, anyone, him.

She hated dieting so much. Since early puberty she had been on diets of one kind or another. After a while it became clear to her that her metabolism was so slow that eating a peanut added several inches to her hips, thighs and stomach. Her relationship with food, with that which could be consumed, was passionate, impetuous, exotic, erotic. She loved eating, she loved to swallow, she loved to taste sweetness on her tongue and her mouth. She would happily have given a month of her life for a mouthful of sherbet or a meaty rib in barbeque sauce.

When Sean proved too much for her she didn't sulk or argue, instead she ate, and the food appeared palpably on her body, each meal became a dimple in her thigh or a part of the warm tyre around her waist.

Underneath all the bullshit she knew that the weight was also her way of trying to make Sean find her less physically attractive. She wanted him to need her for herself, she wanted security. Instead he would stare at her as she lay in the bath or as she tried to get dressed and undressed and he would say, 'You've put on so much weight lately that when we make love it's like fucking a barrel of lard.' Invariably as an afterthought he'd add, 'It's a good job that I like barrels of lard.'

She'd try to smile.

A lot can happen in five months. The first thing they did after saying hello was to move into Shelly's bedroom and have sex. After sex

Shelly got up immediately and went to the bathroom. She had a wash and then came back into the bedroom and started to get dressed.

Sean lay in bed and watched her. He said, 'I've really missed you.' It was almost true; he was sick of living at home and her flat was convenient and she cooked well and he didn't have to try so hard with her as he did with other women.

She smiled as she hooked up her bra and adjusted the material over her breasts. She said, 'I suppose I've missed you.'

He said, 'Why are you getting dressed?'

She grinned. 'I thought you could take me out to dinner. I fancy an Italian or a Chinese.'

He sat up straight in bed and surveyed her thoroughly. Then he said, 'You're looking great, Shelly, do you know that? You've lost a load of weight and it really suits you.'

She nodded, 'I know.'

He was surprised by this new confidence, this calm assurance. In five months she seemed to have changed incalculably. He felt rather piqued by this but also attracted. She seemed so happy.

Suddenly it struck him that she was seeing another man; there was something about her that was so serene and fulfilled. The idea of her with another man made his stomach churn. He said, 'Have you been seeing someone else?'

She laughed. 'Why?'

She was pulling on some jeans which five months ago wouldn't have gone beyond her knees. He shrugged. 'I dunno. You seem different. You've lost weight. Before you'd have never got dressed like this, straight away.'

She went into the bathroom to fix her make-up and brush her hair. As she left the bedroom she looked over her shoulder and said, 'Let's go and eat, Sean, I'm starving.'

In the end they chose Chinese. On their way to the restaurant— along the High Road, next to the Shopping City—Sean noticed how other men stared at Shelly as she walked. She seemed aloof and oblivious. He wanted to hold her hand as they strolled along but she held her handbag in the hand closest to him which made this difficult.

They chatted about work and Shelly asked how his mum was. He said she was fine. It all felt rather odd and unnatural. He had imagined that she would be tense when she saw him but in fact she seemed perfectly relaxed and at her ease. If anything he was the one who felt uncomfortable. His previous role in their relationship had been one of indispensability. The whole point of him had been the fact that she needed him. He knew that she needed someone. He felt nosy and jealous but he said nothing until they were seated at a table in the restaurant.

The waiter flirted with Shelly as they ordered their meal. He noticed their eye contact and it made his stomach contract. After the waiter had left their table with the order (Shelly was hungry and had ordered a substantial meal), he played with his cutlery, making his finger into a flat, straight scale and trying to balance his knife on the finger so that it didn't tip off, then his fork, then his spoon. Shelly watched him with a half smile flickering around the corners of her lips.

Eventually he said, 'Is there someone else?'

She shrugged. 'I don't have another man in my life at the moment, Sean, no. That was part of the deal, remember? It was a trial separation but our view in the short term was to getting back together.'

He nodded. 'I know that, it's just that you seem so different. You're a different person to the girl I left five months back. You seem above it all now, like someone in love.'

Secretly he wondered if she was just in love with him and he had never really noticed before, had never really seen her before tonight. She shook her head. 'I've already told you that I'm not in love, I'm just happy. If I'm in love with anything then it's food.'

He frowned. 'What do you mean?'

His voice was rough and unsympathetic. She smiled at this roughness. 'I mean that I'm happy because I'm using new sources in my life to find satisfaction and contentment. For some people it's drink, for others it's sex, for others it's drugs. Well for me it's food.

Eating makes me happy. Before I thought that I only ate because I was unlucky in love but now I know that I eat because I like it.'

He had never been able to understand her delight in large spoonfuls of raspberry and rum mousse, the condensed glee in a packet of plain chocolate digestives. He said, 'The doctor told you that compulsive behaviour always leads to unhappiness.'

She smirked. 'Fuck the doctor.'

He frowned. 'Are you?'

She laughed. 'Be serious Sean!'

He smiled, but it was the smile of someone who thinks that they understand something when really they understand nothing. She said, 'Compulsive behaviour is to a large extent something that people rely upon to get out of bed in the morning. It's what makes the world go around.'

He shook his head. 'No, that's habit. If something is compulsive it's usually bad for you.'

She smiled at him icily. 'Like sex?'

He smiled back. 'That's pleasure.'

The waiter arrived at the table with the starters, some spring rolls and prawn crackers. Shelly ate a couple of the crackers and then started on a spring roll. He looked down at his plate but didn't feel hungry. She said, 'The more I indulge my compulsions, the less I feel them ruling my life. It's weird. You'd think it would be the other way around but it isn't. Eat up, it's delicious.'

He tried a mouthful and it did taste good.

Her voracious appetite, which had developed two or three years into their relationship, had always violently irritated him. When they had first started going out she ate virtually nothing. When they went to restaurants he would joke about how little she ate as she ordered the salad option and ate very slowly, chewing each mouthful with great restraint and discipline. He thought it appropriate that women should behave this way; women who gained too much enjoyment from food, greedy women, were usually too demanding in bed. They made him nervous.

He stared nervously at Shelly as she chewed and swallowed with great finesse and rapidity. After several minutes the waiter came to take their plates away. Sean had left most of his starter but Shelly's plate was clean.

The waiter smiled at her as he took her plate. 'You enjoyed that?' Shelly nodded. 'It was delicious, but don't worry, I've still got room for the main course.'

The waiter pulled a face which implied that he found it hard to believe that someone who looked as good as Shelly didn't have to starve themselves to keep in trim. Sean was sure that he was staring at her breasts. He nodded curtly and dismissed the waiter with a brisk thank you.

Shelly touched her napkin to both corners of her mouth. She looked around her and studied the other people in the restaurant. Sean stared at her face; her green eyes, her strong nose, her dark black eyebrows and her curling fringe. He said, 'Your hair suits you in that short bob style.'

She dragged her eyes from the couple sitting by the door and focused them dreamily on Sean's face. 'Does it?'

She paused and then before he could answer said, 'Yes, I think it does. It's still too curly. Bobs should be very straight ideally.'

He nodded in silence, pretending that he understood or cared. She reached out one of her hands and caught a droplet of wax that was dripping down the small white candle in the centre of the table on the side of her middle finger. It felt hot on her hand for a second and then solidified. She began to draw her hand back again but before she could properly do so Sean put out his hand and took hold of hers. Their arms were suspended uncomfortably in mid-air. She squeezed his hand fondly and then drew hers away.

The waiter brought the main course. As he dished up his portions Sean said, 'What's going to happen now, between us?'

In his car on his way around to her flat he had imagined this situation but the roles had been reversed. He had visualized Shelly, all tearful and cloying, biting her lip, begging him to come back to her. She'd change, she'd be less possessive, anything.

Shelly didn't answer his question immediately. He repeated himself: 'What's going to happen now, Shelly?'

She frowned and eventually said, 'I don't know.'

She started eating. She had chicken chow mein with mixed vegetables in soy sauce. It tasted heavenly. Sean couldn't eat. Everything seemed to be going wrong. He knew that Shelly needed him, needed someone. He put down his knife and fork and said, 'Shelly, please tell me if there's someone else.'

She didn't reply. He began to feel jealous and angry, bitter. After a few minutes watching her eat he said, 'I bet you'll regret this meal tomorrow. It'll take it's toll on your figure.'

Shelly stopped chewing and looked into his eyes. 'I shouldn't think so.'

He frowned. 'How come?'

She finished her mouthful and curled some more chow mein on to her fork, 'I don't gain weight any more. It's connected to something called symbiosis.'

He grimaced. 'What's that supposed to mean?'

'It means that I don't gain weight any more but I can eat what I like.'

The flame on the candle flickered for a moment as the door of the restaurant opened. His eyes focused on the flame for a second, then returned to her face. 'How is that possible?'

She sighed and put down her knife and fork and then leaned forward on her elbows and whispered, 'I've got a tapeworm.'

He wasn't sure that he'd heard her correctly. 'What?'

She smiled as though what she was telling him caused her infinite joy. 'I've got a tapeworm, Sean, it's symbiosis. We both depend on each other to carry on.'

Sean shook his head in disbelief. 'What do you mean, Shelly? Is this a joke or something?'

Worms disgusted him. He had seen part of a nature programme on television a few weeks before which had featured something about worms that had made him almost physically sick. He had turned it over straight away.

Shelly returned to her meal, unperturbed. After a mouthful she said, 'I got him by eating raw mincemeat. It took a while and obviously I had to specify certain parts of the animal, you know, stomach, offal. I actually told the butcher that I wanted meat minced for my dog. As I said though, it took several attempts.'

Sean's lip curled in disgust. 'You ate raw dog meat?'

She shook her head. 'No, low quality meat, not from a can. Lots of animals get tapeworms. Obviously though there are many different varieties. It's very complicated because I think they reproduce in lots of different ways. I went to great lengths to get mine.'

Sean still couldn't be sure that Shelly wasn't joking. He said, 'What do you call it? Trevor?'

She laughed. It was the first time that she had laughed properly all evening. 'I don't have a formal name for him—I think he's asexual. I haven't read all that much about them.'

The waiter returned to the table to make sure that their meal was all right. Shelly answered, smiling, 'It's absolutely delicious, thank you.' Sean just continued to stare at her face. Once the waiter had moved away he picked up his fork and tried to eat one of the lightly battered prawn balls on his plate. As he chewed Shelly said, 'You see, the tapeworm consumes my undigested food so that it doesn't have the chance to turn into fat. That's my theory anyway. He then uses the food to grow and reproduce himself. He sort of develops another segment which divides away from his body after a certain period. This segment, I'm slightly confused on this point though, this segment then either stays in the stomach, hooking on to a prime place, or it's flushed out with your body fluids.'

Sean said nothing. He was pushing prawn and batter around his mouth but he couldn't swallow. Shelly took this silence as an indication of interest so she added, 'I'm glad you're not a biologist, Sean, because I'm explaining this very badly.'

Sean carried on chewing. On his forehead were slight beads of perspiration. He picked up his napkin and blotted them. Shelly took a sip of wine and said, 'I have to be careful about alcohol. I sometimes think that it must be bad for him so I don't drink very much any more. That's something else good that he's brought to my life.'

Sean pushed his mouthful of well-chewed food into his cheek and said, 'What happens when it grows, Shelly?'

She shrugged and picked up her knife and fork again, 'I'm not absolutely sure. In general I think they just get bigger and bigger until they fill up all your tubes. I think they can grow to an enormous size. They just grow bigger and bigger and reproduce.'

Sean shuddered. 'And what happens then? I'm sure they're harmful.'

Suddenly an image flashed into his mind, an image that he had seen accompanied by the voice of David Attenborough. There had been a snail on a leaf. As it ate the leaf it had consumed some sort of worm the size of a pin head. The worm lived and grew inside the snail, created a home for itself in this new snail-stomach world. After several weeks the maggot had grown rather large. It became visible inside one of the snail's two feelers. It grew and grew until eventually it filled the feeler entirely. After a while it looked as though, instead of a feeler sticking out of the snail's head, it had a large, independent, squirming maggot whose movements were curtailed only by a thin layer of the snail's translucent skin. The maggot moved, squelched, writhed under the snail's skin, eating, growing.

Several days later the snail's other feeler began to fatten up, to grow pale, to move against its own will as another maggot appeared in this feeler. Sean hadn't been able to tell whether this was the same maggot or a different one. They certainly looked like two fully formed and independent creatures. Eventually the snail had no feelers left, just two white maggots sticking out of the top of its head, living on its juices, eating it while it carried on moving and living and breathing. The maggots shuddered and vibrated inside the snail's feelers, its eyes, prisoners in its skin, eating him.

Sean had yelped his horror and had snatched for the remote control to switch it off. He couldn't stop thinking about it afterwards though. He was sure that the snail must've died, but after how long? He felt like gagging.

Shelly had almost completed her meal. She was saying, 'Sean, eat something. It's such a waste.'

He spat out his masticated mouthful into a napkin. She said, 'I haven't been so happy in a long time, Sean. The only tiny way that I notice the worm is when I go to the toilet. Often when I go now a segment of the worm comes out in my urine.'

One of Sean's main rules of love was that women didn't go to the toilet; or if they went they did different things there than men. He refused to have his idealism shattered. Shelly had always been very circumspect about her personal habits in the past. She had always called the toilet the Little Girls' Room. When she said it he liked to imagine that women kept dolls and horses and perfume and lipstick in the Little Girls' Room, that they popped in there for a bit of fun and then came out again, beautiful, perfect and squeaky clean. He was a firm believer in the use of feminine deodorants.

Shelly was saying, 'I think the segment is just part of the worm that is dead because when I've studied it it doesn't move or anything. It's not like an independent life form . . .'

Sean couldn't believe that Shelly was saying these things; he interrupted, 'This is all a tiny bit intimate, Shelly.'

She shrugged, 'I don't know. I think I've really changed in that respect over the past few months. I used to be embarrassed about my body before and the things that it does naturally. My tapeworm has changed all that. It's like I'm now involved in a very natural and obvious relationship. It's like I can see at last how I relate to the world as a creature; to trees and grass and cows and pigs, and the moon's cycles and the sea. We all are alive in a similar way. It's all connected and we all depend on each other, in a sort of chain of existence.'

As she spoke the waiter returned to their table and took away their plates. Shelly smiled at him as he completed this task and said, 'I'd love an Irish coffee.'

He nodded and looked at Sean. Sean said, 'Just a plain coffee for me, please.'

Shelly straightened the table cloth and picked up a few crumbs to put in the ashtray. Sean felt inside his jacket pocket and took out a couple of cigarettes. He offered Shelly one. She shook her head. 'I've given up.' He raised his eyebrows then stuck a cigarette in his mouth and lit it. After inhaling he said, 'Shelly, you've got to get rid of that worm.'

She smiled. 'No.'

He exhaled vigorously. 'Well, what's going to happen when it grows to an enormous size? I'm sure you eat enough to treble its size every other day.'

She ignored this insult and said, 'I'm going to keep this one for ten months then get rid of it. Afterwards I'll get another small one and start from scratch all over again. That means it'll never get out of control.'

The waiter brought them their coffees. Shelly thanked him and took a sip of the hot, sweet, creamy liquid. Sean was momentarily quiet so she said, 'I'm going to have to read up on the whole thing because I'm not one hundred per cent sure how they reproduce. If the little segments that come out in my urine are baby worms then maybe I'll have to try and swallow one of those.' She paused and then added, 'They aren't very big but they've got hooks on them. When I pee they hang on to the lip of my body with their hooks and I have to unhook them myself. It's quite simple when you know how.'

Sean's expression was full of an incredulous horror. She smiled. 'It's all right, Sean, it doesn't hurt and it doesn't bother me.'

Sean's mind was now turning over very rapidly. He was thinking of the sex they had indulged in an hour or so before. He couldn't stop himself; he said, 'I couldn't have caught one earlier, could I?'

She frowned. 'I shouldn't think so.'

Then she smiled. 'I think you would've seen it if it had hooked on to the end of your prick.' She started to laugh. 'Imagine if the entire worm had hooked itself on, all eleven or twelve inches of it. You'd have become rather confused when you went to the bathroom!'

She spluttered with laughter as she sipped her coffee.

Sean was stony-faced. He said, 'You don't give a shit about me any more, do you? About my feelings in all of this?'

She stopped laughing and shrugged. 'You've never given a shit about me in the past, Sean. In fact I think that I can honestly say that I have had more help and support from my tapeworm over the past five months than you have given me in the last four years.' As she said this she tapped her stomach with her left hand and then took a swig of her Irish coffee.

Sean didn't know whether he wanted to live with her any more, whether he loved her, but he was damn sure that he wasn't going to be compared to her tapeworm and come out of this comparison at a disadvantage. He said, 'That thing is eating you up inside. It's a parasite.'

She nodded. 'Yes it is, and the two of you have a whole lot in common. Unfortunately, you didn't improve my self-image like this tapeworm has. It needs me. You never needed me. It's helped me. You never helped me.'

She finished her coffee and he stubbed out his cigarette. She started to put her jacket on. 'I've got a new direction in my life now, Sean. I've learned that I can survive without you, that I can be attractive and desirable and funny and interesting without needing to have you around to tell me what I am or what I can be.'

He shook his head. 'You've got a real problem, Shelly.'

She stood up. 'No, you have, Sean. I'm leaving now and you can pay the bill.'

As she left the restaurant she winked at the waiter.

The
Piazza
Barberini

Tina was doing Rome on a budget. Her companion was horrible. He was called Ralph. She met him accidentally, and he stuck to her like a burr, like a leech, until he grew bored of her. Then he let go, just as suddenly.

He had, she discovered, over seven different ways of describing the rectum. His favourite was ring which he used and used until it was quite worn out. Ironically—she just *knew* this was funny—Ralph was actually an arsehole himself. But she was too polite to say anything. He even looked like an arsehole. Not literally, but he wore dark glasses, a furry trilby—right there, on the back of his head, monstrously precarious—and thick-soled loafers. She presumed that he thought his look was, in some way, Italian. She knew better. Even the Italians knew better.

Ralph was staying at a *pensione* south of Termini. It wasn't particularly salubrious around there. Tina didn't like it. She, by contrast, was staying in Old Rome, in the heart of Rome, close to the fruit market, the best piazza, the better cafés.

Tina had met Ralph while she was queueing for the Vatican Museum. It had been a ridiculously long queue, but she presumed that the wait would be worth it. Ralph had joined the queue behind her, had introduced himself, had asked whether she'd mind saving his place for him while he popped off for a minute, then disappeared. An hour later, when she'd nearly reached the front, he reappeared again. She'd completely forgotten about him by then. She almost didn't recognize him. His glasses were pushed up on to his head. His eyes—bold, empty—stared at her: a mucky brown. Two round hazelnuts. He said he didn't have quite enough money for the entrance fee—'What? You're kidding! That much?'—so she paid for him on the understanding that he'd pay her back later.

He never did. Ralph was from Reading. He worked for British Telecom. He had a smattering of Italian. He could order coffee, ice-cream, several flavours of pizza, without even consulting his guidebook.

Tina felt sorry for him. He wore a Lacoste polo shirt, but it wasn't actually Lacoste because the alligator was facing the wrong way. She knew about these things. She was training to be a buyer at Fenwicks, New Bond Street, London. Ah, yes.

Ralph tried to persuade Tina to have a piece of brightly coloured cotton twine plaited into her hair on the Spanish Steps. Several men, unkempt, like hippies, were offering this service for a small sum.

'I'd rather not,' she said, noticing their dirty hands, their tie-dyed shirts. 'I think I might just climb up to the top of the steps and look at the view.'

Ralph followed her. He was like a naughty spaniel; bored, precocious, snapping at her heels.

The view was fine. When they'd had enough of it, Ralph said, 'I wanna take you somewhere special. It's called the Piazza Barberini. It's not far from here, just down the hill. When she was in Rome, Sophia Loren used to live nearby.'

He took hold of her arm. Tina allowed herself to be led. She followed him obligingly because it was a pretty street, a steep, deep incision into the hillside. Grand houses frowned out on either side of them.

She was too obliging. What kind of girl, after all, takes any trip on her own? A bold girl? A silly girl? Oh, she wanted to be both, for once. Even Ralph, even he was a step in the right direction. A step, and she was on a trip, a voyage. Rome, she knew, held something special just for her: a fresco, a figurine, a shady walkway, an orange tree. If she kept on looking, she would find it.

In the Piazza Barberini she paused for a moment to stare at a fountain.

'I've got fountains,' Ralph said, contemptuously, 'spouting out of my brush.'

Close by was a second, smaller fountain which was covered in big carved bees. 'That,' Tina said, pausing for a moment, 'is very sweet.'

'Yeah.' Ralph walked on.

'And if it was in London,' she said, 'it would be covered in bird dirt. They don't seem to have pigeons here, or if they do, they don't mess nearly as much.'

'In Rome,' Ralph said, conversationally, 'you're only considered gay if you're passive during sex. If you screw other men, but aren't screwed, then you're not gay.'

Tina scowled. 'That's disgusting.'

Ralph grinned. 'In Italy the men are men and the women are glad of it.'

Tina rolled her eyes. She decided that Ralph had been in Rome for too long. He'd been here a week already. She'd arrived a mere thirty-six hours ago. She was glad that she was staying for only five days. After seven days Ralph was bored. He seemed incapable of seeing the prettiness around him. He was growing cynical. He didn't appreciate how good the weather was.

Ralph led Tina towards a church—In Rome, she thought, what else?—and up some steps. At the top, slightly out of breath, he turned and proclaimed, quite seriously: 'Here lies dust, ashes, nothing.'

'What?'

'It's written on the wall,' he said. 'Inside. I kind of liked it.'

She moved towards the entrance. 'No,' he said, turning from her, 'not there. This way.'

Ralph cut to the right, through a small door and down into rock, into a clammy darkness.

The stairs were steep. She followed. 'The friars here,' he said, over his shoulder, most informative, 'had cappuccino named after them.'

'Why is that?'

'Bugger knows.'

It was musty and dusty. At the foot of the stairs lay a cramped, airless, stone chamber. It had been transformed, very badly, in an almost purposefully amateur way, into a shop. There was a till and a rack of cards. Nothing much else.

A friar appeared, as if by magic, silently, out of the stonework. He was draped from head to foot in mud-coloured hessian. He stood in front of Tina and blocked her way. He stood close to her, too close, invading her personal space with the kind of bald insolence and gall that only a religious man could muster. She could tell by his eyes that he spoke no English. *She was a stupid girl.* That's what his eyes said. *She didn't understand anything.* He wanted to compress her, to liquidize her. He hated her.

In his hand the friar held a bucket. In the bucket were coins. He shook the bucket. He had a grey beard. Blue eyes. Tanned skin, like leather. He came from another century. Tina kind of hated him, too, somehow.

She put her hand into her pocket and pulled out some money. 'Give him something small,' Ralph said, materializing next to her but making no effort to contribute himself. 'You have to give a donation.' She threw some coins in. The friar shook the bucket again, more vigorously this time. Tina took out a few extra lire and tossed them in. The friar grunted, still giving an impression of intense dissatisfaction, before turning his back on her.

'This way,' Ralph said, his voice rippling with enthusiasm. 'Through here.'

From the chamber, to the right, was a short passageway. This was a crypt, Tina decided, a real crypt. It smelled of soil. Of course. On the floor was a thin coating of brown earth.

'That's specially flown in,' Ralph said, kicking it up with his loafers, 'from Jerusalem.' He snickered.

Brown. Everything was brown. Everything was wooden. It felt

like a Spanish villa: whitewashed walls and dark bark. All this stuff. Candles, soil, *stuff*.

'Not wood,' Ralph said, as though he could sense what she was thinking. 'Not wood. *Bone.*'

Bones. Hundreds of hip bones, delicate, like oyster mushrooms, arching in an extraordinary design, a beautiful design, across the ceiling. Ribs as lamp fitments. Vertebrae as candelabra. One wall was only skulls. Thousands of skulls balanced one on top of another on top of another.

Tina walked, numbly, dumbly, from chamber to chamber. Some contained friars, like the one outside but recently deceased, still in their hessian, hands suppliant, fingers, fingerbones. Some were newly buried, thinly covered, freshly coated in soil.

Angels hung, corpse-like, soggy, badly, ugly . . . oh dear. Their wings were collar bones. They flew under bone arches. Tina walked, from chapel to chapel, smelling earth and death and candlewax.

'Four thousand!' Ralph whispered. 'Over four thousand dead Capuchin friars in this small place!'

Tina felt full of skin. Full of moisture. Kind of fleshy and watery, but also dead inside. She was walking through Death's rib-cage. The whole world was bone and she was such a tiny part of it. In the final chamber, two arms were hung on the wall. Ready to chastise, ready to embrace. Mummified.

Where was Ralph? Behind her?

'Watch this,' he said, leaning over, putting out his hand, grasping a bone, yanking and pulling. The friar Ralph engaged with was headless, was armless, was a sagging punch-bag of dust and rot. The bone Ralph yanked at emerged from the neck of a rotting cassock, but it could've come from anywhere, originally. It was approximately eight or ten inches long—as round, skinny and hollow as a penny whistle—and when it snapped, it gave out a crunching sigh, like the sound a slightly soggy dog biscuit might make if held in eager jaws.

'Ralph! Stop it! Leave it!'

'Hey! Tina!' Ralph said, dancing in front of her and holding the bone to his lips like it was a little pipe he would play.

He puffed out his cheeks and his fingers flew up and down it. Tina took two steps back. Her eyes were wide. She was mortified. Ralph! She didn't like him, not one bit. She hadn't trusted him all along. She'd never met anyone from Reading before. He was as foreign to her as pesto or tagliatelle or tiramisù. Just as strange and inexplicable.

Tina turned and stumbled away from him, staggered at first but then found her feet, found herself moving faster and faster, picking up speed from chapel to chapel. Wanting, needing, fresh air. *Had to get out. Where was the friar? Nowhere. Was Ralph following? Didn't seem to be.*

Soil flew upwards and outwards in an arc, some of it she kicked with her heels against the back of her calves where it slid and it niggled, down her socks, into her shoes. Soil from Jerusalem. She kept on running.

It was so hot.

Tina was in her hotel room. The window was open. The nets were shifting, shuffling in the breeze.

She had pulled off her shoes and her socks. Her feet were itching. She dusted them with her hands, delved between her toes with the tips of her fingers. Her mind was still dipping and churning.

Where was Ralph? Why had he done that? Should she have intervened? Should she have stopped him? He was hateful. She imagined him, still laughing and grinning, relentless, in his own hotel, south of Termini. She wouldn't see him again.

Tina kept touching her lip, which felt, repeatedly, as if a cobweb was dangling from it, a silky strand, a tiny feather, tickling her, irritating her. She hoped she wasn't getting a cold sore.

She felt lonely. That was stupid. She touched her lip.

'I must stop doing that.' She felt heavy. 'Stop this. You're being silly.'

She clambered on to her bed, fully dressed, lay down flat and closed her eyes. 'Thank God,' she muttered resolutely. 'Thank God I'm not a Catholic. Thank God I'm just a buyer at Fenwicks, New Bond Street, London.' She turned over and sighed.

Tina dreamed. Tina dreamed she was doing Rome on a budget. Her companion was horrible. He was called Ralph. She met him accidentally and he stuck to her like a burr, like a leech, until he grew bored of her. Then he let go, just as suddenly.

And when Ralph let go—this was the good part—Tina met Paolo. In the botanical gardens. Paolo was half-American, half-Italian, a doctor and an amateur botanist. He was dreamy.

The day after the dust, the bones, the dirt and the death of the Piazza Barberini, Tina consulted her guidebook over an espresso and then picked her way slowly and cautiously through the via della Lungara to the botanical gardens in Trastevere.

You see, Tina knew that Rome held something special, just for her—a fresco, a figurine, a shady walkway, an orange tree—and that if she searched for it she would find it.

The weather was temperate. Plants were growing. Everything looked glorious in the Italian sunshine. The trees and the specimens were extremely well labelled. Tina wandered around the botanical gardens, smiling to herself, trying to expel all thoughts of candle-wax and hessian and dark bark from her mind. And Ralph. Him especially.

Inside one of the greenhouses a smart group of horticultural Italians—smelling of starch, scent and shoe leather—were inspecting the finalists in an orchid exhibition. Tina slipped in to take a look.

The orchids seemed alien, like sophisticated intergalactic creatures. They didn't look real. Tina squatted down in front of one, closed her eyes and inhaled. The air was warm and smelled only of soil. *Soil.* She shuddered.

'You know, that orchid is a colour you see nowhere else on this earth apart from in one other place. It is a purple-brown the colour of the human kidney, *sì?*'

Tina looked up.

'I'm Paolo. Hi. I could see you were not with the others. I guessed you were English from your shoes. Am I correct in so guessing?'

'Oh.' Tina looked down at her suede moccasins and then back up at Paolo again. 'Uh . . . The flowers were so lovely . . .'

'Orchids.'

'Yes. They almost look . . . plastic.'

'I suppose you could say that. God is a master technician, huh? I should know, I'm a doctor. I studied in America for several years, in Boston.'

'Your English is excellent.'

'Thank you. I enjoy the chance to, ah, take it out for a test drive every so often.'

Paolo shrugged his strong, square shoulders. Tina smiled.

'Your hair is in such a pretty style,' Paolo said. 'The English are so original.'

Tina put a hand to her pale brown bob. Paolo's beautiful dark eyes clouded over, momentarily.

'You must think me so presumptuous. You have not even had the chance to introduce yourself.' Paolo took hold of Tina's hand. 'Your name?'

'Tina.'

'Forgive me, Tina.' He kissed her fingers, so softly that she barely felt his lips, just his breath, which later, she discovered, was sweet and nutty and flavoured with pistachios.

Was this the thing? Was this the thing Rome held just for her? Not a fountain or a figurine, but Paolo? He took her for coffee and then invited her to collect wild mushrooms with him that afternoon in the Parco Oppio. Tina floated back to her hotel clutching a moist amaretto biscuit in one hand and something that felt suspiciously like the key to Paolo's heart in the other.

The haughty Italian matron who presided over the front desk in Tina's hotel obligingly changed some of Tina's pounds into lire and then announced, in her clipped English: 'A man came for you earlier. He left no name but he was wearing something full of . . . fluff, on his head, a hat,' she grimaced, 'and shoes made of plastic. He is . . .

uh . . .' Unable to find the right word, the woman twirled her finger in a circle and raised her eyes skywards.

'Mad?' Tina tried.

'No.'

'English?'

She shrugged. '*Sì.*'

'Did he leave a message?'

'*Sì.*' The woman offered Tina a folded piece of paper. Tina opened it up. In badly formed letters was written:

> Tina I've gotta see you It's urgent
>
> love ralph

Tina turned the note over, picked up a stray, yellow Bic pen from the desk and wrote:

> Ralph, At last I think I've found what I was looking for in this magical city of Rome. I won't waste your time or mine by describing what it is, but I am quite certain of what it isn't. It isn't a short Englishman in stack heels with a bad haircut and dirty teeth. I know that now. What you did in that church yesterday appalled me. I've decided I don't want to see you any more. You disgust me. Goodbye.
>
> Tina

Tina handed the notelet back to the woman. 'If he comes by again,' she said sweetly, 'will you make sure that he gets this?' Then she slipped the Bic pen, without so much as a second thought, into her jacket pocket.

Paolo pushed aside a bush and whistled to himself. 'Do you see what I see, Tina?'

Tina recoiled. There was something about this fungus, something that made her palms dampen. Paolo put out his hands and gently plucked the mushrooms. 'With strips of pasta, some garlic, hard cheese . . . a touch of single cream.' He kissed the air and then plopped the mushrooms into the basket he was holding.

'They look a little like . . . uh . . . bones,' Tina said. 'Don't you think?'

'They taste like flesh,' Paolo said, standing up and striding off. 'Very rich, very strong, very gamey.'

Tina followed a short distance behind him. She caught up at the next bush. 'This is a nice park. Are we close to the Colosseum?'

Paolo pushed aside the bush but there were no mushrooms underneath, only a used soft drink can and the plastic segment of a syringe. He stood to attention. 'You don't want to come here at night. Homeless people haunt this place. That is why I hunt here for mushrooms, because others don't have the audacity to look in such a venue. So you have to be observant,' Paolo added. 'Especially a woman on her own. That makes you extremely vulnerable.'

He stalked off again. Tina followed. 'Actually,' she said, 'I've found Rome very hospitable. I mean . . .'

'A woman came into my surgery yesterday,' Paolo said. 'She had been mugged while walking through the Jewish Ghetto. They wanted her watch. She resisted. They sliced into her arm with a blade, through the tendons, down to the bone. The blade was rusty. I knew even then it would go septic, get infected, start to swell and rot like garbage in the stinking heat of an Italian summer.'

'My God.'

'You must be wary. To you this is simply a holiday, but to the casual vagabond and thief, you are a perfect financial opportunity.'

Tina, from the corner of her eye, noticed what she thought might be a cluster of wild mushrooms, but they were sprouting alongside something that bore a startling resemblance to a clump of dog shit and she couldn't bear the idea of drawing Paolo's attention to them, not even for the thrill of earning his approbation.

'Have you noticed what I've noticed?' Paolo stood still, like a bloodhound, his nose flaring, his fists tightening. Tina's heart sank. He'd seen the mushrooms. Before she could respond, however, Paolo whispered, quite urgently, 'As I was saying, this place is new to you and so the sights and the pleasures of the senses are here to be enjoyed for the very first time, but I . . . I am more familiar with this environment so can take in the larger view, the periphery. Someone is following us. Did you see him? When I bought you your *gelato* he stood a little distance away. Later he bought one for himself.'

Paolo pointed. Tina followed the line of his finger. She failed to detect anything unusual.

'See?' Paolo asked. 'In the scruffy clothing, with his long face, his dirty arms. He has a pronounced limp. He's ducking behind that yellow flowering bush. He knows I'm on to him. A junkie. Probably a thief.'

Tina looked again. A man with a child and a suitcase. A young woman sitting under a tree reading a magazine. Two teenagers playing with a frisbee. And then she saw him. *Ralph!*

She nearly swore, but she stopped herself. 'Paolo!' she exclaimed. 'Over there! See? Some mushrooms.'

Paolo looked where she'd indicated, strode over, crouched down and plucked them from the soil. 'Such a meal I will make you!' he exclaimed. 'Such a feast!'

By the time he'd straightened up again, Ralph had made himself scarce. Tina blinked and wondered if she'd dreamed him.

She went home to change for dinner. Ralph was loitering outside her hotel. He was holding an open copy of *La Moda* in front of him but he wasn't reading it.

'What do you want, Ralph? Didn't you get my note?'

His face was pale and moist. He seemed distracted.

'Yeah,' he said, 'and to be honest . . .'

'I don't like being followed around,' Tina said, emphatically.

'So who the hell is that guy?' Ralph interjected indignantly. 'Christ, you're a fast worker. Yesterday it was me, today it's some fat Italian with hair sprouting out from his cuffs and his collar.'

'It was never you, Ralph,' Tina said haughtily as she pushed past him and stepped into the hotel's revolving doors. Ralph was nimble though, quick on his feet, and he stuck to her, entering the same little segment of the doors. He was crushed up against the back of her as she pushed and walked. He smelled of Dettol. Then he stopped and the door jammed. Tina tried to keep moving but Ralph was too strong. The glass held fast.

'Stop pressing against me! Let me out of here.'

'Tina,' Ralph said, 'I regret what I did yesterday. And I want to give you that money I owe you from the Vatican Museum.'

'Keep it. I don't want it.'

Ralph put his hand into his pocket and drew out an old tissue, a bus ticket, a couple of lire and a cheese straw. Tina blinked and focused. It wasn't a cheese straw. It was a bone.

'My God! What is that? Did you *steal* it?'

'Uh . . . ?' Ralph looked down. 'It's a cheese straw.'

'Oh.' Tina felt claustrophobic and slightly dizzy. 'I thought it was the bone. I mean, I thought you had the bone.'

Ralph guffawed. 'That's one way of putting it.' He adjusted his position. Tina squinted at him, somewhat perplexed. Close up, she found his white skin, his dead eyes, particularly distasteful.

'My friend thought you were a drug addict,' she said, sharply. 'You look a mess.'

'Fine,' Ralph responded. 'So I'm sorry about the way things turned out yesterday. But that note you left . . . See,' he bared his teeth, 'my mouth is spotless.'

'But your shirt,' Tina smiled back, tight-lipped, jabbing at his chest with her middle finger, 'isn't Lacoste. It's a second-rate impersonation. Which, to be brutally honest, Ralph, seems entirely appropriate.'

While Ralph paused to digest this information, Tina took her chance and gave the door a violent shove, pushed it forward and snapped out of the restrictive glass bubble into the foyer. Ralph was disoriented for a moment but then quickly followed. He didn't let up. He trailed her to the front desk.

'Go away, Ralph.'

'It's only . . .'

She spun around. 'What?!'

He was still holding the bus ticket and the cheese straw in his right hand.

'It's only, I mean . . .' he said, shiftily. 'Couldn't we talk this over in private?'

'Get lost, Ralph.'

Ralph didn't budge. Tina asked for her key and then pressed for the lift. 'By the way,' she said sharply, 'Paolo said Sophia Loren never lived in the Piazza Barberini. She never even lived in Rome. It's just a myth. My guidebook says the same thing.'

Ralph opened his mouth to say something, but before he'd uttered a single syllable, Tina had swept off, up the stairs, taking them two at a time.

The lift arrived. The doors opened. People got out. The doors closed. Ralph remained where he was. He grimaced, looked around him, cleared his throat and then gently, neatly, *carefully*, he folded up his copy of *La Moda*.

'It looks fantastic, Paolo,' Tina murmured. She was sitting in his spotless flat and staring down at a steaming plateful of pasta and mushrooms.

'Tuck in,' Paolo said, turning this little smidgen of colloquial English over on his tongue like an exquisite truffle. Tina picked up her fork. She ate a small strand of the pasta and then smiled. 'It's delicious.'

Paolo beamed at her.

She speared a mushroom. She inhaled deeply and lifted the mushroom up towards her lips. She could smell it. It didn't smell like a mushroom at all. It smelled of old bone. Rotten bone. She paused.

'What's wrong?'

Tina closed her eyes for a moment. Don't blow it, Tina, she thought frantically. This man is a dream. You've arrived, girl. You've arrived! But her brain took no account of these thoughts and projected the unpalatable image of a dog's anus on to the inside of her eyelids. Her gorge rose.

'Tina?'

She opened her eyes. 'Paolo?'

'Is something wrong? Is it the evening light? Is it too bright?'

'The light?' Tina blinked. 'Oh. Yes, it is bright.'

'Easily remedied.'

Paolo sprang up and over to the window to adjust the blinds. While he was distracted, Tina grabbed her handbag from the floor, yanked it open and tipped the mushrooms from her plate straight into it. This whole manoeuvre took a total of four or five seconds. She snapped the bag shut.

'Tina!' Paolo expostulated. Tina squeaked and looked up guiltily. But Paolo was not staring at her. He was staring out of the window. 'Tina, come here for a moment.'

She did as he asked. Paolo pointed. 'It's him, huh? You see him?'

Tina craned her neck and followed the line of Paolo's index finger.

'You see him? The same one as earlier. Next to the street lamp. Smoking.'

Ralph. Next to the lamp-post; bad shoes, bad hair, puffing on a cigarette. Something was wrong, though. It was his hat. It wasn't on his head, perched jauntily, as one might have expected; it was hanging from his belt buckle like a furry codpiece.

'I have reason to believe that man is stalking you,' Paolo said. 'I have every reason to believe it.' Without another word he strode swiftly from the room.

'Hang on a second . . . Paolo?'

The door slammed. Tina returned to the window. After a short time, Paolo appeared in the street. Ralph gave a start, grabbed hold of his hat, turned on his heel and ran. Paolo followed, but didn't venture beyond the end of the road. Tina went back to the table, sat down and picked up her fork.

Of course he insisted on escorting her home. He told her how one of his uncles had been glassed in the Palazzo Nuovo for his cuff-links. 'People see you, Tina, and straight away they can tell you are green. You are green like a dollar sign. A big, green dollar sign walking down the road.'

He frog-marched her into the hotel foyer, watched as she

picked up her keys, called the lift. While they waited for it he arranged to meet her early the following morning for breakfast. He kissed her ear as the lift doors opened. 'Don't leave the sanctuary of the building until I am here to meet you, OK?'

Tina smiled and nodded. Paolo was so *protective*. It gave her goosebumps.

'You are so desirable,' he muttered, 'so damn vulnerable. You are an accident, Tina, just waiting to happen.'

Tina had a shower, wrapped a towel around her midriff and then strolled into her bedroom.

'My God!'

Paolo was sitting, bold as brass, on the end of her bed.

Tina clutched at her towel. 'Paolo! What on earth are you doing here?'

Paolo clucked his tongue and shook his head. 'The window. You left it wide open. I was checking the rear of the building. I came up by the fire escape. You must be more cautious, Tina. I could have been anybody.' He stood up. 'I'm sorry to have to scare you like that. It's just that we can't be too careful, huh?'

Tina nodded.

Paolo returned to the window, swung his leg over the ledge and jumped out on to the escape. 'OK,' he said. 'Tomorrow. Breakfast.'

Tina nodded again.

'The window. Close it tight, *si*?'

'I will. Straight away.'

She closed it. She sat down on her bed.

'Is that guy some kind of a fucking psychopath or what?'

Tina froze and then she yelled.

'*Aiuto!*'

In the short silence that followed an accent that was distinctly English and distinctly Ralph's said, 'And what the fuck does that mean?'

Tina squatted down. A loafer was visible, protruding from the end of the bed.

'What the hell are you doing under there?'

Ralph was silent for a moment and then he said gently, 'I think I'm dying.'

'You're what?'

'Dying. I climbed in. You were in the shower. I needed to talk to you. Then I heard someone else climbing up the escape, so I scrambled under here. Then he sat down on the bed and now I'm stuck.'

'Stuck? How?'

Ralph cleared his throat. 'To put it bluntly, I have an erection and it's stuck inside the mesh on the underside of the mattress. It's like chicken wire or something.'

'You've got a what?'

'I've got an erection.'

Tina recoiled. She grabbed hold of her clothes, her jacket, her shoes, and dashed into the bathroom. She shot the bolt and got dressed. When she'd finished dressing she called through. 'If you've not gone by the time I count to ten, Ralph, I'm going to scream and scream until the police come.'

'One.' She put her ear to the door to listen out for his response. 'Two.' She could hear him speaking but not what he said. 'Three.' She pulled the door open a fraction.

'Four.'

Ralph's loafer protruded, as before. He had not moved.

'Five.'

'What's the guy's name, anyway?' Ralph asked, apparently unruffled by Tina's little display.

'None of your business.'

'Funny name. Must be foreign.'

Tina scowled. 'Paolo.'

'Paolo?' Ralph snorted. 'He's so fucking paranoid. More to the point, he's so *hairy*. Even his ankles. I was staring at his ankles for a full five minutes while you were still in the shower and, I'm not kidding you, the hair was half an inch thick. It was extraordinary. Staring at his ankles was the only thing that stopped me from screaming myself stupid.'

Tina paused and then addressed herself emphatically to Ralph's loafer. 'Paolo has every reason to feel paranoid on my behalf. I have a strange man stalking me, pestering me, hiding under my bed while I'm in the shower . . .' Modesty forbade her to mention the erection.

'And the erection,' Ralph said. 'Don't forget about that.'

He twitched his foot. Tina stared at it malevolently. The thick sole, the scuffed heel. Slip-ons, she thought. So common. They were brothel creepers, really, with a large ornamental buckle glued on the side. Nasty, stupid shoes.

'Anyhow, Paolo's a doctor,' Tina muttered, dragging her eyes from Ralph's footwear. 'Doctors are caring by *nature*. It's an instinct.'

'A *doctor*!' Ralph parroted. 'How *gratifying* for you.'

He was quiet for a while and then he said, 'You wouldn't happen to have a pair of nail clippers handy, would you?'

'Nail clippers?'

'So I could try and cut myself free.'

Tina looked churlish but picked up her bag anyway and was about to open it but then paused. 'I don't know if I want you cutting yourself free. You might be dangerous.'

Ralph snickered. 'Let's get one thing straight between us, Tina. I had no interest at all in ever seeing you again after our little bit of fun in the crypt yesterday. And although I have an erection, that's no reason to think I find you irresistible.'

Tina tucked her bag under her arm and headed for the bathroom. She'd just remembered Paolo's mushrooms and wanted to clear them out over the sink to minimize the mess.

'What are you doing?'

'Finding some clippers.'

'Oh.'

Tina grabbed some tissues and pulled the bag wide. She paused. She stared.

'Oh, shit.'

In her bag, instead of the mushrooms she'd expected, there were ten finger bones. Ten clittery-clattery finger bones. Yellow bones. Earthy bones.

She dropped the bag.

Ralph was still talking. Tina wasn't listening. She backed away from the sink, out of the bathroom, into the bedroom and gently pushed the door shut. When she next spoke her voice was low. 'I couldn't find any clippers after all.'

'Great.' Ralph sighed. 'So now what?'

Tina grimaced. 'If you leave yourself alone for a few minutes maybe it'll have a chance to go down.'

'It won't go down. It has no intention of going down. That's what I've been trying to tell you.'

Tina said nothing, only stared peevishly up at the lamp fitment. Ralph continued talking, undaunted. 'You don't know the half of it.'

'I don't want to know. I'm not interested. I just want you out of here.'

'So I got home to my hotel yesterday,' Ralph said, his voice slightly muffled by the bed and the mattress, 'sat down, dozed for a while and then *ching!* A hard-on. Well that's hardly anything out of the ordinary. So I grappled with it for a while, but the more I touched it the harder it got. And it wasn't a good hard. It was a bad hard. It was angry. I couldn't relax. It hurt if I sat down, it was even worse if I stood up. It *burned.* And it wasn't a sexy feeling, just kind of irritating. Eventually I started to get depressed. Frustrated too. But then out of the blue, after a few hours struggling, I found relief. Want to know what it was that relieved me?'

Tina's lip was tingling. She curled it. 'Desperately.'

'You. It was you.'

She recoiled.

'Funny, huh? As soon as a thought of you flitted into my mind I felt a kind of *loosening*, I mean, it didn't go down or anything but the discomfort eased a bit. But it kept me up all night just the same. And I felt weak. Like all the blood had been diverted from my body and brain into just that particular part of me.'

Tina smirked but said nothing.

'In the morning I walked over to your hotel. I left you the note. In the foyer it stopped hurting altogether. Strange, huh?' He paused. 'So you don't even have some scissors handy?'

'No.'

'Well, can you try and lift the bed then? It feels like I'm being garrotted.'

Tina appraised the bed. It was large and heavy and the headboard was a thick, dark wood. She squatted down. 'There's no way I can lift this thing. It's huge. You're just going to have to untangle yourself.'

Ralph fiddled quietly for a while. The sound of his nails against the mattress wire set her teeth on edge. She stared over at the bathroom door.

'Have you ever had a 24-hour erection before, Ralph?'

Ralph stopped fiddling.

'Nope.'

'Maybe you should go to a doctor or something.'

'Why? Fancy calling Paolo over?'

Tina's thoughts turned to Paolo. She touched her bottom lip with her index finger and dwelt on his pistachio-flavoured kisses. Her fingers, she noticed, after a short interval, smelt very strongly of soil. *Soil?* She stared at her hands. They were clean. They were spotless.

'I'm only saying,' Tina continued, slightly anxious now, 'that you snapped that bone yesterday and ever since . . .'

Ralph chuckled. From under the bed his laughter sounded like a mouse scampering. 'Have you got bones on the brain or something?'

'You snapped that bone and now you have this strange *stiffness*.'

'The penis doesn't have a bone in it, Tina. It's blood that makes it hard.'

After a pause, Ralph added, 'I guess it's just one of those things. We don't much like each other but in some weird way we're destined to be together.'

Tina struggled to stop herself from growling.

'Fate,' Ralph sighed, and then tapped his foot against the mattress.

Tina felt claustrophobic. She walked to the window. 'So why

do I keep seeing bones everywhere?' she asked, almost piteously. 'And why does this whole room reek of soil? Damp soil. Can't you smell it?' She yanked the window open.

Ralph sniffed obligingly. 'Smells of old cum and mothballs under here.'

'We're cursed!' Tina exclaimed dramatically, half meaning it, half not.

'Bullshit!' Ralph sounded utterly unperturbed. 'I don't believe in that stuff.'

'But you believe it's fate that we should be together? That's so stupid. Maybe I should call down for a porter.'

Ralph continued to fiddle. 'Great idea. Try explaining this situation in pidgin Italian.'

'I'm tired.'

'Ring Paolo, then,' Ralph said brightly. 'Explain things to him.'

Tina blinked. 'Paolo? No way.'

'Why not?'

'I'll look stupid.'

'Hardly. I'm the one looking ridiculous here, not you.'

Tina said nothing. Ralph, in turn, ruminated for a while. Then he said, quite softly, almost inaudibly. 'Maybe you're right, though, maybe I shouldn't have taken that bone after all.'

Tina froze. *'What?'*

'Perhaps I shouldn't have taken it. I should have just dumped it.'

Tina's hands formed into fists. 'You *took* the bone? Is that what you're saying?'

'Not exactly.' Ralph tried to stifle a yawn but failed. 'You did.'

Tina's hands flew to her throat. It tightened.

'You nearly slipped, remember. I thought that monk fella was coming so I tossed the bone into your jacket pocket.'

Tina stared down at her jacket. She took two deep breaths, and then slowly, fearfully, she slipped her hand into her right pocket. Inside she found some tissues and a couple of English coins. Nothing else. She exhaled her relief and then steeled herself for the left pocket. She dipped in her hand . . . More tissues, an old bus ticket, and then? Something stiff and slim and potentially fibrous. Gently, gently she withdrew it. The bone. Only it wasn't a bone, it was a Bic pen. Yellow, innocuous.

'You *bastard*!'

Ralph howled. 'Sorry,' he coughed, between gasps. 'I guess that was rather *close to the bone*!' He laughed some more. Tina said nothing. Instead she went and picked up the phone.

Most of it she explained there and then. The remainder she whispered to him outside on the fire escape, away from Ralph's prying ears. Of course he was angry. But there was a slant to Paolo's anger that Tina hadn't anticipated. It wasn't the sacrilege or the invasion of her privacy or even the lie over her former intimacy with Ralph that he minded. It was the erection.

'A 24-hour erection? No way. It is not possible.'

Paolo clambered into the room, got down on to his hands and knees and stared at Ralph and his entrapped member. Ralph shielded himself with an outstretched hand. 'What is this?'

Paolo was undaunted. 'No way. I am a doctor. I have never heard of such a thing.'

Ralph grinned, sensing Paolo's pique. 'Actually, it's been more than twenty-four hours now. It's closer to thirty.'

Paolo swore in Italian and then stood up. 'OK, turn away, Tina, I don't want you seeing anything that might prove unsettling. And you . . .' He kicked Ralph's foot.

'Ow!'

'You, get ready for me to lift the bed. I'll go slowly but prepare yourself for some discomfort.'

Tina turned away. Paolo braced himself, grunted, and then lifted. Ralph cursed and rapidly made some necessary adjustments.

'Right,' he said finally, 'I'm decent. Hold it three seconds longer, Paolo, and I'll roll out from under.'

After exactly three seconds Paolo dropped the bed, unceremoniously. Ralph tried to stand up. But before he could straighten himself Paolo had darted over and shoved him, quite forcefully, in the centre of his chest. Ralph jerked and then wilted. Paolo was at least a foot taller than he was.

'Sit! Over there. In that chair.'

Paolo pointed. Ralph winced, staggered over and sat down.

'Now what?'

'So,' Paolo glared at the significant protuberance between Ralph's thighs. 'I can clearly see that there is indeed some activity in your trousers.'

Ralph looked down at himself, as if to confirm in his own mind that this was true.

'Yes.'

Ralph's penis was stretched and erect under the fabric of his jeans.

'Tina,' Paolo said softly. 'Make yourself comfortable on the bed. I myself will take the other chair.'

Tina did as Paolo had asked. Paolo pulled a chair over to a position directly opposite Ralph's, and then settled himself into it. Nobody spoke. Finally, Tina said gently, 'It's late. Hadn't Ralph better get going?'

Ralph nodded keenly, all previous thoughts of his improbable connection with Tina patently abandoned.

'No, Tina,' Paolo replied calmly. 'Now we wait.'

Tina frowned. 'But what for?'

'We wait until his magical erection goes down. Then I will kill him.'

Ralph's eyes widened. So did Tina's. Paolo just smiled and kept his eyes fixed on Ralph's thighs. Ralph squirmed.

'Ah yes!' Paolo sneered, looking and sounding quite demonic. 'Try and maintain that erection under real pressure, little man. We'll all see how long it lasts, eh, Tina?'

Tina cleared her throat. 'But maybe, Paolo . . .'

Paolo silenced her with an impressive jerk of his eyebrow. 'You called me, Tina, and I came. This is my business now. Keep out of it.' Tina retreated back on to her pillows.

Ten minutes. Twenty minutes. Thirty minutes passed. Nothing moved except for Tina's eyes which turned every so often towards the clock on her bedside table. After forty minutes Paolo was still as watchful and focused as a kestrel in a summer wheatfield. Ralph was pale and bug-eyed and sweating. But his erection remained prodigious.

Eventually Paolo stirred. 'Tina, I need to use your bathroom.'

Tina nodded. Paolo stood, went to the window and fastened it, turning the security lock at its base and pocketing the key.

'The room keys?'

Tina pointed to the bedside table. Paolo picked these up on his way into the bathroom. He closed the door behind him.

In a flash Ralph turned to her and whispered frantically. 'He's a fucking maniac! He's going to kill me. He means it. Why the fuck did you have to go and phone him?'

Tina gaped. 'Me? Why did I phone him? It was your idea in the first place. How was I to know he'd react this way? Anyhow,' Tina pointed, 'the erection's still there, isn't it?'

Ralph unzipped his fly and brought out a cheese straw. Tina stared, dumbstruck. Finally she murmured, 'What is that?'

'What does it look like? I never had an erection. It was a wind-up. I wanted to pay you back for being such a stuck-up bitch the other day. And for passing me over.'

'Passing you over? Are you mad?'

'I was going to run off once you'd phoned him, so that he'd come round and you'd look stupid. But,' he indicated the zip on his fly, 'this fucking thing *did* get caught and I *was* stuck there for a while so then I thought, why the hell not sit this out and be in on all the fun?'

The toilet flushed. Tina gestured frantically. 'Put that back in! He's coming.'

A droplet of perspiration had formed on the tip of Ralph's nose. 'I can't. It's crumbling. It's hot down there.' He waved the straw and it drooped. Tina's hand darted into her pocket and she pulled out the Bic pen.

'Take this. Quickly.'

Ralph snatched the pen and stuck it down his trousers with dispatch. Just in time. Paolo came strolling out of the bathroom. Tina was still staring anxiously in Ralph's direction and so failed to detect that Paolo was holding something in his hands. Her bag. After a cursory glance at Ralph's genitals, he sat down in his chair again and placed the bag on his lap.

'Tina, could you possibly explain something to me?'

Tina glanced over. 'Paolo?'

'Could you perhaps explain why it was that when I went to wash my hands in your sink I found your handbag in there, and it was open, and inside it was the mushroom dinner I cooked you?'

Ralph turned and appraised Tina. His mouth had fallen slightly ajar. Tina looked down at the counterpane. She opened her lips to say something but then Ralph spoke first.

'Actually, Paolo,' he said calmly, 'she throws up everything. It's a medical condition. She's an anorexic.'

'Bulimic,' Tina corrected him, quickly.

'That too.'

Tina chewed on her lower lip. She felt so tired. She could barely call up the strength—physical, moral—to meet Paolo's gaze. 'I'm sorry, Paolo,' she said finally, peering up beseechingly. 'It was no reflection on the meal. Really it wasn't.'

Paolo continued frowning for a few seconds longer and then suddenly he smiled. Tina smiled back. Even Ralph smiled.

'Dear Tina,' he said gently, 'you must think me a beast. I had no right to look into your bag. I'm sorry.'

His face softened and, true to form, Tina's heart—like a lump of semi-congealed butter on a warm hotplate—softened with it. Everything would be all right. She felt it, suddenly. Everything would be just fine. She turned to Ralph. 'This is ridiculous, Ralph,' she said boldly, 'and it's all gone on for long enough. We should tell Paolo about the pen. I'm positive he'll understand.'

'The pen?' Paolo's eyebrows rose.

Ralph's face was rigid. 'I don't think so, Tina,' he said slowly, his eyes fixed on her most expressively.

But Tina didn't baulk. 'It's just got way out of control,' she said firmly. 'Tell him, Ralph. Get it over with.'

'Get what over?' Paolo leaned forward in his chair, his neck extending so that the muscles stretched and pumped with all the elasticity of chewing gum.

Tina took a deep breath. 'It isn't an erection, Paolo. Ralph's got a pen down his trousers. It was all just a stupid joke. He told me while you were in the bathroom.'

Paolo got to his feet, very slowly. 'Ralph,' he said softly. 'Over the past hour I have had the opportunity to scrutinize your clothes and your footwear at some length. Your shoes are very unusual. In Italy we don't have anything quite like them. Perhaps I could take a closer look. Would you mind?'

Ralph, paradoxically, had pushed his body as far back into his chair as it would go. He took a deep breath. He shook his head. 'Of course I wouldn't mind.'

Slowly, stiffly, he lifted up his foot so that Paolo might see one of the shoes without bending down. Paolo took hold of the foot, pulled the shoe off and quietly inspected it.

As he did this, Ralph watched him fixedly, and then, for a split second, his eyes darted sideways, towards Tina. In that instant Paolo grabbed hold of Ralph's jaw, prised his mouth open and rammed the tip of the loafer into it.

Ralph flailed helplessly, his jaw stretched wide, his eyes squeezed tight. Tina sprang up and grabbed hold of Paolo's arm. 'Stop it! Leave him alone! You'll hurt him!'

As soon as she touched him, Paolo let go. He raised his palms to the ceiling. 'See? I've let go. See?'

Tina nodded.

'Are you happy now?'

She nodded again.

'Good.' Paolo smiled. Tina tried to smile but couldn't quite manage it. Ralph? Ralph didn't even try to smile. He was too busy choking. The loafer lay in his lap, bereaved of its fancy buckle.

Tina hadn't yet noticed. Ralph, gagging, threw his shoe at her to get her attention. He tried to cough but his throat was blocked and he couldn't exhale. Tina caught the shoe. She looked down at it and then over at Ralph who was slack-jawed and drooling.

'What's wrong?'

He clutched at his throat.

Paolo glanced down too.

'I think he's choking on something. Ah!' He pointed to the shoe Tina held. 'The buckle's come off. He must have swallowed it.'

'Oh God!' Tina dropped the shoe. 'So now what?'

Paolo shrugged. 'I suppose we should call for an ambulance.'

He walked over to the phone and picked it up. Tina watched as Ralph's complexion rainbowed from red to wine to damson to ivory. Then he fell from his chair and on to the carpet.

Tina felt sick. Ralph was writhing. She was panicking. Paolo, perfectly calm, spoke on the phone for a short interval and then returned to Tina's side.

'An ambulance?'

He nodded. 'It'll be a short while.'

'But he's choking!'

'Sì.'

'Can't you do something?'

Paolo shook his head. 'I am not insured to intervene in this kind of situation. If he dies I might get sued by the family. It could ruin me.'

'If he dies?' Tina gasped. 'You're a doctor, Paolo!'

Paolo cleared his throat. 'Roughly.'

'Roughly? What do you mean, *roughly*?!'

'I'm a chiropodist.'

Tina fell to her knees, grabbed hold of Ralph's head, stared up at Paolo and said, 'So, fine, if you *were* a doctor, what would you do?'

Paolo scratched his head. 'I suppose I would try the Heimlich Manoeuvre.'

'Yes!' Tina exclaimed. 'How does it go?'

'I have no idea. But, uh, after I'd tried that, if it didn't work, I'd make an incision at the base of the throat and push a straw into it so that he could breathe from below the blockage.'

Ralph, meanwhile, was undergoing some kind of spasm. Tina didn't know what kind of a spasm it was, only that it looked almost biblical in its monstrosity. His face was ashen, his eyes were rolling.

Tina exploded. 'I need a knife. But I haven't got one. Do you have one?'

Paolo shook his head.

'I need something pointed. *Anything* pointed.'

Ralph clutched at his groin.

Typical, Tina thought. Even in his moment of crisis . . . But then she remembered. She grabbed at his trousers, yanked down the zip, ripped out the Bic pen and held it aloft. Ralph had started to foam and to slacken.

Tina indicated towards her own throat as she looked up at Paolo. 'Is this the place? At the bottom here? Is this it?'

Paolo shrugged. 'I wouldn't know, but I don't think shoving a bone into his throat is any way to go about it. It looks dirty and it's blunt at its tip.'

Tina scowled down at the pen. It was a pen. It was a pen. It was. She started shaking. She looked into Ralph's face. Oh God, she thought, Rome *was* holding something special just for me. Not a statue, not an orange tree, not even a shady walkway, but Ralph. Ralph!

She stared at him, fixedly. How did she feel? She *hated* him. Ralph opened his eyes. They were the colour of two brown hazelnuts. That did it. Tina shoved his head between her knees, raised the sharp point of the Bic pen skywards, paused for one second, one long second, and then brought it down, forcefully, with as much accuracy as she could muster, into the base of Ralph's throat. It entered so easily. Ralph arched and stiffened, but she kept her hand steady.

'Stay still. Hold on.'

Tina yanked the pen out again, ripped the biro section from its centre and then firmly thrust the hollow pen shell back into the wound.

Glub.

Ralph lay still, corpse-like, flaccid. Two seconds, three seconds, four seconds, five . . . And then his chest started to rise. It rose, it rose, it rose. Air whistled through the pen's shell. In, in, in and then out.

Paolo threw himself into a chair. 'You could've killed him.'

'But I didn't,' Tina said, almost regretfully, and as she spoke she cleared a piece of clotted blood away from the pen tip. The air whistled in and it whistled out.

'Do you hear that, Ralph?' Tina whispered, conspiratorially.

'The pen's making a noise like a penny whistle. Do you hear it?' Ralph's eyes had been shut since the pen had entered him. But now, slowly, gradually, he opened them. His mouth moved, it started to form a word. Tina stared at his lips. What was he saying? Was it 'Thank you'? Was it 'Sorry'? What was it? And then she realized. Chiropodist, he said. Chiropodist! Ha. Ha. Ha.

Tina felt lead in her belly. And rage. 'Take that back, Ralph. I mean it.'

Ralph's lips were smiling. Ha. Ha. Ha.

His head remained clamped between her knees. Tina took her index finger and waved it calmly in front of Ralph's eyes. 'See this?'

He blinked yes. She took the finger and placed it over the tip of the pen shell. The shell stopped whistling. Ralph's eyes bulged. His chest stopped moving. He stopped smiling, finally.

'Want to take it back yet, Ralph?'

Ralph struggled to nod. Tina tightened her knees around his skull.

'Mean it, Ralph?'

Again, he struggled. His hands flailed, helplessly. His brown eyes, not blank, not empty any more, but saying something, emphatically. He was sincere. Just this once. He'd taken it back. He'd meant it.

Tina smiled, nodded, and casually asked Paolo how long he thought the ambulance would be.

'About four metres,' Paolo said, grinning, trying to win back her favour.

'Did you hear that, Ralph?' Tina asked softly. 'Paolo made a joke. He made a joke. Ha. Ha. *Ha.*'

Ralph wasn't smiling.

'I can hear the sirens,' Paolo said. 'Can't you?'

Tina listened carefully and then nodded slowly. 'Yes, I think I do hear them.'

The sirens grew louder. Her eyes filled with tears. They sounded strange and strong and quite beautiful. Tina sniffed, blinked, looked down for a moment, and then, so *regretfully*, and with the sweetest, the softest, the gentlest of sighs, she lifted up her finger again.

Popping
Corn

Oh!' she said. 'If I had her breasts I'd become a topless model or a cocktail waitress, or I'd go to Saint-Tropez and lie on the beach all day.'

'And get cancer.'

Mandy was sitting on the bus with her mother. They had met up outside the gym. Her mother finished work fifteen minutes before the end of Mandy's aerobics class. She waited outside by the bus stop, frustratedly watching the buses go by. Sometimes she waited for twenty minutes, occasionally longer. The gym was in Deptford.

'Breasts are for milk,' her mother said. 'You get pregnant, they fill up, you squirt it out. Like a cow.'

I wonder if it's erotic, Mandy thought, feeding babies.

Her mother added, 'When I had you my nipples cracked. They were chapped and they bled. Every time you sucked on them it felt like I'd shut them in a suitcase.'

Mandy imagined this. Breasts bare, suitcase open, packing for holiday, breasts jut forward, suitcase accidentally slams shut. Whap! Chop! Nipples sliced neatly off. Inside the dark suitcase; two soft, pink jellytots.

Then she remembered Imogen's breasts. She had seen them in the showers, and then after, when Imogen patted them dry on a pale blue towel, 36C. Small tan nipples. No unsightly blemishes or stretch marks. *She didn't wear a bra! No! Not even in the class!* Only a tight, high-cut leotard like the one Jamie Lee Curtis wore in *Perfect*.

By rights they should be down by her knees, Mandy thought, and secretly, in the back of her mind, *I wish they were!*

But the truth of it was this: Imogen could easily have no inkling of how fantastic her breasts were. She probably wished they were smaller, or that her nipples were a different shade.

I hope she thinks that, Mandy thought, imagining how it would be to carry two breasts like those around—light, soft trophies.

Mandy's own breasts were much too heavy and much too round. She wore a bra to exercise in, a terrible contraption like the kind of restraining garment people were strapped up in at mental hospitals. To stop them from hurting themselves. Surgical.

Mandy pictured herself wearing no bra for the class, her breasts bouncing so much that after half an hour the skin holding them to her ribs becomes slack, thin, sticky, eventually tears. The breasts break free and travel downwards in her leotard, eventually settling either side on top of her hip bones, like two fistfuls of cellulite.

Her mother said suddenly, 'When you were a kid, three or four, we were sitting on a bus, on the top deck, close to the front, and a brassy woman came up the stairs and sat close by. She had on a tight skirt, heels, blonde curls piled up high and a low-cut top, with her breasts on display, shoved together, like plums, shoved up. You stared at them for a while, all solemn, and then you turned to me and said, very loudly, "Mummy, why has that lady got a front bottom?" '

Mandy laughed. She had heard this story before, many times. Another breast story. Ha Ha. Funny breasts, tits, boobs, dugs, knockers.

One good thing about my breasts, she thought—focusing on herself again, on the two soft pieces of fat in flesh under her sweatshirt—when I drop off food from my fork, it lands on my chest instead of on my lap. Why was this so good? She couldn't decide, only knew that it was. Her breasts were a buffer zone, they protected her, padded her, covered her heart. If she ate popcorn at the cinema, eating in a scruffy way, fistfuls shoved in at once, to avoid embarrassment, she had to take care to remember to collect and consume the formal white line of fluffy kernels before lights up.

Dual
Balls

Selina Mitchell had never been particularly free-thinking. Since she was fifteen she had been completely under the sway of her dominant and rather single-minded husband Tom and her dominant and rather light-headed friend Joanna. She had always lived in Grunty Fen. If you grow up somewhere with a name like Grunty Fen you never really see the humour in the name, and Selina was no exception to this rule. She never thought it was a particularly amusing place to live. In fact she hated it most of the time. It was physically small, socially small and intellectually small. It wasn't even close enough to Cambridge to bask in any of the reflected glory; but if ever Selina had cause to write a letter to London or Manchester or Edinburgh for any reason she invariably wrote her address as *Grunty Fen, Cambridgeshire.* She hoped that this created a good impression.

The only scandal that had ever caused real consternation, discussion and debate in Grunty Fen was when Harry Fletcher had started to wear Wellington boots to school (in summer) and the school had been forced to alter their uniform rules in order to acknowledge that Wellingtons were a legitimate item of clothing for school wear. The teachers had seen this new allowance as a victory for the environment over the purity of education, a muddying of the intellectual pursuit. The kids all wore wellies to school for a while and then switched back to mucky trainers after their initial *joie de vivre* had worn off.

Selina had been a quick-witted student—by Grunty Fen standards—and had been one of the few children at the village school bright and determined enough to go to teacher training college. At seventeen she had packed her suitcase and had gone to Reading to learn how to be a teacher; to spread discipline and information.

At seventeen she had thought that she would never return to Grunty Fen again, but inevitably she went home during her vacations to visit her parents and wrote long, emotional letters to her boyfriend Tom, who had tried to stop her going to college in the first place by asking her to marry him.

After three years at college Selina had returned to Grunty Fen, 'Just until I decide where I really want to go.' Eventually she had married Tom and had started teaching at the village primary school.

She disliked children and didn't want any of her own. Tom liked children—probably because he wasn't forced into a classroom with thirty of them every day—but he realized that if he wanted to hang on to Selina (she was one of the intellectual élite) then he would have to bow to her better judgement.

Time rolled by. Selina's life was as flat as the fens and just about as interesting. Nothing much happened at all.

Joanna, Selina's best friend, had lived a very similar sort of life except that she had enjoyed little success at school and had never attended teacher training college. She had got married at sixteen to John Burger whose family owned a large farm to the north of Grunty Fen, and had borne him two children before she reached twenty. She had always been wild and mischievous, but in a quiet way, a way that pretended that nothing serious was ever going on, or at least nothing seriously bad. Joanna was the bale of hay in Selina's field. She made Selina's landscape moderately more entertaining.

Joanna didn't really know the meaning of hard work. Most country women throw in their lot with their husbands and work like automatons on the farm. But Joanna had more sense than that. She preferred to stay at home 'creating a friendly home environment' and cultivating her good looks.

At the age of thirty-nine she aspired to the Dallas lifestyle. She spent many hours growing and painting her nails, making silk-feel shirts and dresses on her automatic sewing machine and throwing or attending Tupperware parties.

Joanna was Grunty Fen's only hedonist, but hedonism wasn't just her way of life, it was her religion, and she tried to spread it like a spoonful of honey on buttery toast.

They were in a café in Ely, a stone's throw from the cathedral, eating a couple of cream eclairs with coffee. Selina was making fun of Joanna but Joanna didn't seem to mind. She pulled the chocolate away from the choux pastry with her cake fork as Selina said laughingly, 'I still can't think of that birthday without smiling. My fortieth, and I thought it would be some sort of great landmark. I was so depressed. I opened Tom's present and it was a home first aid kit. Of course I said how lovely it was. Then, trying to hide my disappointment, I opened your present, firmly believing that it would contain something frivolous and feminine. But inside the parcel there were only ten odd pieces of foam, all neatly and pointlessly sewed up around the edges. Neither of us knew what the hell they were. I thought they might be miniature cushions without covers. Tom thought they were for protecting your knees during cricket games, a sort of knee guard. I even thought they might be falsies.'

Joanna smiled. 'This must be one of the only places in the world where a woman of forty doesn't understand the basics of sophisticated dressing. I thought you could sew the shoulder pads into all your good shirts and dresses. It's a fashionable look, Selina, honestly.'

Selina shrugged her non-padded shoulders. 'I will sew them in eventually, I promise.'

Joanna grinned to herself. She looked rather cheery. Usually before, during and after the consumption of a cream cake Joanna panicked about its calory content and moaned about its probable effect on her midriff.

As Selina waited for the inevitable outburst she said, 'If we didn't come to Ely every few weeks for a chat and a break I'm sure I'd go mad. Ely. Imagine! This small, insignificant town has come to symbolize freedom and independence to me. It's rather sad; it's like the Americans symbolizing freedom with a sparrow instead of a bald eagle.'

She looked into Joanna's face. Joanna was smiling. It was as if she was listening to a song that no one else could hear. Selina stared at her in silence for a minute or so and then said, 'What is it, Joanna? I'm sure you're up to something.'

Joanna's eyes were vaguely glassy. Selina frowned. 'You've not been taking those tranquillizers again, have you?'

Joanna laughed. It was a sort of throaty, gutsy laugh. 'Oh Selina, if only you knew. If only! What's Tom like in bed at the moment? Has it improved since our last little chat?'

Selina shrugged and her cheeks reddened. 'Nothing much has happened in that department. Are you enjoying that cake?'

She had finished hers several minutes before, but Joanna was still (uncharacteristically) pushing her cake around her plate. Selina added quickly—to distract Joanna from intimate territory— 'School's been awful. Felicity has been sitting in on classes. It's to do with the new assessment rules from the education authority. The classroom is no longer my kingdom. It's been taken over by men in little grey suits. Of course Felicity loves it all. She even had the cheek to offer me a few tips on my teaching technique the other day. I'm surprised she was capable of taking any of the lesson in. Most of it she spent fiddling with her hearing aid. Anyway, everyone knows that Heads are incapable of controlling classes and that's why they become Heads in the first place. Maybe I'm just bitter, but the thought of that old crone deigning to tell me how to handle a class! She said something like, "Be freer, Selina, be more adventurous, take risks!" I tried to tell her that the syllabus had destroyed all elements of spontaneity in the classroom. If the kids want to cope with the workload nowadays it's all blackboard, chalk and copying.'

As Selina finished speaking Joanna shuddered slightly. Selina smiled. 'Ghost walk over your grave?'

Joanna shook her head and then giggled furtively. 'Look Selina, it's not that I'm not interested in what you are saying about school— God knows, my two did well enough under your tuition and they thought you were a great teacher—it isn't that I'm not interested, but I just must change the subject for a moment.'

As Joanna spoke, she leaned towards Selina conspiratorially and her voice dropped to a whisper, 'Selina, I'm wearing Dual Balls.'

Selina frowned. 'What do you mean? Is it a girdle of some kind, or some sort of skin ointment?'

Joanna never ceased to amaze her with her violent enthusiasms with frivolity. She pushed a slightly greying brown curl behind her ear and thought abstractedly, 'I must have my hair cut, it's almost touching my shoulders now.'

Joanna's chair scraped along the floor as she pulled it up closer to Selina. Selina could smell her perfume—something heady like Opium—which flushed through the air like bleach through water. Joanna whispered again, 'I've got Dual Balls, Selina. I've had them in since I left the house. It's been incredible.'

Selina shrugged, 'You're going to have to explain this to me, Joanna. I don't know what Dual Balls are.'

Joanna bit her lip and stared at Selina through her heavily mascaraed lashes for a moment, then she said, 'I got them from an underwear catalogue. I ordered them and they came in the post. John doesn't know anything about them.'

Selina cleared her throat nervously, 'Are they something rude, Joanna?' Joanna winked saucily. 'I should say so. They're like two small round vibrating grapes. Battery operated.'

Selina took a sip of her coffee to try and deflate the tension, then said, 'Have you got them in your bag?'

Joanna snorted loudly and several people at other tables turned and stared at them both for a moment. Selina felt slightly embarrassed. Joanna soon recovered from her fit of hilarity and whispered, 'They're not in my bag, stupid. I've got them in my fanny.'

Selina was not initially so much shocked by the idea of Joanna's little vibrating grapes as by her casual use of the word 'fanny'. It was an old-fashioned word. She had once had a great aunt called Fanny, a gregarious, light-hearted aunt who had always seemed very old to her as a child; old, frail but charming.

She didn't really know how to reply to Joanna, how to disguise her intense unease and embarrassment. Luckily Joanna had other things on her mind. After a few seconds silence she squeezed Selina's arm and said, 'I'm going to nip into the toilets and take them out, then you can have a proper look at them.'

Selina's expression was querulous. Joanna noticed as she stood up, and grinned. 'Don't worry, Selina, I'll give them a good wash before you have to have any contact with them.'

Selina sighed. 'Joanna, please be discreet. This is only Ely after all, not San Francisco.'

Joanna didn't reply.

Once she'd gone Selina relaxed and drank a large mouthful of her coffee. She stared out of the window at the cathedral. She thought, 'God, I feel old. Maybe it's teaching. It just beats all the enthusiasm out of you. I'm sure I never used to feel this way. The kids are no better or no worse than they were twenty years ago. It must be me that's changed.' She sighed and waited for Joanna's return.

After about five minutes Joanna emerged from the toilets looking furtive but self-satisfied, like a large tom cat on the prowl, about to spray an unsuspecting territory with his rank odour. Selina thought, 'This room belongs to Joanna. She doesn't give a damn about anything.'

Joanna sat down next to her again and Selina said straight away, 'I don't know where you get these ideas from—or your nerve for that matter—look at you, as bold as brass!'

Joanna smiled and patted her chestnut perm with one of her bright-pink-fingernailed hands, 'Don't look at this hand, look at the other one under the table.'

Selina moved backwards slightly and stared down at Joanna's other hand which held the Dual Balls like a couple of freshly laid eggs. Selina said, 'They're bigger than I thought they'd be and attached to each other. I imagined that they'd be a sort of flesh colour, not that strange off-white.'

Joanna raised her eyebrows, 'Flesh *is* off-white, Selina. Are Tom's balls a very different colour to these?'

She smiled provocatively. Selina shook her head disapprovingly. 'Tom's . . .'—she couldn't use the word—'Tom's aren't anything unusual, Joanna, and I certainly don't make a habit of trying to use them like you've just used those. Also, his don't use batteries and they aren't attached by a small piece of cord.'

Joanna smirked. 'You wish Tom's balls were like these. They're very effective, and so discreet. I think the thrill of using them is trebled by the fact of wearing them out. It's so arousing.'

Selina grimaced. 'Walking can't be easy with them in. Why don't they just drop out?'

As Selina spoke Joanna switched the balls on. She waited for Selina to finish talking and then said, 'Why don't you try them and see?' The balls vibrated vigorously in her hand. They sounded like a quieter version of an electric razor. Selina was sure that everyone could hear. She whispered frantically, 'For God's sake Joanna, switch them off.' Joanna frowned. 'I worry about you, Selina. You're becoming very old-maidish, very schoolmarmish. You don't have any spirit of adventure any more.'

Selina didn't rise to the bait. 'I've never had any spirit of adventure and you know it.'

Joanna nodded. 'I suppose that's true. No backbone, no spontaneity. No interest in what's state of the art . . .'

Selina raised an eyebrow. 'Where did you come across that little phrase? Something on television, something American I suppose?'

'You wouldn't have the nerve to wear these out, no way,' Joanna interrupted.

Selina smiled. 'I'd have enough nerve, Joanna, just too much sense. I don't need something like those. I think they're horrible. Now switch them off.'

Joanna turned and stared out the window at people passing by. An old lady staggered past pulling her shopping trolley. Joanna pointed at the woman, 'I bet she'd wear them out. I bet she's got more spunk in her little finger than you've got in your entire body.'

Selina almost smiled at this but then stopped herself. 'Possibly. Look, the waitress is coming over with the bill. Please turn them off.'

Joanna didn't turn them off, but started instead to lift up the hand containing the vibrating balls until they were almost at a level with the surface of the table. Selina was excruciatingly embarrassed. 'Joanna, switch them off and put them away. You're embarrassing me.'

Joanna was staring at the Dual Balls rather thoughtfully. After a moment she said, 'I dare you to wear these when you're teaching one of your classes. Just for one lesson. I dare you!'

Joanna loved dares. This was principally because she always thought of them and didn't therefore usually do them herself. 'Go on Selina, I dare you!'

Selina laughed. 'You've got to be kidding. Those horrible little things are having no contact with my intimate body whatsoever.'

Joanna lifted the balls slightly higher than the table and said, 'If you don't accept the dare I swear I'm going to put these into your coffee cup when the waitress comes to clear the table. That should be in about twenty seconds.'

Selina saw a couple of people at the nearest table to them discussing something and laughing. She was sure that they had noticed. She said, 'Joanna, put them down, please.'

Joanna held them even higher. The waitress started to walk towards them. When she was about five steps from the table Selina said, 'OK, I promise to wear them, I promise, all right?'

Joanna switched the balls off immediately. It seemed very quiet without their buzzing.

On her way home Joanna passed John in the tractor. He stopped so that she could overtake him then waved his arm so that she would pause for a moment. She wound down her window. 'Yes?'

He shouted from his high seat, not bothering to switch off the tractor's roaring engine, 'Did she take them?'

Joanna nodded emphatically. 'Yes. It worked like a dream. She was really shocked when she thought that I was wearing them. It was a real effort not to laugh.'

He smiled. 'You must be a great actress then.'

She shrugged. 'I did all right.'

She crossed her fingers down by the steering wheel. He

frowned—although he couldn't see her hands— 'Joanna, you were just acting?' Joanna guffawed. 'Don't be ridiculous. I'd probably have crashed the car if I'd worn them driving . . . Of course I wouldn't dream of wearing them anyway, why should I?'

She winked. He smiled. He obviously believed her. She uncrossed her fingers, waved at him and then drove on.

She negotiated the turn into their driveway with special care; she'd almost driven off the road there on the trip out.

One of the favourite pastimes in Grunty Fen is Chinese Whispers. People whisper gossip like it's going out of season. They also discuss what's happened in all of the major soaps and mini-series on television. Mostly though they prefer to gossip because it's a tiny place and everyone knows everyone else's business.

John got pissed in the local pub on Saturday night and told several of his cronies about Joanna's dare. The men all laughed loudly at the notion of someone as staid and strait-laced as Selina experimenting with sexual gadgets. They knew she wouldn't do it, but they enjoyed thinking about it just the same. A couple of them went home in their cups and told their wives. The women were shocked, interested and surprised on the whole; a small proportion were slightly jealous.

After Sunday lunch Selina was doing the washing up in the kitchen and Tom was sitting at the dining table in the next room doing the *Sunday Telegraph* crossword. Occasionally he read out loud to Selina any of the clues that had completely eluded him.

Selina washed the soapsuds from the final plate and placed it with the others on the drying rack. Tom seemed busy and preoccupied so she took this opportunity to clean out the sink and refill it with very hot water and a squirt of bleach. She went and found her handbag and took out the Dual Balls which she had placed inside, wrapped up in a tissue. She opened the tissue and removed the Dual Balls then placed them in the hot water and bleach, still wearing her rubber gloves. As she rubbed the balls with her hands she felt like a fetishist.

At the sound of Tom's voice from the next room she jumped

guiltily and her heart lurched; then in a split second she had grabbed the washing-up cloth and had dropped it over the balls, covering them completely. Tom was saying, 'Thirty-one across. Vulgar Cockney squeezes ends of these into tube. Six letters. I think it's an anagram. Any ideas, Selina?'

At this exact moment, a mile or so away, Joanna and John were still eating their lunch of beef and roast potatoes. John had a slight hangover. Joanna had prepared a meal for four but neither of the children had bothered hanging around for it. This made John even more ill-tempered and grouchy. He kept saying, 'It's such a waste of good food. Those two don't know what it's like to do without. You spoil them.'

Joanna ignored him. She was thinking about Selina and the Dual Balls. She wondered whether she would use them or not. Selina rarely broke her word, if ever.

She cut into a potato and watched the steam rise from its hot centre. She speared a bit of it on to her fork and prepared to put it into her mouth. Before she had done so, however, John said, 'I told a couple of the fellas about your joke with Selina last night.'

Joanna stared at him, dumbstruck. 'You did what?'

Her voice was sharp and strident. He shrugged. 'I know I promised not to but it sort of slipped out.'

She put down her fork. 'I don't know why I tell you anything. You're totally unreliable. I'm sick of you spreading my business about and sticking your nose into everything. This was none of your affair in the first place.'

He frowned. 'Well, why did you tell me about it then?'

She pushed her chair back from the table and stood up. 'I didn't tell you about it, you opened my bloody mail. You have no right to open letters and parcels that are addressed to me.'

He shook his head, confused. 'You don't have anything to hide from me, Joanna. What's the problem all of a sudden? This isn't like you.'

Joanna slammed her hand down on the table, rattling the plates and glasses and cutlery. 'I am a woman, John, women have secrets. That's one of the few good things about being a woman as far as I can see. Now that you've told everyone about this thing with Selina she'll be a laughing stock. She's my friend, for God's sake.'

John stood up and moved around the table towards Joanna. His head ached with every twitch of his body. 'Everyone knows that Selina won't use those things. She's not like that. It was a silly idea in the first place really.'

Joanna felt tearful. She shouted, 'Well, it seemed like a good excuse at the time!'

Then, grabbing her plate, she marched off into the kitchen, where she threw her lunch into the bin.

John sat down at the table again. He felt somewhat confused.

Felicity Barrow received a telephone call from her friend Janet Street on Sunday afternoon. Janet was extremely excited because she had a bit of amusing gossip to impart about one of the teachers at Felicity's school. Felicity liked to call it 'my school,' even though she was only the headmistress.

Janet had a rather puffy, breathy, light voice, and the scandal in her news almost extinguished it altogether. She gasped down the phone, 'Jim told me that Selina Mitchell has been wearing some sort of sexual device to school and using it while she's teaching classes.' Felicity interrupted, putting on her best head-teacherish voice. 'What on earth are you saying, Janet? And do speak clearly, I haven't adjusted my hearing aid yet.' On concluding this sentence she sipped her tea and took a large bite out of a mint-flavoured Viscount biscuit.

Janet gulped. This noise travelled all the way down the telephone line and into Felicity's ear. Then she whispered, 'Well, Jim said that it is a sort of vibrating machine which is shaped like the female sexual organs, but convex. It is attached by elastic to the two thighs, I think the elastic goes around the buttocks at the back . . . anyway Jim says it's very discreet. What happens is that it is battery-operated and it presses into the vagina while methodically rubbing at the clitoris. Apparently after several minutes this stimulates a sexual climax.'

Felicity tried to suppress the impulse to laugh, but finally gave into a throaty chuckle. 'Janet, I think what you're saying is untrue. We both know Selina Mitchell, we've both known her for years. I was headmistress at Grunty Fen Primary when she was a pupil at the school herself. There has never been anyone in the school whose dignity, discretion and professionalism I have held in higher regard. Just the other day I sat in on her class and assessed her performance. My only advice to her was that I thought her techniques too staid, perhaps a jot unimaginative . . .'

Janet interrupted. 'That's all well and good, Felicity, but you know what they say, there's no smoke without fire. She did go away at the end of the sixties, after all. Who knows what sort of habits she picked up then . . .'

Felicity's initial amused indulgence at Janet's news suddenly evaporated. She snapped, 'Stop talking such absolute rubbish, Janet. I'd certainly have expected that you of all people would be the last to surrender your credulity to the clutches of vicious and totally unfounded gossip. I don't want to hear anything more about this subject, and if I do hear anything from a different source I will be forced to presume that it originated with you. Do I make myself clear?' Janet answered breathlessly in the affirmative and the conversation ended abruptly shortly afterwards.

Felicity had been headmistress at Grunty Fen Primary for almost thirty years. The time had come and gone for her to retire but she had ignored suggestions from various departments—chiefly from her husband Donald, who was several years into retirement himself—and had carried on giving her all to the young children of the district.

She took her vocation very seriously. Her main problem was that she couldn't be convinced that anyone else she knew would be suitable for her job. The ideal candidate would be a woman—she thought that women made the best Heads because they were much more frightening than men—and preferably they would originate from Grunty Fen or the surrounding area. She believed that Fen children had to be taught by people who were familiar with the various interests, problems and subtleties of their character. She knew that

Selina Mitchell was keen for promotion. She had been coolly vetted for a favourable reference from Selina herself on several occasions, but nothing had come of it.

Felicity put her feet up on to her foot-stool, took out her hearing aid, leaned back in her chair and took another bite out of her biscuit. She had resented Janet's news because she felt that anything bad said about her staff reflected badly on the school and ultimately on herself. She was rather proud and vain but disliked these qualities in other people. Selina, she believed, was far too proud and vain for her own good. She was too closed, not sufficiently free-thinking. Felicity found her distant and arrogant. Selina found Felicity interfering and arrogant. Neither side would bow down to the other. They weren't destined to be good friends, but Felicity often regretted that they had never even managed to become formal friends.

She took another sip of tea and decided to call Selina into her office for a serious chat first thing in the morning. She picked up a copy of the *People's Friend* and ran her finger down the list of contents, muttering. 'No smoke without fire, indeed!'

Selina didn't dare carry the Dual Balls to school in her teaching bag in case any of the children poked around in it looking for a pencil or a book and came across them. Instead she wore a smart blue blazer with a deep inside pocket in which she carefully placed the Dual Balls before breakfast.

On arriving at school she went straight into her classroom to enjoy five minutes of quiet contemplation before the start of the day. She was keen to avoid Felicity and other members of staff, who on a Monday morning always seemed to try extra hard to be sociable and community spirited. Selina hated all that 'bonding' business. It wasn't her style. She rarely went out for drinks on a Friday night with her colleagues; even so, she always saw them over the weekend because Grunty Fen and the surrounding areas were so sparsely populated that a trip to the shops usually meant a trip to meet everyone from your past, your present and your future that you were keen to avoid.

She sat at her desk and put her hand into her inside pocket to feel the Dual Balls. They felt cold and smooth; highly unerotic. She looked around the classroom and thought, 'I'm so bloody sick of this routine. I'm sick of teaching. I just wish that it was heading somewhere or that something would come of it, but nothing will. I've vegetated, stultified.'

The room smelled clean but of chalk and paper and dust. Her mind turned to Joanna and their conversation at the weekend. This raised a smile. She thought, 'Of course she's right. I don't have any real spirit of adventure.'

The bell rang and the day began.

Felicity had popped into the staff room at the beginning of the day to ask Selina into her office for a chat. Unfortunately Selina didn't materialize so Felicity had to content herself with the idea of meeting her during lunchtime. She checked the wall chart in the staff room to make sure that Selina wasn't on play or dinner duty.

It was a hot day. After several hours Selina became uncomfortable in her blazer and took it off so that she could cool down, hanging it carefully over the top of her chair and keeping a firm eye on it. The morning droned on and eventually it was time for lunch.

All morning she'd had half of her mind on the Dual Balls. A part of her really wanted to fulfil her dare and show Joanna that she was a woman of her word. Another part of her baulked at the idea of using the balls in principle. They were crude and revolting. Secretly she was rather interested to know how they would feel, but only in a silly, inquisitive way that took no account of what was right or for the best.

As the last child left the classroom Selina made a firm decision. She resolved to go and 'try on' the Dual Balls and to try them out for several minutes in the privacy of her classroom at the beginning of her lunch hour. Then, if Joanna asked, she could say in all honesty that she had in fact worn the balls at school in the classroom.

The day was very still and warm. She opened the top button on her shirt to let the air circulate more freely around her throat then strolled to her chair and put on her blue blazer. It felt heavy and made her skin feel sticky. She felt ridiculously tense and strung-out.

Luckily the toilets were close to her classroom. She worried about walking with the Dual Balls in; Joanna hadn't cleared up that little chestnut during their coffee and eclairs.

The toilets were empty. She chose one of the two cubicles and locked herself in. She was glad that she had opted to wear a skirt and sheer stockings for easier access.

Inserting the Dual Balls gave her a feeling of youthful mischievousness, as though she were one of the children in school doing something secretive and wrong like puffing on a cigarette.

The Dual Balls felt cold, bulky and stupid. She pulled the string that switched them on. In her hyper-sensitive state the buzzing of the Balls seemed like the violent crashing of cymbals. Although the toilets were empty apart from herself, she coughed loudly with embarrassment to try and hide the initial shock of the sound.

After a few moments of acclimatization Selina rearranged her clothing and stepped out of the cubicle. The balls felt like an inordinately large blue-bottle whizzing around, lost inside her knickers. She took a few experimental steps around by the sinks—where she fastidiously washed her hands—and the Dual Balls stayed firmly in place. She breathed a sigh of relief, then steeled her resolve and nerve as she headed for the door.

Once out in the corridor, surrounded by screaming, sweaty, excitable, break-enjoying children, Selina was able to relax. She felt less furtive and guilty out in the public sphere. She reached her classroom without misadventure; though her variation on a John Wayne swagger may easily have aroused interest in any but a child's mind. She pushed open her classroom door and went in.

Her heart sank. Sitting in the front row of desks, dead centre, was Felicity Barrow.

Smiling broadly, Felicity said, 'Oh good, Selina. I was just about to give up my search and return to the staff room.'

Selina's entire body felt stiff and immobile; only the Dual Balls continued on moving naturally inside her. She tried to negotiate the walk to her desk as freely and casually as possible. To distract Felicity's attention she said, 'Lovely day isn't it?', and pointed towards the window. Felicity turned towards the window and stared out through it at the blue sky. 'Yes, it is lovely.'

She was pleased that Selina was trying to be friendly. Selina took these few seconds' leeway to trot over to her desk and plop herself down on to her hard wooden chair. She noisily cleared her throat so that Felicity's silent contemplation of the day's glory wouldn't emphasize the jubilant buzzing of the Dual Balls. Felicity's gaze returned to Selina's face. 'You're looking very well, Selina, if I may say so, very bright.' Selina smiled. 'I think I'm actually just a bit warm. Perhaps I should take my blazer off.'

She performed this simple action with as much 'involved noise' as possible, concluding with the scraping up of her chair closer to the table. Her hands were shaking slightly, so she took hold of a pencil and tapped out a tiny, slight rhythm with it on the table top.

Felicity watched these adjustments very closely, then said, 'You seem unusually tense today, Selina, any particular reason?'

Selina shrugged. Inside she was boiling with embarrassment and unease but she endeavoured not to let this show. 'I don't know, Felicity. I feel all right really, just a bit, I don't know, a bit frustrated, rudderless . . .'

She didn't really know what she was saying, but after she had said it she felt as though she was talking about sex, as though she was an actress in a dirty blue film. She pinched herself and blinked her eyes, then looked over at Felicity.

Felicity was still smiling at her. 'Maybe you're upset about all that ridiculous gossip that was circulating this weekend?'

Selina was still recovering from the tingling pain of her self-inflicted pinch. The pain seemed rather arousing, and the discomfort too. She asked automatically, 'What gossip?'

Felicity's cheeks reddened slightly. She had hoped that Selina would have been willing to make this conversation easy and un-embarrassing. She cleared her throat and to hide her discomfort adjusted the position of her hearing aid in her ear. 'Apparently someone has been spreading a rumour about . . . about your purported use of sexual stimulants during school time.'

Selina's face flushed violently and her jaw went slack, 'I . . . I don't know what to say Felicity. What can I say?'

At that moment in time she felt as though her head was clouding over, clouding up, as though she were in a plane that was going through turbulent clouds. She felt quite willing to admit to everything.

Whatever doubts had clouded Felicity's mind evaporated immediately when she saw the strength of Selina's reaction. She had expected Selina to keep her cool and to utter a cold, cynical, stinging reply. Instead her reply was so unguarded and natural, so loose and out of character, almost intimate, that Felicity could not stop herself from smiling warmly at her. 'Of course I knew it was untrue. I just thought you should be aware of the kind of things that a couple of nasty people are saying.'

Selina couldn't meet Felicity's gaze. She looked down at her desk and tried to call on an inner reserve of strength. Unfortunately this moment of introspection only re-emphasized in her mind the furtive activities of the Dual Balls. She was so tense that her body had become extremely dynamic and excitable. The hard wooden chair wasn't helping matters either. She shuddered, and suddenly her brain felt like sherbet.

The strength of Selina's reaction made Felicity's heart twist in sympathy. She bit her lip for a moment and said nervously, 'Selina, I'm sorry. I didn't think that this would affect you so badly.'

Selina felt as though she was on a roller-coaster ride. She said, 'I feel as though I'm on a roller-coaster ride, Felicity. I don't know what to say.'

She was all gaspy and uncontrolled, her insides churning with a sort of ecstatic violence. In the silence of the room she heard herself breathing heavily. Felicity sat quietly, saying nothing.

After a minute or so Selina began to gasp. She was totally out of control. She threw her head down on the table and shuddered until the shudders turned into enormous, violent, gasping, wracking howls.

Felicity froze. She had never seen such a forthright display of uninhibited emotion before and from, of all people, Selina

Mitchell. She felt a terrible sense of guilt that she should have provoked such a display, but also a sense of pride that Selina should have chosen to share this wild moment of release and abandon with her, Felicity. She stood up and went over to Selina's side and placed a gentle hand on her back which she moved up and down, up and down, as though comforting a small child or burping a baby.

Selina felt Felicity's hand massaging her back but felt too far gone to respond coherently. She just said, 'Oh God, oh no, oh my!'

Felicity moved her hand from Selina's back and grasped hold of one of her hands. She said, 'Selina, listen to me. This isn't as bad as it seems to you. It doesn't affect the respect and regard that I have for your teaching abilities. You are one of my best members of staff, in fact you are my very best member of staff.'

Selina heard Felicity's words but their sounds washed over her and made very little sense. She was at the edge of a precipice and in the next moment she was falling, flailing, floating. Her ears tingled as the wind rushed by. She steeled herself for a crash landing, but instead her landing was cushioned by a million feather eiderdowns, each as soft as a poodle's belly. Everything solidified again.

Felicity was pleased to note that after a minute or so her piece of encouragement had appeared to get through to Selina. She was calming down. After a while her breathing returned to normal and she raised her head slightly from the desk. Several seconds later she said quietly, 'Felicity, I feel terrible about this, but it was just out of my control. I feel so embarrassed.'

Felicity clucked her tongue and shook her head, 'Don't be silly, Selina. I know how these things build up. I'm just glad that you were able to let go of all that anguish and to share it with me.'

Selina felt as though she was floating in the Red Sea, lifted above the water by the sodium chloride, the sea like a big marshmallow. She blinked several times and sat up straight. She noticed that Felicity was still holding her hand. She smiled at Felicity and said, 'Things have been building up inside me for a long time. I feel so much better now, so buoyant.'

Felicity gave Selina's hand one final squeeze and then let go. She said, 'I know that you are a very controlled person, Selina. I've known you for most of your life and you've never let your emotions rule your head. I think you very much deserved this opportunity to vent your feelings.'

Selina was now fully recovered. She felt stupid but also surprisingly smug. She said, 'I hope you don't think that this silly outburst will have any bearing on my discipline and dignity before my classes.' Felicity shook her head. 'I know that I can always rely on you, Selina. I'm certainly quite positive that you are an indispensable asset to this school.'

Inside Felicity's head an idea was turning. It was as though a light had been switched on or the last piece of a jigsaw puzzle snapped into place. She said, 'Trust me, Selina, you have a great future ahead of you at this school. I'm going to see to that.'

Selina began to smile. She said, 'Felicity, you've been very kind and very understanding. Thank you.'

Felicity shrugged, 'It was nothing. Now clear up your face. Here's a tissue. A bit of spit and polish should do the job.'

Selina took the proffered tissue and applied it to her running mascara. Felicity walked towards the door. 'This has been an invaluable chat, Selina.'

Selina nodded and pushed her hair behind her ears, 'It has, Felicity, and thanks again.'

Felicity smiled and opened the door. Before she closed it behind her, however, she turned and said somewhat distractedly, 'I'm sorry to rush off like this, Selina, but my hearing aid is playing me up. I think it's dust or the batteries. It's been driving me mad with its buzzing for the last fifteen minutes or so.'

Selina smiled. 'That's all right.'

As the door closed, she stuffed Felicity's tissue into her mouth and bit down hard.

Water
Marks

You think just because you're getting married you can say that word in this house? You think that?'

Susan had repeatedly pronounced the synonym for 'copulate,' loudly, unashamedly, with emphasis, and Margaret, her mother, wasn't pleased.

'For heaven's sake, Mum!'

'Fine. That's it.' Margaret picked up Susan's breakfast tray and took several steps towards the door. 'If you want to speak like that in this house then you can go and eat your breakfast in the garden.'

'Mum!' Susan started to wheedle. 'It's my wedding day. I can't eat in the garden on my wedding day.'

A sheen of perspiration had appeared through Margaret's make-up. She hadn't yet had time to apply powder. *That's* how hectic it had been all morning.

Susan added, 'Anyway, I'm not stepping outside with my hair like this. Call Leanne.'

Margaret held on to the breakfast tray, eyeing the half-finished glass of Buck's Fizz, and then swallowed down her irritation. It is her wedding day, she thought. Let her get away with it. She dumped the tray down on to Susan's bed and went to call her second daughter.

Leanne was downstairs giving Dad his pep-talk. Scott, her son, was playing on the stairs, bumping noisily up and down, one step at a time, on his skinny, bony rump. He came when Margaret called. He popped his head into Susan's room, took stock of the situation and said, 'Why does Aunty Susan's hair look so funny?'

Susan slammed her hair brush down on to her dressing-table. 'Mum, get that little sod out of here before I wring his neck.'

Margaret placed a firm hand on to the top of Scott's head. Her fingers could almost grasp his crown in its entirety. His head felt cool, like an ostrich's egg. She applied pressure, twisted him around, his head first, his body following like a small spinning top. After she had turned him 180 degrees, she pushed him gently with her knee out of the room.

'Go,' she muttered. 'Go find Grandad. Ask him if the cars are sorted.'

'OK.' He didn't seem particularly bothered.

Leanne passed him on the stairs. 'Watch out,' he said, 'Aunty Susan's got a cob on.'

Leanne stopped. 'A cob,' she said, 'is a kind of loaf, a round loaf, sort of twirly. Or it's a male swan. That's a cob.'

Scott continued his descent. 'Grandad said Nan had a cob on this morning when the champagne cork went through the kitchen window.'

'Fair enough.' She turned and climbed up, making her way into Susan's room.

Margaret was standing in the doorway, her hands on her hips. Leanne squeezed past her.

'Now what?'

'Guess.'

Susan turned to face her.

'Susan, I'm sorry, but that's exactly what you asked for.'

'What?'

'You wanted it Elizabethan.'

'I wanted Elizabethan, but I didn't want it looking like I'd shaved three inches off the hairline. It looks like I'm going bald. The top's like a bloody . . .'

'It's a bouffant,' Margaret interjected. 'That's what you'd call it.'

Leanne added, 'It's like Glenda Jackson in that film about Elizabeth I.'

'Bloody great. She looked like an old sow in that film. I hated that film.'

Margaret sighed. 'I quite liked it.'

'You would.'

Susan put up a savage hand to her hair, but only patted it. Leanne said, 'Maybe it'll look better when the veil's on.'

'Piss it.'

Margaret picked up the tray again. 'Are you going to eat any more of this?'

'No. I've got indigestion.'

Susan turned and stared into the mirror. She didn't, she decided, look anything like *herself*. Maybe that had been the idea in the first place, to look *unlike* herself. My face, she thought, looks like a bee sting. Red and puffy.

A beautician had called around first thing to do her hair, her skin, her make-up. Even her nails. She inspected her hands. The nails, at least, looked pretty and polished. She said, 'My face is still all red.'

Leanne had been pilfering the breakfast tray. She was holding a large, brown sausage between her finger and thumb, readying herself to take a bite. Susan's comment distracted her. The sausage wasn't yet quite cold.

'A facial,' she said, 'wasn't a very good idea. I mean, you should've had it two or three days ago. A facial brings out all the impurities. As soon as I have one I always get loads of spots.'

'I was spotty before.'

'You look fine.' Margaret managed to sound convinced of this, adding with equal certainty, 'This is your day.'

'You should've got married in hot-pants, like me.' Leanne grinned, remembering.

'Yeah, well, I wanted to be a traditional bride. I wanted a traditional wedding. Now my face looks like a cow's arse, I don't suppose that's going to happen.'

Margaret said, 'You'll be wearing a veil. You'll look fine.'

'Where's the dress?'

Leanne was eating the sausage. It was pink at its centre. Downstairs she could hear Scott slamming the glass-panelled door between the living room and the kitchen. He's going outside, I bet, she thought. He'll mess up his suit. She said, 'I told Scott about holding your train again this morning. He promised to try and be more careful with it.'

Susan scowled. 'The little sod'll probably sit on it and have me dragging him down the bloody aisle. Where's the dress?'

'On my bed. It only arrived an hour ago. I'll go and get it.'

Margaret took the tray downstairs, knocked on the kitchen window at Scott, who was poking around in the pond with a twig, then returned upstairs to her bedroom to fetch the dress. She had laid it out on the bed earlier. It was covered in plastic but glossy inside; a pale creature in its transparent chrysalis. She picked it up carefully and took it through.

Leanne was fiddling with Susan's hair. She was saying, 'If you just leave the back down then it'll look like it always does.'

'Well, do a French plait or something, then.'

Margaret interjected, 'Simon doesn't like it when you do it that way.'

Leanne smiled. 'Last time I did it for you he said it looked like you had a randy armadillo clinging to your scalp.'

Margaret tutted. Her tongue stuck to the roof of her mouth. That's strange, she thought, I must be nervous. She lay the dress across Susan's bed and then checked her watch. 'Fifteen minutes before the car comes. I've not even powdered yet.' She put her hand up to the front of her fringe to check that she'd taken her curler out.

Leanne said, 'Don't worry, I'm doing a pleat.'

Susan grimaced at her reflection. 'Make sure it doesn't stick out. I hate it when they stick out. Makes you look like one side of your head is bigger than the other.'

Inside Susan, waging a battle with her irritability, was a little voice saying: It's going to be fine. It's going to be all right. She said, 'Leanne, switch the radio on. They always do dedications and a song for people getting married on Radio One at this time on a Saturday. Gary Davies or someone.'

'Let me pin this in first.'

'I'll miss it.'

She yelled, 'Mum! Can you come back in here? Can you come and switch the radio on?'

Scott wandered in. 'You want the radio on?'

Susan nodded. Leanne almost dropped the pieces of hair she was holding. Scott sat on Susan's bed and fiddled with the small radio on her bedside table.

'Just switch it on. Don't mess with the tuning.'

He switched it on. A voice said '. . . *especially Mandy and John in St Albans from the gang down at the rowing club. This is for all of you.*' The dedication was followed by the opening few strains of 'Endless Love.'

'I don't believe it. I bloody missed it. I waited twenty-four years for this moment and I missed it.'

Leanne pushed the final hairclip into the pleat and then stood back. 'Rubbish. You hardly ever listen to the radio any more.'

Susan kicked at the leg on her dressing table. 'I bet there was a request for me and I missed it.'

'I don't think anyone sent a request in. Simon didn't mention it either.'

'Maybe everyone in the office or down the pub . . .'

Leanne laughed. 'You never even mentioned it before now.'

Scott switched the radio off. Very tactful for an eight year old, Leanne thought. He then said, 'Only gits listen to Radio One.'

'Go and look up "git" in the dictionary.'

'I did earlier. It means . . .' He considered the word he was about to use. 'A comptemptible person.'

'Contemptible.' She thought about this for a minute. 'I bet it means more than that.'

Leanne was doing an evening course in Old English. She was reading 'The Nun's Tale.' Lately she'd become fascinated by the origins of words. She was considering a course in linguistics, but wasn't absolutely sure whether linguistics had anything to do with the history of language.

'Give me the bloody dress.' Susan raised her voice so that Leanne should realize that this was *her wedding day*. As a bride she had authority.

Leanne picked up the dress. Susan watched her. She took hold of the dress, bending over to grasp it, holding it in her arms like a dancing partner. When Susan snatched the dress from her, it was like she was stealing Leanne's partner in a Ladies, Excuse-me. She yanked the plastic off.

Leanne joined Scott who was standing next to Susan's small bookcase looking for a dictionary. She said, 'You must've had a dictionary for school, Susan.' Then she saw one and pulled it out. 'Git,' she said. 'Look it up again.'

Scott was grouchy but did as he was told.

'G-I-T,' she said.

Susan was surrounded by a broken blancmange of cream taffeta. She was fiddling with the seed pearl buttons.

'A hundred sodding seed pearl buttons,' she said furiously. 'Traditional my arse.'

Leanne said, 'Do you want a hand with those?' As she said this she noticed a strange stain, like a water mark, on the back of the dress. 'Scott?' She spoke casually.

He said, 'I haven't found it yet.'

'Why don't you go downstairs and let Grandad help you look? Aunty Susan's got to get dressed now.'

Scott sighed, exasperated, but closed the book and left the room. Susan was still grappling with the buttons.

Leanne inspected the stain more closely. It was seven or eight inches in diameter. It did look like a water stain. This was bad news, because water, as a consequence, probably couldn't be used to remove it. If I tell Susan, she thought, she'll go mad. But if I don't tell her . . .

'What the hell is that?'

Too late. Susan had seen it.

'I think it's a water stain or something.'

'Call Mum.'

Susan dropped the dress and sat down on the bed, thoroughly disgusted.

Leanne was accustomed to the rapidity with which Susan responded to things. For Susan, everything happened immediately—it *had* to—or not at all. If she had been a flower—her dad regularly said this—she'd be a passion flower. She'd bloom for a single day and then die. Passion flowers are beautiful, Leanne thought, but when it comes down to it, I'd rather be a lilac. The little flowers start off a dark, rich purple, fade into a lovely mauve, then turn into a bright white. Three flowers in one.

Leanne called Margaret. Margaret came in after several seconds, only half-way into her suit. She wore the skirt, a searing shrimp pink, on the knee, a nice length, good fabric.

'What?'

'The dress.'

Susan pointed. Leanne had picked the dress up. She indicated towards the water mark.

'I don't believe it. It must've been like that when they sent it.'

'I'm going to sue them.'

'You only tried it on two days ago. I didn't notice a stain then.'

'Phone them and tell them I'm going to sue.'

Leanne said, 'Is there any way of getting out a stain like this?' Margaret didn't really have a clue. She didn't know much about stains on the whole. What sort of a mother does that make me? she thought. Susan was glaring at her as though it was all her fault. She was the oldest. The oldest person was always responsible. Susan said quietly, 'I'm not going. Ring Simon. Tell him it's off.'

Leanne stared at Susan. Her nose and chin were red and her eyes were doleful. This is like a game of Mouse-Trap, she decided. Scott had the game at home; a brightly coloured plastic contraption with a large silver ball. She couldn't remember how you played it, what the rules were, but she did know for certain that once the silver ball had started to roll, the course of events was pretty much determined. She said, 'You can't hardly notice it, really. There's so much material. Once your veil's on it'll stretch down way below . . .'

'Phone them and tell them I'm going to sue.'

Margaret said, 'You could probably pin a couple of folds together if the veil didn't cover it.'

Leanne watched Susan's face. This could go either way, she thought. Anger or self-pity. She hoped it would be the latter. The corners of Susan's mouth began to turn down. Her chin trembled.

'It's a botch-up. It ruins everything.'

Secretly, Susan was almost pleased. The hair, the radio ... these things hadn't been a sufficient cause for dejection, but the dress ... well!

Margaret stopped herself from uttering platitudes. She wanted to say, 'It doesn't matter,' but, of course, it did matter.

Leanne said, 'Simon asked you to marry him that day you vomited in his car after Alton Towers. Remember? It won't make any difference to him.'

Scott rushed in. He was now wearing a button-hole. Margaret said brightly, 'The flowers have arrived. That's something.'

Scott shouted over the top of her words, 'Git. A bastard. In the sense, to beget. Hence, a bastard, fool.'

Damn, Leanne thought, that wasn't very successful.

Susan matched his yells with her own. 'Scott, bugger off!' Every time I get some attention, she thought, that little brat ruins it.

Scott stuck out his bottom lip, looked from Susan to his mother and then back again. Margaret snatched hold of his hand and led him out of the room. She's my daughter, she thought. It's her wedding day.

Leanne said, 'Susan, just because you're the bride, doesn't mean you can get away with being rude to everybody.'

'Well, what the hell does it mean then?'

Leanne scowled. 'It means that you can get away with throwing a tantrum, but that if you're a decent person you'll decide to behave well, even though you know that you don't absolutely have to.'

Susan said, 'Leanne, you're full of shit.'

Leanne held up the dress. 'Put this on.'

'No.'

'Don't be stupid.'

'It's ruined.'

'It won't even notice once the veil's on.'

Leanne watched Susan's face. *Will she, won't she, will she, won't she?*

Susan stood up and held out her arms. Leanne helped her pull the dress on. Dad shouted upstairs, 'Nearly time now. The flowers are ready. The cars are here.'

Susan twirled in front of the mirror. The dress looked fine . . . But the stain? Once the veil was on . . . The veil was long. For a moment she understood exactly what Leanne had meant about the bride choosing to be nice. That, too, was a kind of power.

Margaret came in, fully dressed now. 'See?' she said. 'I told you it'd look just lovely.'

Susan saw herself as a scale. In her mind things were delicately balanced. She was outside herself, looking on. Things are very carefully balanced, she decided. A small weight of irritation, frustration, fury, was outweighed, only just, by a supreme equanimity. This is as it should be, she thought. I'm a bride. I'm going to church. This whole day is about . . . love.

Margaret handed Susan her bouquet. Next she picked up the veil and helped Leanne to pin it on to Susan's head. They adjusted its pale folds. This is that special moment, Margaret thought, where a mother gets all emotional.

Susan burped, then put her hand over her mouth and said, 'I could do with a Rennie or something. My gut's all acid.'

Leanne said, 'I'll get you one after I've found my shoes and my bag. I won't be long.'

Scott was sitting on the bottom stair looking petulant. Leanne said, 'Don't get any fluff on your suit.'

He said, 'I don't like Aunty Susan.'

'She's uptight, that's all. She didn't mean to be rude.'

'What did she mean, then?'

'It's complicated.'

Scott wasn't satisfied with her answer. He said, 'So sometimes it's all right to be rude?'

'Sometimes, but only if you've got a good enough reason. We'll talk about this later, OK?'

Leanne looked around for her bag and located it on the hall table. Her shoes were neatly placed on the front doormat. She slipped her feet into them and then made her way through to the kitchen, past Dad, the flowers, the chauffeur, who was having a cup of tea. She found some indigestion tablets. Scott was trailing around behind her. She said, 'It's nearly time to go.'

'Is Aunty Susan allowed to be rude because it's her wedding day?'

'No. Yes. She's only rude because she's upset. That's all.'

She swept past him and up the stairs. Scott watched her. In his mind he was working out a simple equation. It went: Wedding= Upset=Nasty=Fine. He smiled to himself. Right.

Susan processed down the stairs. Leanne and Margaret darted around behind her like a couple of frantic swifts. Susan felt almost too grand for this house, like a misplaced princess. Her mind had been quietened by meditating solely on the letter I. I'm looking forward now, she thought. I am the present. I am the future.

The chauffeur led the way to the main car. A Rolls. White. Margaret followed, then Leanne, next to Susan, who had agreed, just this once, to hold up her own train. Grandad locked the front door.

Scott stood in the path behind Susan as they waited to arrange her comfortably in the car.

'Aunty Susan,' he said, his small voice chiming out as clearly and purely as a perfect crystal bell.

'What?' She barely turned.

He said, 'Aunty Susan, it looks like you've wee-weed all down the back of your dress.'

Susan's good intentions flew out of her mouth like a big, fat, red, angry robin.

Back
to
Front

Nick was back to front, but only on the inside. When he was born, the midwife held him up by his tubby, bloody legs, cleared out his mouth and his nasal passages while the doctor, holding his stethoscope, aimed it like it was a dart and Nick's heart the bulls-eye, listened, blinking, holding his own breath, for the infant's heartbeat.

But he heard nothing. Just the faintest scuddering; a faraway, dreamy sound, something so distant from the white, harsh delivery chamber, the long, tiled hospital corridors, the clatter of trolleys, the banging of doors; something so soft and fragile, so remote, that it sounded like the peripheral scuffle and bicker of two wagtails arguing over a berry in a holly bush.

He tried not to panic. Nick's mother, propped up on four pillows, whipped and battered, noticed in an instant.

'What's wrong?'

'Nothing's wrong.'

'Tell me!'

'If you'll just quieten down for a moment . . .'

The young doctor held his breath until his eyes began to water. Still that rattling noise, and very indistinct. But the child was as fresh and ripe as a little cherry, a boy, breathing and gurgling and thinking about squealing.

'I'm just going to take him off with me for a minute,' the doctor muttered, grabbing Nick's legs and righting him. The midwife caught the doctor's eye. Nick's mother caught the midwife catching the doctor's eye. As Nick was carried from the delivery room, she struggled to count the number of his fingers and the number of his toes. Ten of each. Before he was gone. And so it was. Nick was set apart. He was different. Outwardly, not a sign, but inside, everything back to front.

'Everything,' the doctor told the midwife, five minutes later, full of wonder, 'the opposite way around from how it should be. I couldn't hear his heart at first but it's beating well enough, except it's on the right-hand side of his body instead of on the left. And all his other organs too. Topsy-turvy. There's a name for it.' But he didn't know the name because Nick was his first.

Nick's mother, Grace, told all the other mothers how her Nick was back to front. 'I called him Nick,' she said, 'because he came along in just the Nick of time.'

The other mothers cackled. Although, in truth, there was nothing medically dangerous about Nick's condition, and time, or the lack of it, was of no consequence whatsoever.

Nevertheless, every day she counted his fingers and his toes just to make sure. Ten. Ten. She was a pernickety mother. As Nick grew older, if he complained about her coddling she'd tell him how he was taken from her on the day he was born, set aside, examined, and all the while she hadn't known what was wrong, had only imagined. And there's nothing worse than imagining. Not a thing.

So Nick was set aside and he was special, but only on the inside, and that kind of difference, the invisible kind, can be very hard to live with.

At school, his teachers found him to be a small, sharp peak; slippery and unassailable. He was so convinced of his own superiority. And the other children had no interest in anatomy, or where exactly the heart was located. It would be a long time until that particular juncture—third form biology, maybe, but certainly not yet.

It was hard for Nick to understand his own apparent insignificance. At first he'd emphasized his difference and this had made the other children hate him. So he wouldn't fit. Didn't want to either. And then they teased, insulted and derided him. So then he couldn't fit, even if he'd cared to. But finally they began to ignore him. He became a blank. A nil. A nothing.

When Nick was aged fifteen, Grace remarried. His stepfather, Thomas Siswele, was Nigerian by birth. Grace thought Thomas was different, not ordinary like she and Nick were but, oh so special. He taught Grace how to cook groundnut stew with plantain.

And so it started. Each day Thomas would bring home the local paper and read out titbits to Grace as she prepared their dinner. He'd read out news about fêtes and fairs and infestations, an award-winning garden on the eighth storey of a tower-block, a fight, a rape, arson, theft.

You'd almost believe, Nick thought, standing in the doorway, unheeded, that he'd gone and written that paper himself, with all the fuss she makes over it.

One Friday afternoon, Nick turned himself in at the police station for shoplifting.

'What did you steal?' they asked. He told them.

'Where did you put the stolen goods?'

'In my bedroom.'

They searched Nick's house and found nothing. So he had to tell them how he'd stolen a car.

'What's the registration? The car type? The colour?'

He told them, details he'd seen in the paper. But then they found the missing car in a lock-up in Walthamstow and covered in someone else's prints.

Nick told them how he'd set fire to a factory in High Barnet. 'Why? What fuel did you use? Whereabouts and how much?'

'Petrol. Everywhere.'

But the specialists told the police that the fire had started because of an electrical fault. There were no traces of petrol.

After a while the police got sick of Nick. His timewasting. Nick was excited by this. He kept on wasting their time hoping it would lead somewhere, but instead of charging him for it they decided to ignore him. They told him he was the boy who cried wolf. And you know what happened to the boy who cried wolf, they said, don't you? Nick prayed it would happen.

Back to front, back to front, back to front. Had to mean something.

Then he met Lyndon, in a police cell.

'What you up for?' Lyndon asked.

Nick struggled to remember. 'Armed robbery,' he said. 'Jewellers.'

'H. Samuel's?'

'That's the one.'

'Did you do it?' Lyndon already knew the answer. His question was merely a matter of form.

'Yes, I did it,' Nick said.

Lyndon eyeballed Nick while rubbing his chin. You see, this was *his* crime Nick was appropriating.

'You didn't do that job,' Lyndon said eventually. 'I did that job.'

Nick merely shrugged.

'I did that job,' Lyndon reasserted. And this was the act he'd been denying and recanting, in his own mind, to the coppers, for hours now, for days now.

'What you in for?' Lyndon asked again.

'Robbery,' Nick said, 'H. Samuel's.'

'Fuck you, man. I did that thing.'

Nick shrugged.

'Don't fuck with me, man. I did that thing.'

Lyndon was no great respecter of lies, except of his own. He squared up to Nick. Nick sighed and turned to the wall.

'What you in for, man?'

Nick said nothing. His mind was miles away, thinking about the distinction between *being* different and *doing* different. He didn't have to be, only to do.

Lyndon had no interest in distinctions of any kind. He had a small knife secreted in the sole of his trainer. He drew it out.

'What you in for?'

Nick was busy deciding in his own mind whether a plantain and a banana were the selfsame thing.

Lyndon calculated that if he stuck his knife in, just so, in that place where nothing particularly important was stationed . . . He knew the distinction, it must be admitted, between grievous bodily harm and murder. Nick had his back to him. Lyndon's knife was so sharp it slid in with ease.

Nick had arrived, finally. This was his moment. He was so happy because everyone was shouting and looking and touching and pushing and staring. Finally the crowds cleared and a doctor stood before him.

'Let's see,' he said, swabbing Nick's wound with cotton wool, assessing its relative anatomical insignificance. This was Casualty. He was busy.

Even so, Nick was losing an unusually large amount of blood. The doctor felt Nick's pulse. It was weak. He used his stethoscope. He could hear almost nothing. The faintest of sounds.

Nick stared up at the doctor, full of joy, and debated whether to tell him his secret. He opened his mouth, he breathed in, he was just about to, and then something wonderful occurred to him. Wouldn't it be great, wouldn't it be just the best thing ever, if he left the doctor to find out for himself? How exciting that would be. What a revelation!

After Nick died, the doctor spent a long while marvelling over his peculiar insides. And the coroner did, too. And the student working alongside the coroner. He'd never seen anything quite like Nick before. All back to front! Nick was his first. Nick was very special. Yes, he was. He was.

Limpets

Davy swore to himself, that day on the New Plaistow Road, that even if he lived to be one hundred years old, he would never ask a woman out again. Not like that. Not *cold.* 'Next time,' he decided, 'I'll be in a disco. I'll ask her to dance, I'll offer to buy her a drink . . .' A series of small questions. She could turn any single one of them down and he wouldn't be irreparably injured. No matter how fine she was, how pretty.

Inside the café on the New Plaistow Road, Jodi, the girl he had asked, was wiping down a table. There was only one other person in the café. He was a short, squat man, a heavy drinker. His name was Leonard.

'You bitch!' Leonard said. 'You turned him down flat, just like that. Do you know how much pluck it takes for a man to ask out a girl?'

Jodi had her back to him as he spoke. 'Are you married, Leonard?'

She knew that he wasn't. He wore a gold ring, like a wedding ring, very plain, but he was not married. Never had been. Brown and bitter was his poison. His father was Greek, his mother Italian. Both dead now. He was sixty-two years old, unemployed.

'I am not married.'

She turned and faced him, one hand held aloft, clutching a moist cloth tightly so that no crumbs should fall from it, her other hand, open below, ready to catch.

'Can you play chess, Leonard?'

He rubbed his nose, which was puce and bulbous. She thought his nose looked as if it was riddled with woodworm. Pores both full and black or gaping.

'No chess. Dominoes.'

'Well,' she said, having established her position in her own mind very comfortably with these two questions, having justified herself quite adequately, 'butt out.'

Davy opened his packet of cigarettes, removed one and stuck it between his lips. He squinted down at it as he fumbled in his pocket for his lighter. In his head her voice reverberated. She said, 'D'you want a can of anything to take with you?' She always said this to him when she totalled up his lunch on the till.

'Not today,' he said, breaking with tradition. 'Actually . . .'

'OK.' She was about to tell him how much he owed her.

'Actually I wanted to ask you something.'

She looked up.

'Yes?'

It occurred to Davy, at this moment, that most people would have said *what*, but she had said *yes*. Why is that? he thought. What does it mean? And then: Ask her, you fool.

'I wondered if you'd come out with me some time. I mean tonight, maybe. Or Saturday.'

Jodi put her head to one side and stared at him. Her hair was carefully arranged in the strangest style. The first time he had gone to the café he had been confused by it, suspicious. Since then, however, quite spontaneously, he had decided that he liked it. Her hair was thick, straight, black, parted viciously, pulled into two fat plaits and these plaits curled into little, neat bundles on either side of her head; thick, black limpets. It was a weird, wretched, ridiculous, Germanic hairdo.

He was fashionable himself, did his hair in a self-conscious quiff at the front, at the back, a duck's-arse. Fashionable he could understand, but strange? Had her hair been loose and straight, he would have propositioned her two weeks earlier.

Of course, Jodi hadn't even noticed him. He was only another bloody customer.

Eventually she said, 'I honestly don't think it's worth it.'

'What?'

'Put it this way . . .' She paused. He waited for her to tell him that she had a husband (no ring), a boyfriend, a sick mother. He wanted to say, 'I work as a runner for a film company up West. I'm twenty-two. I'm actually very interesting . . .'

'Imagine,' she said coldly, 'if people were like . . . if their faces were like television screens, and when any one person looked at another person they could see everything they were thinking and everything they had ever thought or said about each other. Well, if that were the case, you'd be looking at my screen, and let me tell you, right off, my screen would be completely blank. Just empty.'

Davy was silent for a moment and then he said, 'How much do I owe you?'

'Two fifty.'

He handed her the money.

'Thanks.'

She opened the till and put it inside, then picked up a damp cloth which she kept behind the counter to wipe down the tables.

He said, 'A simple yes or no would've been perfectly adequate.'

Jodi ignored this, ducked under the counter, walked to the table that he'd used and began to wipe it down.

She was too thin, he decided, and those stupid black plaits on either side of her head looked like Mickey Mouse ears.

'See you.'

He walked out, relieved that only one other person had been present in the café to witness his humiliation. An old geezer who was always there, sitting at the corner table, smoking, half-pissed. Sweaty.

It was good and cool outside. He stopped next to the edge of the kerb and scrabbled around in the pockets of his jeans for his cigarettes. Screw her! he thought. Never-a-bloody-gain. No way.

* * *

'You bitch!' Leonard said.

Jodie listened to Leonard's comments and responded appropriately. She then returned to the till, picked up a copy of *The Times*, turned it to the correct page and then folded it down to a manageable size before lounging against the counter and studying it.

Leonard stood up. She didn't raise her eyes from the paper. He was an old bastard but a regular. She trusted him.

He staggered to the door, pulled it open and then stepped outside.

'Hey. You, boy. You still hanging around here? Still after something?' He coughed quietly, drew a glob of phlegm from his throat, into his mouth and then swallowed it down. Davy was inhaling on his cigarette. He turned and looked over his shoulder at Leonard.

'Who, me?'

Leonard moved towards him. 'Tell me something,' he said, 'How come women are so fucking stupid?' He tapped the side of his head with a plump, yellowy forefinger. 'No logic.'

'What?' With my luck, Davy was thinking, this fat old git'll turn out to be her father.

'Ask me about her,' Leonard said. 'Anything you like. I know everything about her.'

'How come?'

Davy eyed Leonard side-on. His gut, his pate, his white stubble.

'I've been going in this place for years. I know all the girls who ever worked in there.'

Davy felt little inclination to have any kind of conversation with Leonard, least of all a conversation of a personal nature. He said, 'I don't think there's much point in discussing it.'

'OK,' Leonard said, 'I'll tell you one thing, though.'

'What?'

'Women do not have logical minds. You hear me? No matter what they do, no matter how they try. That's just the way it is. I mean, how many great thinkers do you know of that are women? Any?'

Davy shrugged. 'I dunno.'

'None.' Leonard folded his arms across his chest. His expansive gut bulged out under the weight of them. He continued. 'This girl

hates men. Why? Because nature has cursed her and given her a
fanny. Because men can think in ways that she can only dream of.
Ways that she can't. So she hates men.' He stabbed at Davy's arm
with his finger. 'So we must all suffer.' He paused and then added, 'I
see it every day.'

'How's that?' Davy was interested, in spite of himself. But already Leonard's mind was elsewhere.

'Here is the picture I have.' He drew a square, mid-air, with his
hand. 'Here is my information. She buys a paper every day. Does
she read it? No. Only turns to the back and looks at the sports.'

He swivelled around and peered in through the window of the
café, towards Jodi, who, true to form, was still leaning against the
counter and staring at her paper. Davy stared too. He noticed that
she was reading a big paper, not a tabloid.

'She has a large family. Four brothers. Hungarian. All older.'

'What's she reading?'

Leonard rolled back on his heels.

'Chess.'

'In the paper? I've never seen chess in the paper.' As he spoke,
however, he had a vague recollection of having seen a black and
white chess board on the back pages of proper papers.

Leonard said, 'See how she does her hair? See how her uniform
is? All neat. Clean shoes?'

Like a bloody Fascist, Davy thought, feeling ashamed of the
impulse in himself that had caused him to find her attractive.

'Everything is as it should be.'

Davy interrupted. 'She can't hear us out here, can she?'

Leonard shook his head. 'Wouldn't notice if I took out a gun
and shot you. See her face.'

Davy turned and peered in through the window again. Jodi
stood by the counter, as before, reading, but her face, he noticed, was
white, pointed, tensed, focused, bloodless.

'What's wrong with her?'

'Sex.'

'What?'

Davy laughed sharply, with embarrassment. Leonard pummelled the palm of one hand with the fist of his other, a gesture that needed little interpretation.

'Know what I mean? All those brothers. She wants to be like a man. All straight and neat and everything clear in her head. Silly bitch.' He licked his lips before adding, 'Ripe for the plucking.'

Davy noticed that Leonard's fringe, originally white, had been stained a sickly yellow from nicotine. Also a small funnel on his upper and lower lips, on the right hand side of his mouth where he characteristically held his cigarette. This man, he thought, is a bloody animal.

Jodi was still leaning against the counter. She was memorizing several of the moves in the Short/Timman match. Originally she had believed that chess was a game that invited skill, wit, spontaneity. But now she knew that the only way to contend at a serious level was to learn, to revise, to memorize, to plan and to structure. Prepare as if for war.

Jodi had three brothers. Her parents were Romanian. All had played chess from a very young age. Her father was an exceptional player. None of the other brothers had ever beaten him. Only she, Jodi, had managed this once, aged thirteen. It had been the best and the worst day of her life.

Her father had said, 'Do you know how you beat me, Jodi?'

'How?' She smiled up at him, exultant.

'Puberty. You have turned into a woman under my very nose but I didn't notice. When you moved your knight and left your Queen unprotected I thought: she's lost it, she's not concentrating. I let my guard down. I didn't see the move for what it was: sensuous, ridiculous, gregarious. Very, very feminine.'

Jodi had stared at him, unsure how to react. She thought, is this good or is this bad? She still asked herself this question: *Good or bad?*

Leonard nudged Davy in the ribs with his elbow. 'Once I listened about how she went to a pub to play chess with this famous English champion. Crazy man, long hair, glasses. I forget his name. Anyway, all the tables in the pub had boards. He played five games all at once,

ten games, just walking between tables. She played four moves . . .
one, two, three . . . and he beats her. Just like that. Easy!'

'So what happened?'

Leonard laughed and shook his head. 'She says, "I'll learn every
move it's possible to make. I'll read every book. I'll see a whole game
in my head before it's even played." Now she says she can play a
game without even looking at the board.'

Davy felt suddenly ashamed. I asked her out, he thought, and I
didn't know any of this. Imagine, all these things going on in her
head and I couldn't even have guessed at them. He stepped away
from Leonard and moved back towards the doorway of the café. He
saw Jodi through the glass in the door. He felt a sudden, incredible,
horrifying desire to consume her entirely, to take her and to make all
those strange, abstract, alien parts of herself his own. He wanted to
drink her down in one, like she was the liquid in a can of fizzy drink
that could quench his thirst and bite into the back of his throat all in
a single, thorough, rushing gulpful.

Jodi sensed a figure hovering around just outside the café, near the
door, a blur beyond the edge of her paper. She had ten moves
worked out in her head, one after the other. She *had* to keep them in.
Order. Symmetry. Design.

Her own private moves were there, too, in the back of her mind.

I will never dance with a man.

I will never make love.

I will never marry.

I will never bear children.

She sighed as she put down her paper and glanced up towards
the figure in the doorway. She sighed but she felt not the slightest
twinge of regret.

And then she noticed that it was Davy standing in the doorway.
Davy? Was that his name? And then she noticed that he had bright
green eyes. It was her move.

Bendy-Linda

Belinda was well acquainted with the fact that the tortoise was a protected species, but this information could hardly be expected to improve her opinion of these silent, shelled, sly, *old* creatures.

She had joined the circus at eighteen, when she was awarded an E grade in her history A Level and an F in physics. Six years ago. Now she travelled the length and breadth of the continent, performing her gymnastic feats. She could start off doing a back-bend and end up with her head sticking out from between her own thighs. People at the circus called her Bendy-Linda, and the single question that she was asked more than any other was: *What is it like to perform cunnilingus on yourself?* To which she would usually reply, 'Depends how long it's been since I had a bath.'

Bendy-Linda also had chief responsibility for the performing parrot troupe: seven parrots which she dressed anthropomorphically and had taught to don and doff hats, hold up miniature papers, kiss each other—birdy, beaky kisses—and dance in time to specified tunes. They also talked. They said, 'Hello there,' 'Milk and no sugar,' 'May I have the pleasure?' and 'Great weather we're having.' She believed that these few sentences and phrases offered the key to a perfect life. A parrot utopia.

Belinda's main problem with the birds was to keep circus people, and others, from using inappropriate language in front of them. One bird had learned how to say 'Bloody Hell' and had been forcibly retired from the troupe as a consequence. Swearwords were like fireworks: much brighter and louder and sparklier than other language. Both children and parrots—those tiny sensualists—were irresistibly drawn to them, couldn't wait to wrap their tongues around them.

There were nine acrobats and tumblers at the circus, all told.

'The turnover of staff in this field has always been rapid.' This was Alberto, circus ring master and manager.

Belinda stared at him, unsmiling. 'I suppose that goes with the territory.'

Alberto nodded, not truly comprehending. *Turnover*, Belinda felt like saying, it's a joke.

Alberto was introducing her to a new tumbler. He was tall, thickset, blond; physically unlike your average acrobat. Alberto said, 'This is Marcus. He's French.'

'Hi.' Belinda offered him her hand. He took it and squeezed it gratefully, but said nothing, only smiled. Belinda smiled back and said, 'We usually all go out for a meal when a new acrobat joins. Pizza or something. It's a tradition. Are you keen?'

He nodded eagerly.

'OK, I'll arrange it.'

The following evening, a large group of them were filling out a significant portion of a local brasserie. Belinda sat to Marcus's left. On her left was Lenny, who in her opinion was a workaholic and a bore. He was analysing one of their routines. 'The first set of tumbles,' he said, his tone rigorous, 'come from nowhere. It's like the floor exercises in a gymnastic competition, lacking a certain fluidity, a certain finesse. I mean, there are no hard and fast rules in this business.'

Belinda looked at him, her blue eyes sombre and unblinking.

'Anyway, the tempo's all wrong.'

Choosing her moment carefully she said, 'Lenny, let's not talk about work all night, OK?' She turned and took a glass from a tray that was being proffered by a waiter. 'Pernod. Excellent.'

She focused on Marcus. 'How've your first couple of days been? I haven't seen you around much, apart from at practice and the show.' She had seen him at practice in his slinky French lycra garments. At least a foot taller than any of the other men, but gratifyingly agile.

Marcus took so long to respond to her enquiry that she almost came to the conclusion that he spoke no English at all. But eventually he said, 'It was . . . all fine.' He spoke slowly and laboriously. The effort of it brought tiny specks of perspiration to his upper lip. Belinda stared at him, wide-eyed. He's drunk, she thought, and it isn't even an hour since the matinée.

The waiter moved over to Marcus and offered him the tray. Marcus selected a bottle of beer, glad of this distraction, and drank down a hurried swig of it. Belinda said coolly, 'You're unusually tall for a tumbler.'

He nodded. 'Yes . . . I am.' After an inordinately long pause he added, 'Five foot . . . nine.'

He seemed to be relishing his words and observations with a drunk man's delight. Belinda had been tipsy herself on several occasions and was well acquainted with the feeling of intense gratification that the performance of everyday feats accorded one while in this condition. The brain works so slowly, she thought, that opening a door or saying hello are transformed into tasks of terrible complexity.

Marcus put his beer down next to his plate and started to say something else, but before he could complete his sentence, she had turned away, towards Lenny, and had begun to discuss the rudiments of their early tumbling routine with him in some detail.

Later that night, when Belinda attempted to enter her trailer, the door wouldn't slide back smoothly, but jammed when it was half open. She stopped herself from saying anything worse than 'Darn!' adding, 'Needle and thread,' for good measure. (The parrots were tucked up next door, covered for the night but ever vigilant.) She then groped around blindly in the doorway until her hand located a tortoise shell. You little swine! she thought, tucking the tortoise under her arm and reaching inside her pocket for a lighter to ignite one of the lamps.

Once the lamp was lit she kicked the door shut behind her. The tortoise was still under her arm, tucked snugly there, held dispassionately, like a newspaper or a clutch bag. His head and feet were completely drawn in.

This creature had once belonged to her grandmother and was called Smedley. Belinda dumped him down on to the floor again. He scuttled away instantly.

When Belinda had taken possession of Smedley, two years ago, she had been misguidedly under the impression that tortoises were no trouble. They hibernate, she was told. They're one of those creatures that don't need any attention. She couldn't reconcile this description with her own particular specimen. He certainly didn't seem to bother hibernating. In fact he appeared to have difficulty in sleeping at all. Most of his time was spent powering around inside her van, his head fully out, stretching on scaly elephant's skin, his feet working ten to the dozen. He took no interest in things, only walked into them or over them. Even his food.

Belinda's grandmother had owned Smedley for thirty-five years. He had lived in her garden during this time, as happy as Larry. Belinda had been given him, in accordance with the will, and a small financial sum concomitant in quantity with thirty-five more years of carrots and greens. Interest linked.

Twenty-four and thirty-five. She calculated these two numbers every time she caught a glimpse of the tortoise, scuttling from the kitchenette to her bedroom, emerging from under her sofabed. Fifty-nine. I'll be fifty-nine years old, she thought desperately, when that bloody creature finally kicks the bucket. It was as if the tortoise had already stolen those years from her. I'll be sixty, she thought, I'll be retired. I won't even have the parrots any more. I won't be able to do back-flips or walk on my hands. Smedley had taken these things from her, had aged her prematurely, had, inexplicably, made her small trailer smell of Steradent and mothballs.

It had been ten thirty when she'd returned. At ten forty someone knocked at her door. She pushed her slippers on, pulled her dressing gown tightly around her and yanked the door open. It was Marcus.

'What do you want?'

She stared into his face, slightly taller than him now, standing, as she was, on her top step. He said nothing, only handed her a note.

'What?' she asked again, taking it.

He bowed, low and formal, then walked off.

Belinda sat down on the top step and unfolded the note. It was written on onion paper. She always found onion paper quite peculiar. So light, so oniony. Very French.

The note said:

> Good evening Belinda,
> Eugenie told me that you thought I was drunk at dinner. Alas, no. I suffer from a speech impediment, a stammer, which in times of social tension can become terribly pronounced. I apologize if this minor problem irritated you in any way. I can assure you that it irritates me in many ways, but, as they say, such is life. N'est-ce pas?
> Marcus

Although the tone of Marcus's note, the night of the dinner out, had been anything but hostile, Belinda spent the following five days trying and failing to apologize to him and to worm her way back into his affections. She found it extremely difficult to talk things over with a person who was virtually monosyllabic.

Because Marcus spoke so very little, he gave the appearance of listening much harder than your average person. Did he listen? Belinda couldn't decide. It felt like he did. She noticed how he became a kind of father confessor to all the tumblers, the acrobats, some of the clowns, the most beautiful tightrope walkers. He didn't strike her as particularly French. His accent—the rare smatterings that she heard—didn't sound especially Gallic.

In fact, both of Marcus's parents were English. They were a couple who had taken advantage of the Eighties property slump in France and had emigrated when he was eight. He was now eighteen. His stammer in French was much less pronounced than in English, which struck him as rather strange.

One thing his stammer had taught him, however, was never to waste words. In general he tried only to say things that were incisive and pertinent. He preferred to avoid chit-chat. When others spoke to him, he slashed out gratuitous noises and phrases in his mind, analysed what they said, not with the gentle, non-judgemental sense of a confessor, but with the practised, cool, steady calm of a surgeon. For instance:

Larry says: 'Marcus, tell me straight off if you think I'm out of line here, but I bet you'll find that the double back-flip after the hand-walking stuff isn't strictly necessary. I mean, it's great and everything but just a little distracting.'
Marcus hears: 'Don't upstage me, new boy.'

Eugenie says: 'Wow! Those lycra things are fantastic. They look so comfy. They really do. I just love blue. I love that shade. It's my favourite colour. Are they durable? I suppose they must be French. The French are *so* stylish.'
Marcus hears: 'Let me get into your trousers.'

Belinda says: 'You really must come and meet my parrots. How about it? Tonight? After the show. If you're busy though, don't worry or anything. I mean, don't worry if you can't.'
Marcus hears: 'I'm sorry.'

In fact, Marcus was slightly off the mark with his interpretation of Belinda's babblings. The truth of the matter was that Belinda found him to be both aloof and disarming. She, too, wanted to charm the pants right off him.

Marcus had, however, noticed several worrying characteristics in Belinda's behaviour that did little to endear her to him. The first was that she jumped—too easily, too freely—to conclusions. This implied a certain amount of self-righteousness, a nasty, bullying bullishness. Secondly, she completed his sentences, which was something that he especially loathed. He guessed that people who were prone to doing this thought that they were helping him in some way, but it only made him feel useless, gratuitous, inadequate. He'd think: What is the point of *me*, if it's so easy to predict what I want, so easy to complete everything I begin?

The third and final thing that Belinda had done which had both shocked and disturbed Marcus, had occurred in the pub several nights after the meal out. Alberto had taken Marcus to one side, late that afternoon, shortly after the matinée, and had raised with him the possibility that he and Belinda might perform together during Belinda's contortionist routine. Since hitherto Belinda had been the only contortionist at the circus, this slot had always been solo. Alberto was keen to have Belinda partnered during this section, and although Marcus was no contortionist himself, Alberto felt that his leonine good looks and strong physique would make him the perfect foil to Belinda's dark skinniness.

That evening, in the pub, Marcus started to mention this new possibility to Belinda as she sipped daintily at her Pernod. He said, 'Can we . . . talk about . . . your . . . contortions . . . ?'

Oh yeah? Belinda thought, and what's he up to?

Alberto had said nothing to her about his plans. She was none the wiser.

She stared at Marcus coolly, vaguely disappointed in him but unsurprised. He was trying to talk again, but she saved him the trouble.

'Cunnilingus,' she said, baldly. 'Unfortunately, my tongue is the only part of my body that isn't double-jointed, otherwise I'd dispense with you boys altogether.'

She took another sip of her drink and eyed him over the top of her glass. He blushed. He tried to say something, but it wouldn't come out. He stood up, drank down his drink in one large gulp and left the pub. Now what? She stared after him, profoundly flummoxed.

Eugenie was lounging against Marcus's trailer, waiting for him to return. She was a small, pretty acrobat with long, red ringlets. She was thirty, single, an old hand at the circus, sexually voracious. As Marcus made his way towards her he was thinking: Damn Belinda!

Damn her! She's the strangest, coarsest, crudest woman I've ever met. She just seems to enjoy frightening me, on purpose.

'Hello,' Eugenie grinned at him. 'I've come around to borrow a cup of sugar.'

'Sure.'

She wasn't holding a cup. He unlocked his trailer and went inside, then emerged within seconds, holding a teacup full of sweet, white granules. He offered her the cup but she didn't take it.

'You're so literal,' she said, still smiling. 'I like that in a man.'

'Thank . . . you.' He inclined his head graciously. After a pause—not thinking to invite her in—he said, 'Be . . . linda.'

'What about her?'

'She's . . . rude.'

'She is?'

'I find . . . her so.'

Eugenie shrugged. 'You must just bring out the worst in her.'

Marcus considered this and then said, 'You think?'

'Maybe.'

'Why?'

She took the cup of sugar from him and said, 'You want to come and have some tea with me? Or coffee?'

'No . . . I . . .'

His stutter was so pronounced that Eugenie didn't wait around to listen to the reason for his refusal. She didn't mind. 'OK,' she said, phlegmatically, handing him back his cup. 'Some other time.'

Marcus sat down on his top step and stared into the cup. Thousands of grains. Mixed in with the pure, white granules were two extraneous tea leaves. That's me and Belinda, he thought. The world is full of millions of people, all friendly, all benign, the same. Then there's the two of us, destined not to get along. Belinda and Marcus. Both in the circus, this small circus. Both tumblers.

He felt relieved that his early and mid-teens had involved a longstanding but secretive intimacy with American *Playboy*. He was prepared for Belinda's lewdness, her crudeness. His father had kept an entire suitcase full of them in the attic which he had pilfered whenever he felt the inclination. Also, he had taken Latin at school, which in certain situations he found to be an invaluable linguistic tool. *Cunnus*—vulva. *Lingere*—to lick. Like choking on an oyster.

'Hi.'

Marcus looked up and almost dropped his cup. Belinda smiled at him. 'Look, I wanted to apologize. I guess I must've shocked you earlier.'

'No . . .'

'Well . . .' She focused on the strong, firm line of his jaw, its determined progression from behind his ear to the tip of his chin. 'I just saw Alberto.'

'Ah.'

'I don't suppose you want to come and see my parrots?'

'I'm . . .'

'Allergic?'

'No . . . I'm . . .'

'Busy?'

'No.'

'Go on, they're very friendly.'

Inside the parrots' trailer it was cool and dark. Belinda lit a lamp but kept the flame down low. 'It's bed-time for them really. I like them to be well rested. Otherwise they get cross and uncooperative.'

Marcus had seen the parrots already, in the big top. He thought them quaint but unnecessary. One day he hoped to work in a human circus, a wild circus where the performers did stunts on motorbikes and didn't use animals—camels with lopsided humps, sad, fleshy elephants, poodles with full wardrobes. Parrots.

'You like them?'

'I . . .'

'You don't like them?'

'No . . . I . . .'

'You like animals?'

He sighed. 'Yes.'

She said, 'My trailer's adjoining. We could have tea if you like.'

He shrugged.

Belinda opened a door and led him through. Her trailer was identical to his, only full of stuff: posters, trinkets, an extra wardrobe. 'Sit on the bed,' she said. 'I don't ever bother making it into a sofa. Too much trouble. Watch the legs are out properly. It has a tendency to collapse.' She filled the kettle.

Marcus didn't sit down immediately. First he inspected some of the photographs on her pinboard. 'These are . . .'

'Me. Yes. When I was a kid. I got gymnastics medals. I was nearly in the Olympics but I sprained my wrist very badly two weeks before. I cried for a month.'

The pictures were eerie. Belinda at eight, ten, fourteen. Belinda doing headstands, handstands, flying on the high bar. Belinda with no breasts, mosquito bites, breasts like tiny buds under the thin fabric of her leotard.

Little girls; gymnastics. He always found this combination vaguely unsettling. On television, with their stiff backs, pointed toes, determined visages. Obscene. Tumbling was different. Better.

'Coffee or tea?'

'Coffee.'

He sat down. The bed collapsed.

'Merde!' This word slid out of his mouth as quickly, as smoothly as an angry cat escaping the arms of its owner.

Belinda stopped what she was doing, turned around and then started to laugh at him, at his clumsy disarray. She said, 'You aren't hurt, are you?'

He shook his head and dragged himself up, then tried to rearrange the coverlet and cushions. Belinda turned back, still smirking, to complete her coffee-making.

This bed reminded Marcus in its construction of the deckchairs his parents had used at home; space-efficient but impossible to set up and make secure. He pulled out the metal bar that acted as the front legs and pushed up the springs and mattress. As he lifted he saw the tortoise.

Initially, it looked to him like an exotic seashell, or a lump of wood, centuries old, glossed up by the touch of many fingers, many hands. Then he saw it shudder, noticed a head, four feet. He reached out towards it, expecting a reaction. None came. One of its eyes was open, the other shut. That couldn't be right. He tapped its shell. Nothing.

I'm going to have to tell her now, he thought frantically, that I've killed her tortoise. How will I tell her? After several attempts, he said her name.

'Belinda . . .'

'Yeah?'

She had put two cups on to a tray. She picked up the tray and walked towards him. 'You haven't managed to get the bed up properly yet?'

He stared at her helplessly, as endearing and muddy-eyed as a golden retriever at tea-time. He pointed towards the tortoise. Her eyes followed the line he was indicating.

'Smedley!'

She quickly slid the tray on top of her dresser and crouched down. 'What's happened to him?'

'The . . . bed . . .'

'He looks all squashed.'

Marcus thought this an exaggeration, but took into account the fact that he hadn't seen the tortoise before its misadventure.

'Is he dead?'

'I . . .'

'He looks dead.' She reached out her hand as if to pick him up but then shuddered and withdrew. 'I can't stand the idea of something being not quite dead.' She added tremulously, 'If he wasn't dead and I touched him and he moved . . .' The thought of this made her feel queasy.

Marcus was staring at her. She saw his face—his expression a mixture of guilt and horror—and realized that these few seconds were crucial.

'He's dead!' she said, and burst into tears.

'I . . . I . . .'

For once he couldn't think of anything to say. Usually he could think of things only couldn't say them. Eventually he said, 'Sorry.'

'Tortoises,' she said, 'are protected. Did you know that? I never really knew what it meant, though. Protected. I never really knew. He was my grandmother's. He lived in her garden for thirty-five years. He was called Smedley. He didn't hibernate, only ran about in my trailer. He wasn't terribly demonstrative, but he seemed . . . happy.'

Marcus stood up. He was eighteen. He didn't feel sufficiently senior, sufficiently adult, experienced enough, loquacious enough, to be able to cope with this situation. He felt like phoning his mother, packing and leaving, joining that other circus, that *human* circus, that un-animalled circus. He could see it already, how good it would be.

Belinda sat down on the bed. It promptly collapsed again. Marcus had only propped up the bottom leg, he hadn't got around to securing it properly. Belinda scrambled up. 'Christ! If he wasn't dead before, he is now. Christ!'

She was still crying, but was already sick of crying. Her tears weren't sufficiently effective. He wasn't hugging her yet, wasn't comforting her. Why am I crying? she thought. To seduce him? That was the sum of it. She wondered idly if you could go to hell for emotional blackmail.

Marcus took a deep breath. 'The tortoise could be hibernating.'

Belinda stopped crying in an instant and said, 'Five words all in a row! Well done! Five words, just like that!' She then burst out laughing. 'Hibernating? *Please!*'

He was mortified by her laughter. She's evil, he thought. Absolutely insincere. Absolutely unprincipled.

He's only eighteen, she thought kindly. Poor bastard.

Marcus turned to leave, so furious now, so angry that he felt like fire, like liquid. 'Your face . . .' he said, struggling, choking, '. . . Chinese Dragon!' Then walked out quickly.

Belinda stopped laughing after he'd gone, stood up, walked over to the mirror. Her face was still mirthful but tear-smattered. Chinese Dragon?

He was right. She looked like one of those brightly coloured, finely painted Chinese masks, the dragon faces, covered in tears, but grinning, grimacing. A frightening face, apparently, but only, she supposed, if you were Chinese.

Belinda went over to lift her mattress, pulled up the bed and kicked Smedley out from under it. He slid about on the floor like the puck in a game of ice hockey. Click, slither, thud.

Oh, well, she thought, this could've been sad, but I really don't care. I could've shocked myself by caring, but I don't care.

She started to laugh again. Laughing was good for you. A kind of internal aerobics. Then she heard a voice, and it was not her own. 'Merde!' it said, and cackled. 'Merde! Merde! Merde!'

Belinda stopped laughing, her eyes tightened, and her mouth—quite spontaneously—performed a sudden, gorgeous, perfectly inadvertent back-bend.

Gifts

Jennifer, 42, had a special gift which God had given her—out of the blue—to compensate for all the things that had happened to her in the past. All the awful things.

Jenny had the gift of knowing that something had occurred—either nice or nasty, but usually nasty—straight after it had happened. If she trod on a dog's foot and it yelped, if the milk boiled over on to the oven, if she dropped a glass and it smashed. Well, then she would *know*. This was the gift that God had given her and she thanked God for it.

Jenny lived in a small complex of sheltered housing close to the big Safeways in Stamford Hill. She lived independently, but if anything bad happened she had a cord she could pull in her hallway, next to the door, so that someone else—the warden, Peter—would come along and sort everything out.

The only problem with this set-up was that Jenny refused to pull the cord. She would not. She referred to it as 'that fucking cord' and she would not pull it. It was a matter of principle. Instead, her neighbour, Naomi, would pull *her* cord on Jenny's behalf to call Peter over if she felt Jenny was in some kind of difficulty and Peter was needed.

Naomi was seventy-six years old and had a bad hip and could, occasionally, be clumsy and hurt herself. Sometimes she had to be taken to hospital when she scorched her hand or slipped over when climbing out of the bath.

At these times, when Naomi was absent, Jenny knew that if she got into trouble then she would simply have to sit down and think very hard about all the terrible things that had happened to her and how God had given her a gift so that she should *know* about them.

Naomi called this type of behaviour 'self-indulgence' but Jenny was content to feel that she knew better. To see things clearly, to register, to comprehend, well, that was surely a great blessing.

Jenny had a temper. Of course she did. And when she saw things clearly, they had to be seen properly, and everything had to happen in a certain way. She had her routines. A break from a routine was always a bad thing. Any kind of hindrance or interruption was considered by Jenny to be unacceptable. Any kind of intrusion, unpalatable.

Chad, 38, of no fixed abode, had a problem with rejection. But like Jenny, God had given Chad a gift too. His gift was that he would see things of no value, things that other people did not want, things that others misguidedly considered 'rubbish' and he would immediately love them.

God had chosen to give Chad his special gift because Chad had had everything—a home, a family, a good education—but he had rejected them. God understood difficult equations. God understood that Chad had been offered everything on a plate but that Chad had tipped the plate over. That made him special.

Peter, the warden, 23, was very familiar with Chad, his comings and goings, his shopping trolley, his stink, his pilfering, his cold sores.

Naomi knew Chad too. She liked to watch him picking through the rubbish, early on a Wednesday morning. The bins and the bags were put out the night before—a shiny black cluster, buzzing and rancid, ready for collection.

Jenny knew nothing of Chad. This was probably for the best.

Unfortunately, in October, when the leaves on the trees were starting to crisp and golden, Jenny's doctor decided to change her medication. He cut it down. He expected her to try to get through the night without her extra tablet.

So now, in the dark, she'd hear the clock ticking. So now, before dawn, she'd hear the birds singing. So now, after sunrise, she'd hear the cars on the main road close to her flat and the vans pulling into the unloading bay at the back of Safeways.

She even thought she could hear the drivers having a morning smoke, taking their fags out, the click of the lighter, the deep inhalation and the tinkle of the embers as they took their first drag. She convinced herself.

Wednesday morning, six forty-three precisely, Jenny heard something else. Much closer.

Outside, beyond the hawthorn hedge, Chad was carefully undoing the plastic knot on the top of a refuse bag. At first Jenny thought he might be a local stray, a cat, but when she listened more intently she decided that his technique was too deliberate, too careful for a creature with claws, too guided and thorough. So she threw off her blankets, clambered from her bed, walked to the window and gazed out. Beyond the hawthorn she saw Chad. Chad had gained access to the bag's contents. He'd found a broken saucepan which Jenny had snapped the handle off the day before. He was staring into it and he was thinking: is it big enough to use as a planter? For a small tomato plant? Shall I store it in my trolley? Shall I?

Jenny rapped on her window with the back of her knuckles.

'Oi!'

Chad looked up. Jenny stood at her window wearing a well-worn winceyette nightdress. The top two buttons were undone. Her navel was visible through a gap between the third and fourth. She had blue rings under her eyes. She hadn't slept properly for almost a week.

Chad stared at Jenny for several seconds, grimaced, returned to the bag, as though its contents held infinitely more interest for him than she did. Inside he found a wafer-thin slither of soap. In his trolley he had a self-assembled soap-cluster-ball which he'd created from just such soap remnants. It was almost as big as a cabbage.

Jenny opened her window and leaned out of it.

'Oi! Leave off!'

Chad looked up again, focused on Jenny, drew his lips back away from his gums and showed Jenny his teeth. They were brown and slightly peggy. It was an ugly expression, like the kind of face an ill-natured cur might pull. A snarl but nothing special.

Jenny gasped, slammed her hands on to her hips, marched into the hallway, appraised her emergency cord. Her fingers twitched but she didn't touch it. Instead she walked back into her bedroom, pulled on her dressing gown and returned to the window.

Chad had completed his dalliance with the bins and was now beating a slow retreat, disappearing from view, pushing his trolley with a combination of dignity and finesse, his back straight, his matted head held at an assured, an almost saintly angle.

Jenny slammed her window shut, piqued and disgruntled. Chad, she just *knew*, was a thief and a parasite.

'He's a magpie,' Naomi said, hours later, somewhat bemused by Jenny's fury. 'Don't get so worked up over it.'

'That's my stuff he's picking over,' Jenny retorted. 'My stuff.'

'Don't get so angry,' Naomi whispered, hoping to calm Jenny by speaking quieter. 'He doesn't mean any harm. He's only a tramp.'

'It's mine!'

'Shall I call Peter?' Naomi wondered out loud.

'My stuff. Private stuff. You know . . .' Jenny thought of something and stopped scowling for a moment. '. . . You know, sometimes people go through your bins when they want to find things out about you. And then sometimes the people whose bin it is calls the police.'

Naomi smiled patiently at Jenny who was still wearing her dressing gown and pink mules.

'Michael Barrymore!' Jenny yelled triumphantly. 'They did it to him! Going through his bins to find out stuff! All his leftovers and everything covered in tea-grains and bits of potato peelings.'

'You mean newspaper people, Jenny,' Naomi said. 'That boy's only a tramp. He's been going through our bins for as long as I can remember. You couldn't call the police. They'd laugh at you. He's not breaking any law.'

'He's like dirty vermin,' Jenny said, 'a rat or something.'

Naomi went into her kitchenette for a glass of water. She returned and handed it over to Jenny. 'Taken your pills yet today, Jenny?'

Jenny took the glass but didn't drink the water, only stared off into the distance.

'Coming for how long?' she asked tremulously. 'How long?'

'As long as I can remember,' Naomi reiterated, then added, 'I'll tell you what he's got in that trolley of his. He's got a ball of soap almost as big as your head.'

'What?' Jenny's eyes refocused. 'Huh?'

Naomi made the shape of a ball in the air with her hands. 'He gets all the soap, see? All the last bits of soap from the bins and he presses them together to make a big, round ball.'

Jenny was confused, Naomi could tell, so Naomi went into her own bathroom and brought out her soap. 'See? When soap gets wet for a while the bottom goes soggy, then if you push it on to another piece they get stuck together when they dry, and that way he's made a big soap ball from all the last, little bits. I've seen him take it out of his trolley. Big as a football.'

Naomi looked up from the bar of soap she was demonstrating with. Jenny's expression was stiff and cold, frosted with disgust.

'Not *my* soap,' she said, shuddering involuntarily.

Naomi rapidly backtracked. 'No,' she said, 'of course not.'

Jenny's eyes widened as the full implications of the big soap ball had their impact in that special Soap-Ball part of her brain. She imagined how intimate a thing a bar of soap was and also, this dirty man, and then the rubbing of the soap into one ball. It triggered something in her. 'Never!'

She sprang up from her chair, spilling water on to Naomi's carpet.

'Never!'

Naomi went and pulled her cord.

* * *

She'd been thinking about it, at night, when she couldn't sleep. The Soap Ball. Her privacy. That saucepan he'd taken.

She kept remembering all the things that had happened with the saucepan. How she'd bought it from Argos. A set of three. How she'd liked to boil eggs in it and cook spaghetti hoops. She kept going over the pan's history in her head; it was bought, it was used, it was broken. All in that order. And now he had it. What had he done with it? Her pan.

Wednesday morning she was up at five. Sitting on a chair next to the window, overseeing her rubbish bags in the pile next to the hawthorn. During the week she'd packed them so carefully. She'd kept thinking about what was rubbish and what was not, what she could throw out and what she could not. Only food and packaging and broken glass. Old newspaper.

Anything potentially useful, anything personal, she kept back. A threadbare face-cloth, a used toothpaste tube, an old hairbrush, an empty moisturizing cream bottle. Anything personal. These things she stacked on her kitchen table in a sad, useless little pile.

Six-forty on the dot, Chad trundled with his trolley into the crescent, pulled up next to the pile of bags, paused, chewed his lower lip, inspecting them. Jenny pushed her face so close to the window that she steamed it up with her breath and had to pull back to wipe it clear. Chad kicked one of Jenny's bags gently with the toe of his boot.

Chad knew about bags. He was an expert. He knew that the best kind of bag for his purposes was the kind of bag that jutted and stretched, that fought to contain something within that fought just as hard not to be contained. Jenny's bag felt soft and soggy, like it was full of bits of food and slush.

Naomi's bag, however, seemed distinctly more interesting. He untied it. Naomi's hands were frail and so Chad found her knots less difficult to negotiate.

Inside, on top, Chad found a mug tree. Natural pine, one of its branches missing, the base stained with something that looked like cod liver oil. He held it aloft. He smiled to himself.

Jenny had been intending to bang on her window as soon as

Chad touched one of the bags, but when he didn't touch hers—only kicked it—she felt a loosening of her resolve.

Instead, she watched him inspecting the mug tree and enjoying a snout through Naomi's bag. Chad reknotted Naomi's bag, after placing the mug tree in his trolley. Might use it at Christmas, he was thinking. Paint it green or something.

He left Jenny's bags alone. As if he knew! she thought, furious. Almost as if he knew! She stood up and tossed the chair she was sitting on against the opposite wall.

Chad heard the commotion emerging from Jenny's first-floor flat, glanced up for a moment, raised his eyebrows, sniffed, muttered 'Slag!' under his breath and then moved off.

Naomi, next door, eating her breakfast, chewing on a piece of bacon rind, heard the chair smash, jumped up and bolted towards her front door.

Peter looked at the growing pile of 'useful' rubbish on Jenny's table. 'So what's going on, Jenny?' he asked softly. Jenny had made him a cup of tea but she was too angry to speak, almost. 'I can see that you're very uptight over something,' Peter added sympathetically, sipping his tea and wishing she hadn't added Hermesetas instead of sugar.

'Naomi's worried,' he said, pushing aside an eggbox and an empty cornflake packet so that he could rest his cup on the table.

'What's his name?' Jenny asked, her throat so taut she nearly growled.

Peter stared at her blankly.

'His name! Him!' Jenny yelled, picking up the eggbox, tearing it in half and then smashing it on to the kitchen lino.

'You know what I think, Jenny?' Peter said brightly. 'I think you and I should take a trip over to see Dr Eric this afternoon. Maybe cutting down on your pills wasn't such a good idea after all.'

'His name,' Jenny repeated, softly.

Peter took another sip of his tea. 'I don't know,' he said gently, after swallowing.

Later, Naomi told Jenny—in passing, not connecting anything with anything—that Chad's name was Chad. Jenny digested this information silently. I *knew* it! She told herself, victoriously, I just knew his name would be Chad.

Jenny was quiet for the rest of the day. In her mind she was thinking, Chad, Chad, Chad, Chad, Chad.

When she went to see Dr Eric, she purred and she simpered like a friendly kitten.

That whole week Jenny assembled all the best things she could find. Her favourite Catherine Cookson novels, her best lace tablemats, a sturdy teapot she'd not yet had occasion to use, a packet of felt-tips which she kept in a drawer for when her nephew called, a full bag of rice, a tin of Heinz baked beans. She lay out her array of goodies on her living room carpet. Then she placed them, one by one, into a black refuse bag.

Chad was late that Wednesday. He'd drunk a bottle of Tia Maria the night before which had left him feeling drugged and sweet and dumb. He was slower than normal as a consequence. And sticky.

It was almost seven when he turned into Jenny's crescent. From a distance he stared up at Jenny's window. He was fully aware of Jenny. He was sensitive like that. He had to be. He knew that for years he'd been looking in her bin and for years she hadn't cared but that now she did care. He knew that people were very prone to chucking things out and then feeling like the things that they'd abandoned still *belonged* to them in some sense. Stupid.

He saw Jenny's outline etched in charcoal against the window-pane. He didn't like being watched. Even so, he drew close to the bags, let go of his trolley, appraised the bags. One bag had been piled up on top. It had an interesting shape. He knocked the bag with his foot, kicked it aside and inspected some of the other bags below.

Jenny was dumbfounded. She was incredulous. All those good things in her bag, all her best things, and he had kicked it aside. If she squinted, she could see that he had opened another bag and was now cradling an old telephone directory in his arms. It was doused in something that looked like beetroot juice. Something cerise. Ugh!

Chad put the directory into his trolley, returned to the bag, pulled out an empty chocolate box, inspected it, put it back, tied up the bag.

He opened another bag, close to the bottom. From within this bag he withdrew an old mop head and a plastic packet of carrots which hadn't been opened. He turned the packet of carrots over in his hand to double-check that they hadn't been touched, grimaced, noticed some mould on one of the carrots. He tossed the mop head into his trolley, tore open the plastic wrapping on the carrots and took one out. He bit off the mouldy end, spat it out, into the hawthorn, then proceeded to crunch his way through the remainder.

Jenny's eyes were wide, her mouth gaped. Those were *her* carrots. That was *her* mop head. This bag, her second bag, her rubbish bag, had been put at the bottom of the pile, specifically, so that Chad wouldn't get at it. How did he *know*? How?

Jenny raised her fist as if to knock on the window but stopped herself, froze, just in time, as Chad, at last, turned to the special bag, the kicked-aside bag.

As he untied it he was muttering to himself. He was saying, 'Something funny here. There's a reason. Something funny. That slag. Something up. Doesn't smell like rubbish. Bag's clean.'

He opened the bag. He pulled out a couple of lace tablemats. He folded them carefully and put them on the pavement to his right. He took out a Catherine Cookson novel and did the same. He took out the bag of rice, the felt-tips—these he held for a moment, he liked them, clearly—he took out the beans and the teapot. He liked the teapot, too.

Jenny sat at her window, watching him. She was very pleased indeed. This was right. This was good. She just *knew* this would happen. Absolutely.

What was her motivation? What was her plan of action? She didn't know yet. Hadn't decided. But it would be big when it came, and decisive, and when it happened she would *know* it had happened. Just so.

Jenny waited impatiently for Chad to put the stuff into his trol-

ley. Everything was piled neatly on the pavement now, all correct
and complete.

Chad appraised the pile of stuff. He then peered up at Jenny in
her window through his lashes. He made a quick decision. He unzipped his fly, pulled out his penis, urinated strongly and freely on
to the little pile of objects. He shook himself, put himself away, did
up his zip. He walked over to his trolley. He departed.

Oh, Jenny was angry now. Oh, she was angry. 'I knew it!' she
shouted out, through the window, through the wall, through the
front door, at the emergency cord. 'I just *knew* he'd do that. I knew
he would. I did! I did! 'Course I did!'

But a voice in her head said, 'Did you know? Huh? Did you?' So
she ripped off a wide strip of wallpaper with her bare nails to prove
to herself that she did know. She then discovered that she was having difficulty breathing. She felt dirty. Almost like he'd urinated on
to her directly. Into her mouth. Her mouth! It was too much. She
screamed and kicked her slippered foot against the wall again and
again until she heard her toes snapping.

Problem was, Naomi—in her rush to get to her emergency
cord—slipped on a plash of egg fat which had spat, seconds before,
out of her frying pan and on to her kitchen lino.

At ten o'clock, when Peter called around to find out if she
wanted any shopping, he discovered Naomi, crashed, incapacitated,
bruises already flowering on her head and arms like bright kisses of
cranberry. She'd fractured her fibia and sprained her wrist. She had
slight concussion.

Jenny watched the ambulance departing from her bedroom
window. Naomi's hurt, she thought. I just knew that would happen.
Chad did it. Chad, Chad, Chad, Chad, Chad.

She made splints for her toes out of toilet rolls, Sellotape and
toothpicks. She's nursed a bird once with a broken wing in just this
way so she guessed that this process would be adequate. Her toes
swelled. It hurt when she walked.

That night, while she slept—her foot propped up on a special
pillow like a crown on a velvet cushion—Jenny dreamed of Chad's

cold sores. She dreamed she was licking them with the tip of her tongue. They felt bumpy, like the head of a broccoli spear. They tasted like cough candy. She awoke, sweating, got up and drank four glasses of water in succession.

Thursday morning, Peter came to see her. Jenny did not make him tea. She was sitting on her sofa with a blanket over her legs. She said plaintively, 'I think I've got a chest infection. Bad catarrh.'

Peter came back later with some herbal lozenges, two lemons and a packet of Anadins. Jenny thanked him cordially.

It was a long week. Her toes hurt. The big toe especially. It remained swollen. The nail was cracked, but gradually Jenny found she could negotiate the hurdles and obstacles in her flat without too much duress.

She was waiting for Wednesday. She was waiting for Wednesday to come. Waiting, aching for Wednesday.

Chad almost didn't turn into the crescent. An instinct. Something warned him. Even so . . .

There were fewer bags out than usual. Chad let go of his trolley, stepped back a bit and peered up towards Jenny's window. The window was bare. Jenny wasn't there. He was so surprised that he whistled to himself under his breath. *Toot-teet-toot!* He stepped forward and bent over to pick up a bag.

Jenny had always *known*, in the pit of her stomach, that some day her thick volume of Mrs Beeton's Cookery Classics would come in handy. The sound of Chad's jaunty little whistle was still resounding in her ears as she stood up from her position behind the hawthorn and smashed it down hard on to the back of his head.

He staggered left, he staggered right, tipped forwards, whoops! Clump. Jenny *knew* that Chad would fall over in just this way and she also knew that he would come to after a minute or so, open his eyes, blink rapidly and rub his forehead like he didn't know what the hell had hit him. Jenny planned to be back in her flat by then, Mrs Beeton stashed carefully among her other cookery books on her kitchen cabinet.

Unfortunately Chad didn't stir, didn't shudder or twitch for several minutes. After five minutes Jenny became slightly perturbed. She stared at him from her bedroom window. She pushed her window open and yelled down.

'Oi!'

Chad didn't move.

'Oi!'

Nothing.

Jenny's heart started racing. She didn't think this would happen. She didn't *know* this would happen. She didn't. She didn't. Nope.

Ha *ha*! Chad was awake but lying still as a corpse. He was so happy. He could hear Jenny's voice, low and then fluting, calm and then jumbled with fear and fright and mortification. He lay as still as he could without stopping breathing. He pretended he was a piece of driftwood lying on a beach. He was full of mystery.

Jenny went into her hallway and stared at her emergency cord. She could not. She could not. Her hand . . . ooohh!

Peter came. Jenny was outside by now, struggling to pick Chad up and he was as limp as a broken wrist. Without asking any questions, Peter took hold of Chad's feet and Jenny held him by the shoulders. Between them they carried him upstairs, to Jenny's flat, into her bedroom, on to her bed. Chad felt the mattress give under his weight, could smell lavender water and cheap talc on the pillow.

Peter knew his first aid. He gave Chad the once over. Chad was enjoying being limp and lifeless, still driftwood, still inscrutable. Through his lashes he glimpsed Jenny standing in the doorway, chewing her nails. He was laughing inside.

'Do you know what happened, Jenny?' Peter asked, eventually.

'Uh.' Jenny had been wondering whether cold sores were contagious, whether to get a tea-towel and prop it under Chad's head so that he didn't infect her pillow.

'I saw him,' she said slowly, then quickening up. 'I saw him bend over and then just fall, like. I *knew* something bad would happen. I could tell from the very first time I saw him.'

Peter sighed. 'Maybe I should call an ambulance—' He paused and then added, 'What happened to your foot, incidentally?'

'Uh.' Jenny looked down at her foot as though this was the first time she'd noticed anything amiss with it.

Chad sat bolt upright. 'You lying cow!' he spluttered. 'Is this any way to treat a man?'

Peter and Jenny both turned and stared at Chad, agog. Before either of them could say anything, Chad said, 'I had a wife and a home and a good education. I had them. I gave them up.'

'Get off my bed,' Jenny said, 'you dirty piece of shit.'

'If I'm a piece of shit,' Chad said, not moving, 'then what does that make you?'

'You try and stop me!' Jenny yelled, turning on her heel and sprinting from the room.

Chad stared at Peter, frowning. 'What? Where's she think she's going?'

They heard the front door slam and the sound of Jenny's feet clattering down the stairs. Chad's eyes widened for a second and then he sprang up from the bed and ran to the window. Outside he saw Jenny lumbering over to his trolley and plunging her hands in it.

'The bitch!'

Chad spun around and ran for the door. Peter walked to the window and peered out. Down below, Jenny was elbow deep in Chad's trolley, pulling out pieces of clothing, coffee jars, blankets, old books, dried flowers, three bottles of brightly coloured nail varnish. Eventually she found the thing she was searching for and held it up, held it aloft like the most precious trophy. The Soap Ball! Chad's Soap Ball! *The bits of soap, where they've been, private places, him all dirty, a bit wet and then rubbed, and then rubbed, and then . . .*

Chad charged into the street. Peter saw his lips moving. *Give me that!* Jenny held the Soap Ball to her chest, with both hands. *Nope. It's mine!* Chad lunged at her. Jenny stepped aside. Jenny said *Keep away from me with your dirty hair. All this soap and you've never even used it.* Chad said *Give it me! It's mine!* Jenny said *You had a wife and you had a education, so you say, and now you go in everyone's bins taking their private things and their soaps and everything.* Chad stopped then, stood stock still. He stared at Jenny with an odd expression on his face. Like she was worthless and he'd only just realized it.

Peter turned away from the window. Suddenly he felt quite sick, a curious feeling in his stomach. He sat down for a moment on Jenny's bed to try to collect himself. You see, he'd just had a premonition and it had struck him with such sharpness, such clarity. He'd just had a vision. It was the future. Ten years. Chad and Jenny, living together in this small flat. The walls a different colour. Everything dirtier. Jenny had a broken arm. Chad had a drink problem. They were happy together. Happy! She was defective and he loved her and she *knew* that he loved her. She did. She did.

Peter stood up, gingerly.

Jenny held the Soap Ball. It was all she'd imagined. Heavy and spiky, like a deep sea creature, like one of those puffer fish that sometimes you saw dried and suspended in dusty old museums near to the coast.

Parker Swells

The first thing she noticed was his handwriting. She was taking classes, you see, in handwriting analysis. His name was Parker Swells. She thought it was a silly name, not a name she could believe in. And his handwriting sloped to the left, wasn't confident, was ill-constructed. There were breaks where there should be joins, no flow, no coherence.

Under Previous Experience—when she checked his application form—he had written: *Builder.* In one glance she saw how he'd left school at sixteen with no exams, but now . . . one two three . . . now he had eight O levels and four A levels. Maths, economics, sociology, physics.

But he was a builder. And you'd think, she thought, that if he was a builder then he'd consider how he wrote things, keep straight on the line, not dip below, and make sure that the overall effect was clear and true. You'd think so.

She'd only met him briefly, when she'd sat in on the interview. They'd liked him. He came over well, seemed nervous but didn't fidget. He had a habit of blowing his fringe out of his eyes. What could that mean? She scratched her ear. Maybe he needed a haircut.

Her name was Bethan and she was a personnel officer. She was responsible for the second interview, the recall. And in this arena she brought to bear all the things she'd learned at college and at night school, and on the job, naturally, about the corporation and the kind of person who'd fit best. The corporate man. Or woman.

Tell me, she'd said, on her quiz form, *which you would prefer if given the choice: a well-crafted gun or a beautiful poem?*

Tell me, she said, just underneath, *in your own words, what was the best thing that happened to you last weekend?*

Parker Swells was not his real name. He'd done things he'd regretted in the past thirty-three years, and he had a child in Norfolk that he didn't want to answer for to the CSA. No way.

It was a desk job he was after at one of the four big banks. He'd passed three lots of accountancy exams. He'd walked the first interview and this was his second. Filling in a quiz form full of patronizing psychological pish.

After inspecting the form for the third time, Parker wondered whether to write what he really thought or whether to write the kinds of answers he knew they'd like to hear. But how in-depth were these things? Could they tell he was lying if he did lie? Could they ascertain by the way you dotted your *i*s and crossed your *t*s that you weren't being wholly sincere? What exactly were they capable of, nowadays? His pen wavered.

Bethan had withdrawn to her office, through a door to the left. The door was ajar though and Parker could see her ankle and the toe of her black patent leather shoe. She had dark hair and brown eyes and she was going somewhere. No wedding ring. A lambswool polo-neck which clung at her throat as tight and sure as the skin of a banana. She was slim. She was untroubled. She could afford to think about why people behaved as they did. To judge. Her life had been exemplary. She needed no excuses.

Tell me, the paper read, *which you would prefer if given the choice: a well-crafted gun or a beautiful poem?*

He'd been a builder. He liked tools and a gun was a practical thing. He had no moral objection to firearms. But his hand, his right hand, had been badly damaged in an accident, and so, realistically, unless he could learn to aim and shoot with his left hand—as he'd learned to write, and that had been a battle—then it would be of no real use to him.

He was shy about his right hand. It was fingerless, supporting only a thumb. He kept it in his pocket or behind his back. People rarely noticed.

Parker picked up his pen with his left hand. He reappraised the sheet of questions. What did they want him to write? In a company this big and this brutal, he supposed the gun, really. And the way the place had been built, out of steel and glass, all smooth edged and modern. A gun.

Even so, he was only one person in this whole corporation, one piece, one part. And he had a gammy hand. And he had no real use for a firearm. He wasn't afraid of anything. He had no scores to settle. He didn't like loud noises, nor did his neighbours. Maybe the poem.

But Parker couldn't remember ever reading a poem. He'd read limericks. He listened to songs and memorized the words.

> My old hen, she's a good old hen
> She lays eggs for the railway men.
> Sometimes one, sometimes two,
> Sometimes enough for the whole darn crew.

He liked that.

Bethan picked up Parker's quiz form. In the gap under the question about the gun and the poem he had written:

Depends on what the company wants. If they want a trouble-shooter, I can do that. Give me the gun. If they want someone with flair and sensitivity, I can do that too. Pass me the poem. I can be both of these things. I can be all of these things. I want everything. I want nothing. I am adaptable.

She pushed her hair behind her ear. He was evasive, she decided, and yet assertive. He was confident. But at the same time, he didn't feel sure enough of himself to opt for one thing or the other. Maybe he didn't like making choices. Maybe he didn't enjoy making decisions. He was slippery.

Her eye travelled lower. She sighed at the way he'd mixed upper case and lower case letters. She started reading again.

What was the best thing that happened to you last weekend?

Here he had written:

Good things often come out of bad. Last weekend I got a message from a friend of mine. His name is Josh and we met at night school. During the day he works for a tool-hire company. Josh is friendly with another mate of mine, Sam, and sometimes we kick a ball around together in the park on a Saturday.

Three weeks ago we were playing and I accidentally fouled Sam. I kicked his shin with my spikes and grazed it. It bled a little. We parted on bad terms, but worse things have happened, so I didn't think anything of it and waited with Josh down at the park for him the week after.

But Sam didn't show. The week after that, either. It started to bug me. Maybe he was angry with me. Maybe he thinks I'm too bullish on the field. Maybe he really hates me. All stupid thoughts, but I was so cut up about it, this falling out, I even tried to ring once but he wasn't in. I didn't have the balls to try again.

Anyhow, Saturday morning, Josh phones me. He tells me Sam's dead. They found his body in his flat. He'd been dead for almost three weeks. He'd had a brain clot or something, a massive haemorrhage. And sure, I was cut up about it, but at the same time I was happy because I knew, in my gut, that Sam hadn't been angry with me about the penalty after all, not really. We hadn't fallen out in the end. He bore me no grudge.

Afterwards, though, when I went to his flat with Josh to help sort through some of his stuff, I couldn't help imagining how the phone must have rung that time I'd wanted to speak to him, and Sam, sitting close by, on the sofa, dead, the TV still on, the phone ringing.

Actually before I run out of space . . .

* * *

Parker had drawn an arrow and had continued this answer on to an extra piece of paper.

'Tea or coffee?' Bethan asked, strolling into the room.

Parker looked up. 'Tea, white, two sugars. Thanks.'

When Bethan returned with his tea, she placed the cup on the desk to his right. She had small hands, he noticed, and on her wrist was a little charm bracelet. The ornaments hanging on it were all connected with animals—fish, mainly, but a ladybird and a robin, too.

Parker thanked her for the tea, watched the curve of her hip pushing against the black fabric that contained it as she walked from the room, picked up his pen, smiled to himself and then started writing.

I must just get to the point. I was helping to sort through some of Sam's things. Me and Josh and Sam's mother. We were all cleaning and packing and clearing out his flat. This was Sunday. I was in the kitchen, mainly, and the first thing I came across was a bag of shopping which had been dumped, on the floor, next to the fridge, still not unpacked. Stuff Sam had bought at Spitalfields market the day after our last match together. The day he died. Some sourdough bread, mouldy now, some beetroots, raw, a lettuce—slimed up—and a box of free-range duck eggs. White eggs, like hens' only bigger.

I was about to throw the eggs into the bin with the other food but then Josh came through and said, don't chuck them, take them home if they're still fresh. And they were. So I did. Imagine that. A dead man's eggs.

I took them home and I was unpacking them from their box and into my refrigerator. For the most part they came easily, but then one of them had cracked and the juice that had escaped had dried like adhesive and stuck part of the shell to the box. I yanked it up but when it pulled free the egg was heavier than the others had been and felt odd in my hand. I looked at it, closer. I held it on my open palm and it was shaking. That little egg. Jerking and warm on my palm.

I sat down and I watched it. For two, three hours. And slowly, very gradually, it hatched.

Bethan turned over the sheet, ready to find something on the other side but the other side was blank. She had become quite engrossed. What an odd man, she thought, and stared fixedly at the sheets before her while using her free hand to fiddle, unconsciously, with the little charm bracelet on her wrist.

She tried to work out what the answer Parker Swells had given her meant. What did it say about him? His friend had died. He was sensitive—worried about the possibility of having injured or offended him—but how did that relate to a work context? Could it relate?

She bit her lip. Parker's reaction to Sam's death had been curious, kind of dispassionate. But he went along to clean his flat, to help out, so he was handy. Good in an emergency? And then finally . . . the eggs. That was strange.

Bethan reread the additional material Parker had added on the second page about the duck hatching. This was the part of his story she found most interesting. Again, she messed with the bracelet on her wrist, looked down at it for a moment: fish, fish, robin, shark, fish.

Sometimes Bethan felt she had to be like a private detective in her line of business. To discover things, to unearth people's secrets, to pluck at threads and see what she could unravel. To read significant signs and signals into the apparently superficial.

Parker Swells had confused her. She felt all fogged up. She inspected his writing again, the slope, the mis-links, the way he didn't close his *a*s and his *o*s. She delved into her bag and took out her college notes. She checked back on a couple of references. There were signs here, definite signs. Below the line, sloping left, the *o*s . . . He was a liar.

*　　*　　*

Parker didn't get his third interview. The letter they sent him—the people from personnel—said very little, only that they'd had plenty of applicants and they hoped he'd find success elsewhere.

By a strange coincidence, a week to the day after Bethan had dispatched her rejection letter to Parker Swells, she met him on the platform at Canary Wharf, waiting for a train. It was five thirty. She was on her way home to Bow. As she walked past him he said hello.

'Hello,' she said, and looked at him askance.

'Sorry, you probably don't remember me.'

'I remember you.' She smiled. 'The duck.'

He chuckled at this but added nothing. 'I was here,' he said, by way of explanation, 'on another interview. With another bank.'

'Oh yes?'

'Yes.'

He was handsome, she thought, in his own way. He had gappy teeth and green eyes and skin which had seen the sun. Leathery. But he was a liar.

The train arrived. The doors opened. Parker was actually in front of Bethan, but he stepped back and held out his arm. 'After you.'

She thanked him and moved forward and then she saw it. His right hand, completely mangled. He caught her expression. 'An accident,' he said, 'at work.'

She nodded. They climbed on to the train. 'It's ugly,' he said, with apparent unselfconsciousness.

'Were you left-handed originally?' Bethan asked, shocked and momentarily stuck for something to say.

'No. Right-handed, always. I had to learn to use my left hand. To write, to eat and everything. After the accident I found I couldn't work so effectively in a manual capacity. That's why I decided to go to college. To qualify for something else.'

Bethan nodded. 'I get it.'

She felt guilty. She was normally so perceptive. That was what she was trained for and paid for, after all. That was her job. To notice things. But she hadn't noticed this. It was down to her, finally, that Parker hadn't got the third interview. Down to her, reading too much into things. But was that it? Maybe the problem had actually been a *lack* of information.

He should have told her about his hand. This was the kind of detail the company needed to be acquainted with. Doubtless, she told herself, stroking and smoothing her own ruffled feathers, too little information and not too much had been her stumbling block.

'Are you still working as a builder?' Bethan asked, eventually, praying for the affirmative.

'When I can.'

'What kind of things do you do?'

'Laying patios, retiling, making paths, that sort of work. And building ponds.'

Bethan blinked. 'I've got some ponds,' she said, 'a big one and a little one. Two ponds.'

'I know. You keep fish.'

Bethan was beguiled. 'How could you know that?'

He pointed to her wrist. 'Your bangle. Full of fish charms.'

She chuckled. 'I gave myself away.'

'Not at all. I'm simply interested,' he said, 'in details.'

'Me too. Actually . . .' She looked out of the window to check where they were. Three stops still to go. 'Actually,' she said, fiddling with her bracelet, 'I wish I'd known about your bad hand. That might've affected the conclusions we reached on your second interview.'

'What kind of fish do you keep?' he asked, like he hadn't really heard her.

'Carp. Koi carp. Beautiful ornamental carp.'

'And what was wrong with my second interview?'

'Um . . .' She paused. 'We felt that your answers on the quiz were slightly unconventional. Like, uh, like, well, like my pond at home . . .'

'Your pond?'

'Yes. My main pond at home has my three best fish in it, but it's hard to see them because it gets greened up a lot. Algae and plants and what-not. I bought a filter for it, to keep it cleaner, but I haven't installed it yet.'

'And my answers . . .'

'Like the pond. There was something good in there, deep down, something interesting, but it was difficult to see, to decipher, and your writing . . .'

'Scruffy.'

'Yes.'

'I know.'

'I'm sorry.'

'That's OK.'

She cleared her throat. 'And the duck?'

'The duck?' he reiterated, looking surprised. 'Oh, the duck. The duck. It's doing fine.'

Parker lay on Bethan's bed with his arms crossed behind his head. He stared up at her light fitment. A heavy, glass lamp, yellow, the wiring, he noticed, coming slightly away from the cornice and the ceiling. He made a fist out of his damaged hand. He'd lost count of the number of women who had taken him into their beds simply because of this one, small, gorgeous imperfection. Sympathy was a powerful emotion. Might not seem it, but it was. And guilt.

Bethan strolled back into her bedroom. She was carrying a packet of biscuits and a couple of apples. She was naked. She bit into one of the apples and handed Parker the other. She sat down on the bed.

'We missed dinner,' she said, and grinned.

'How big is your garden?' Parker asked.

'It's tiny, really.'

'Do the ponds take up most of it?'

'Come and look,' Bethan said, and pulled on a T-shirt.

'I didn't build them, they were here when I bought the flat, so I thought I might as well put in some fish. Initially I just had goldfish and then one day I saw some carp at a garden centre and I thought they were so beautiful. So big. They come in every colour. See him? The gold one? Gold and white. He's called Samson. He's the oldest. The biggest too: I feed them by hand.'

Parker stared into the water. The ponds were antique and grand and well-established.

'That's a beautiful pond,' he said. 'Is it deep?'

'Very deep. Too deep. Sometimes the fish swim under and I don't get to see them for days. And see how murky it gets towards the bottom? That's why I bought the filter.'

'It's good, though,' Parker interjected, 'not to see the bottom. The fish must like to dive and disappear.'

'Only I haven't been able to set it up myself,' Bethan said, like she hadn't heard him, 'the filter. Too complicated. I'll show you it, if you like. It's in the shed. You might be able to give me some tips.'

She stood up.

It was late and Parker was pulling on his coat. She had given him the key to the side gate.

'I'd give you the house keys,' she said, 'only I've not got an extra set.'

He smiled at her. He found it strange that she'd have sex with him, let him inside her, but the keys to her home she couldn't quite trust him with.

'I wish you could bring the duck along while you're fixing up the filter,' she said, out of the blue, as he was walking through her front door.

'What?'

'The duck. He'd do well on my two ponds but I don't think the fish would like it.'

Parker laughed. 'There is no duck,' he said.

'What do you mean?'

'No duck. I made it up.'

She stared at him, her mouth open, barely comprehending. Eventually she said, 'But the duck . . . that was the best part of it.'

'Of what?'

'The story. The duck . . .' She looked flabbergasted.

Parker put his head to one side, still smiling. 'While I was filling out that quiz you brought me in a cup of tea, remember?'

She nodded.

'And I saw the bangle you were wearing, full of fish and birds and stuff. I thought the duck story would appeal to you. That was all.'

'So you lied on your application form?'

'Doesn't everybody? Didn't you?' Somehow, though, he thought he already knew the answer to this question. 'It doesn't matter,' he said. 'It's only a question of telling the right kind of lies.'

'Doesn't matter? Of course it matters.'

'You really want the full picture?'

His smile was strange, suddenly, and full of pain. 'You don't want the full picture,' he said, answering his own question. 'You wouldn't recognize the full picture if someone sat down and painted every tiny stroke of it straight on to your pretty hands and your silly face.'

'What's that supposed to mean?'

'You didn't know I was disabled but you came to certain conclusions about me because of my writing, you read into what I'd written things I hadn't said. It was kind of . . .' he paused and considered for a moment, 'kind of despicable.'

'Was it all lies?'

'Only the duck.'

'So you are a liar. I was right. I was right about you.'

He ignored this. 'Was I a liar,' he asked, 'before I filled in your stupid quiz form?'

She stared at him in silence for a while and then she put out her hand. 'Can I have my key back?'

'Why?'

'I don't want you fitting my filter any more. I feel weird about this now.'

'Don't be foolish. I'll fix the filter.'

'Give me the key.'

He laughed and handed her the key. She closed the door on his smiling face. She wrapped her arms around her breasts and shuddered.

It took almost an hour for the police to arrive. The constable who finally turned up was thickset and blond-haired and held his hat under his arm like it was a baby. He had a habit, Bethan noticed, of wiping his palms on the side of his thighs. She invited him in.

He took out his notebook and waited for her to say something.

'I came home from work,' she said, 'to discover that someone had broken into my property, through the back gate . . .'

'Did they force the lock?'

'No. I think they broke the lock and then replaced it. I found some new keys posted through my letterbox.'

'Someone changed the locks and then posted the new keys through your letterbox?'

'Yes.'

'Do you happen to know who might have done such a thing?'

'Yes. I know who did it. He's called Parker Swells.'

Bethan spelled Parker's name out loud and checked as the constable wrote it on his pad.

'I have his address and all the details you could want about him, only everything's still at work . . .'

The policeman nodded. 'And what, exactly,' he said, 'apart from changing the lock on your back gate, did he actually do?'

'Come outside.'

Bethan took the police officer into her back garden. She pointed. He looked around him. There was little to see. A neat lawn, flowerbeds, nothing amiss.

'He stole my ponds,' she said, her voice cracking.

'Your what?'

She pointed. He saw five, large, beautiful fish in a curious selection of small, clear-glass containers.

'He stole my ponds.'

Ponds, the policeman wrote down in his book. Stolen.

Bethan watched as he wrote this. His writing, she saw, was round and girlish and immature. She wished they'd sent someone else. He clearly wasn't going to prove competent.

'And why do you think he did this? Why did he steal your ponds?'

Bethan didn't know. She couldn't answer. She felt so ridiculous.

'He had a duck, a pet duck,' she said, eventually. 'Maybe he stole them for his duck.'

She glanced up and saw the policeman was smiling at her. She looked away.

'Those are beautiful,' he said, indicating towards the fish. She nodded. Her fish hung, suspended, in their small, plain glass bowls; tight and bright and golden. Their gills moved; in and out, in and out. Bethan could clearly see every tiny little detail now.